A NEW HOME AT THE WARTIME HOTEL

MAISIE THOMAS

Boldwood

First published in Great Britain in 2025 by Boldwood Books Ltd.

Copyright © Maisie Thomas, 2025

Cover Design by JD Design Ltd.

Cover Images: Shutterstock and Paul Thomas Gooney/Figurestock

The moral right of Maisie Thomas to be identified as the author of this work has been asserted in accordance with the Copyright, Designs and Patents Act 1988.

All rights reserved. No part of this book may be reproduced in any form or by any electronic or mechanical means, including information storage and retrieval systems, without written permission from the author, except for the use of brief quotations in a book review. This book is a work of fiction and, except in the case of historical fact, any resemblance to actual persons, living or dead, is purely coincidental.

Every effort has been made to obtain the necessary permissions with reference to copyright material, both illustrative and quoted. We apologise for any omissions in this respect and will be pleased to make the appropriate acknowledgements in any future edition.

A CIP catalogue record for this book is available from the British Library.

Paperback ISBN 978-1-83633-242-8

Large Print ISBN 978-1-83633-243-5

Hardback ISBN 978-1-83633-241-1

Ebook ISBN 978-1-83633-244-2

Kindle ISBN 978-1-83633-245-9

Audio CD ISBN 978-1-83633-236-7

MP3 CD ISBN 978-1-83633-237-4

Digital audio download ISBN 978-1-83633-239-8

This book is printed on certified sustainable paper. Boldwood Books is dedicated to putting sustainability at the heart of our business. For more information please visit https://www.boldwoodbooks.com/about-us/sustainability/

Boldwood Books Ltd, 23 Bowerdean Street, London, SW6 3TN

www.boldwoodbooks.com

In memory of
Gordon Harrop (1910–1981)
and
Lily Harrop (née Dunbar, 1912–1998)

1

MANCHESTER, END OF APRIL, 1928

Kitty Dunbar lay wide awake in her bed in the darkened hospital ward. She was sore and exhausted but she had never felt happier or more excited in her whole life. She was a mum! A brand-new mother – a whole six weeks earlier than expected.

It had been scary to start with. Scary? Downright terrifying. She had been out at the shops when pain sliced through her and she had dropped like a stone to the pavement. She'd been brought to hospital in the back of an ambulance, its bell clanging. She had never been more frightened in her life. Yet now – now none of that mattered–and never would again. All that mattered was being a mother.

'Mummy,' she whispered, and her heart fluttered.

She yearned for her baby, but all the babies spent the night in cots lined up in the nursery. In fact, they spent much of their day there too. Not that Kitty had been here long enough to become any kind of expert, but she had already gleaned that much. The babies were brought to their mothers at feeding times – oh, and in the evenings, so their fathers could admire them.

Bill had done that in spades.

'Here comes Baby Dunbar,' the nurse had said, smiling as she brought Kitty and Bill's baby to Kitty's bed.

Instinct had made Kitty hold out her arms to take her child, but the nurse had placed the tiny infant in the cot at the foot of her bed. Did you only get to hold your baby at feeding times?

Rising to his feet, Bill had moved to lean over the cot. Kitty witnessed the moment when the strong lines of his face softened and his blue eyes had assumed a misty expression.

'No touching, thank you, Father.' The nurse spoke in that mock-jolly voice some people used on children.

She walked away. Bill continued to gaze at his daughter, breaking off for only as long as it took for him to grab his chair from beside Kitty and plonk it down beside the cot, and that was where he stayed for the rest of visiting time. He was a big chap, tall and well-built; he might well be thickset in later life. It was deeply touching to see him so evidently in thrall to this tiny new person.

'Abigail,' he said. 'Let's call her Abigail.'

'I thought we'd agreed on Louise,' said Kitty. Actually, she had wanted Eloise but Bill had thought that too fancy-sounding. Kitty still wasn't sure if that was his opinion or his mother's.

'It means "father's joy". One of the tea-ladies told me. It was her mother's name.'

'You want to name our daughter after the tea-lady's mother?'

'No. I want to call her "father's joy" because that's what she is. I'd no idea she was going to have such an effect on me. I know you're supposed to love your children, but I'd no idea it would be like this. So... instant. So *complete*.'

And just like that, little Louise had become Abigail. What a good thing Kitty hadn't been asked earlier by the nurses what her baby's name was. Now she came to think of it, the staff never used the babies' first names anyway, always referring to them as Baby Smith, Baby Jones... Baby Dunbar.

Baby Dunbar. Abigail Dunbar. Excitement shimmered its way all through Kitty as she lay now in the darkness, senses heightened. Every now and again she wanted to utter a laugh of sheer joy and had to turn it into a little gasp instead.

One of the other mothers stirred, turned over without waking and settled down again. Another snored. How could they sleep? How could they – when they were the mothers of new babies?

Maybe all the others in the ward had been mothers before; maybe their new babies were their second, third, fourth. Maybe Kitty was the only brand-new mum and that was why she was the only one who was wide awake. Perhaps it was partly the shock. This time yesterday, she'd still had six weeks to go – and now here she was in hospital, along the corridor from her new daughter. Abigail. The name had taken root. Abigail Dunbar.

When the babies were brought in for their next feed, Kitty was sitting up in bed ready while the other mothers were still being roused. The other women had lightweight shawls to drape over their shoulders above their naked breasts to protect their modesty, but Kitty had nothing of the sort. It had never once occurred to her during her pregnancy that she might end up in the maternity ward. She'd had everything ready at home, including the promise of Mrs Carter's cradle because little Nellie Carter should have outgrown it by the middle of June when Kitty's baby was due. Instead, here she was in hospital at the end of April without any notice or preparation.

She ought to be in a flap, fretting about the six weeks' worth of getting ready that had been torn from her, but she wasn't. She was too happy. Besides, everyone would rally round. Mam and Naomi wouldn't know whether to make more fuss of her or of the baby. Having a little girl was special too, after Naomi's three lads. Kitty couldn't wait to get home and show her off, but that would have to wait. She'd been told she needed bed rest, which was a joke, because she wouldn't have got that if she'd been at home.

She was allowed to take Abigail home on Saturday afternoon. She was such a sweet little thing, as dainty as a doll, with deep-blue eyes and wisps of hair the colour of vanilla ice cream, though both her parents were dark. Kitty loved the way she scrunched up her tiny fingers and toes – and Bill's adoration of their child melted her heart.

'I'm taking you home in a taxi,' Bill declared when she was ready to leave, Baby Abigail in her arms.

'I was expecting Mam to fetch me and we'd go home on the bus.'

'On the bus!' Bill's laugh rumbled deep in his chest. 'D'you think I'd let my two special girls go home on the *bus*?'

'Honestly, Bill,' Kitty protested. 'A taxi – the cost.'

'Let yourself be spoiled, woman,' Bill answered jovially. 'You gave us all a terrific scare when you were carted off in the ambulance. Can you imagine how I felt when I received the message at work? A journey by taxi is the least you deserve. We want our daughter to arrive home in style.'

Burying the niggle about the price, Kitty surrendered to the moment. This was a special occasion and Bill was so transparently proud of their beautiful daughter. It would be mean to begrudge him this small extravagance.

She laughed. 'Will you still want a taxi when we have baby number four?'

Bill grinned. 'You bet I will.'

* * *

The taxi turned the final corner and Kitty, cuddling Abigail, tilted her face to look out at the line of terraced houses with a shop on each corner. Just think: the last time she'd been here, she'd had an aching back, swollen ankles and six weeks to go, or so she'd thought.

A few of the neighbours were out. Old Mrs Tierney, dressed in the black she'd worn for as long as Kitty could remember, was sweeping the flagstones in front of her house, sending dust and grit and a few twigs into the gutter. Mrs Bulstrode and Mrs Pearce, dressed in wraparound pinnies and turbans, were nattering on the doorstep. Others, pinnies and turbans replaced by coats and felt hats, had baskets over their arms as they set off for the shops.

One and all, the women turned to watch the motorcar drive along the road. Kitty caught their looks of surprise and her face and neck felt impossibly hot as embarrassment flooded her – but only for a second. The next moment, the women were smiling and she smiled back, discomfort replaced by delight. Sure enough, when Bill helped her from the taxi, an audience crowded round and Kitty was all smiles as her neighbours cooed and admired.

Bill was fairly puffed up with pride. 'Excuse us, ladies. I'd better get my wife and daughter inside.'

'Aye, you do that,' said Mrs Bulstrode, and the other women nodded. There were a few chuckles as well and Kitty realised the women were indulging Bill in his status as new father.

He unlocked the front door, saying, 'I feel as if I ought to carry the pair of you over the threshold.'

Kitty used her fingertips to draw down the edge of the shawl Abigail was wrapped in. It had ridden up and covered the tiny rosebud mouth. Kitty touched her daughter's cheek ever so gently with one finger. Looking at Abigail had become her greatest pleasure.

'Let's get you indoors, little one,' she murmured, 'so you can settle into your new home. You'll like that, won't you?'

'She'll love it,' said Bill.

Walking into the narrow hallway, Kitty wondered what he meant by that; she didn't suppose he meant anything, really. Then she entered their cosy parlour and knew exactly what he'd meant.

She turned to face him as he came into the room behind her.

'Bill—'

'Don't make a fuss, Kitty.' His handsome face clouded with frustration and hurt. His dark eyebrows tugged together below the broad forehead.

Kitty felt frustrated too. Here they were, bringing their darling daughter home. They'd not been in the house two minutes – and Bill had done it again. Splurged out on something brand new. Oh, *why* did he feel the need to do these things?

'Don't you think it's beautiful?' Bill's voice rang with satisfaction.

Kitty wanted to say, 'It doesn't matter how beautiful it is. How much did it set you back? How much did it set *us* back?' She was annoyed with him for putting her in this position when today everything ought to be perfect.

She said, 'But I'd arranged to borrow Mrs Carter's from up the road. You know I did.'

Bill chuckled. 'That was when we were expecting a June baby. Now we've got an April baby and Nellie Carter presumably still needs her cot.'

Kitty couldn't argue with that – but honestly, a drawer would have sufficed.

'You haven't really looked at it yet,' Bill said encouragingly.

It was beautiful, there was no denying it. Kitty had never seen a cradle before, not a real one on rockers. She'd seen cots – oblong, sturdy. Her own mam always laughed when she said that her children had all started off in a laundry basket lined with blankets.

But this – this was a real, true cradle, woven in basketwork, with elegant rockers curving beneath it and even a basketwork hood at one end. Not that the basketwork was the be-all and end-all. No, the cradle was covered by delicate, transparent muslin, with ruffles all around. It looked like something out of a fairy tale.

'Well, yes, it is lovely, but—'

'Don't you think our daughter is worth it?' Bill asked. 'Worth the very best? Don't you want the best for her?'

Kitty was stung by the unfairness of the question. 'Of course I do.'

'Well then.' Bill's features relaxed. 'I've told you before, love, I want to give you the best. Now I want to provide Abigail with the best as well.'

'I understand that,' Kitty began.

'Do you?' Bill asked. 'Because you don't sound as if you do.'

'We have to be able to afford it,' Kitty said in a quiet, reasonable voice.

'The same old refrain,' said Bill, but he laughed, too happy to be impatient. 'Don't you fret about the cost, Kitty Dunbar. This cradle is bought and paid for. Now for heaven's sake, settle Abigail so we can see what she looks like in it – or do you propose standing there holding her all day?'

Kitty carefully placed Abigail in the cradle.

'Bill, this bedding is new. What about the baby blankets and so forth in the linen chest?'

'That's all second-hand. You can't have a new cradle and not have new linen.' Bill gazed lovingly at his daughter. 'There – doesn't she look like a little princess?'

He slid his arm around Kitty's waist as they stood side by side, looking down at their little girl. Warmth spread through Kitty's body. Abigail's tiny form was adorable in the froth of baby-linen.

Kitty leaned against her husband. 'I'm grateful that you want to give Abigail and me the best of everything, but, please, no more extravagance after this.'

Bill stiffened. 'Are you saying I don't know how to manage my money?'

'No, not at all,' she answered quickly. 'I just want us to live within our means. We mustn't be lavish.'

Bill pulled her closer and kissed her temple. 'It isn't lavishness when it's done out of love.'

2

'You've got fair hair and blue eyes just like your Auntie Naomi,' Naomi said in a cooing voice.

Sitting comfortably in her parlour, Kitty was aware of her heart swelling with love as she watched her sister gently rocking Abigail in her arms.

'It's a shame you'll never be able to make anything of your wedding anniversaries,' said Naomi.

Kitty stopped with her cup of tea halfway to her lips. Lowering it, she stared at her sister. With her face bent over the baby, Naomi was apparently unaware of having said anything devastating.

'You what?' said Kitty. 'Why can't we celebrate our anniversary?'

Naomi looked up, regarding Kitty with mild surprise.

'Because of this little one being so early, of course. Think about it. You and Bill got wed last September and five minutes later you were expecting.'

'Abigail is a honeymoon baby.' Kitty couldn't think of anything more romantic.

'She should have been born in June,' said Naomi, 'but she surprised us all at the end of April.'

'I'm just grateful she's all right,' said Kitty.

'So are we all. She's perfect,' Naomi said sincerely. She smiled down at her niece. 'You're a perfect little angel, aren't you?' She was still smiling when she looked up at Kitty. 'Don't you see? A so-called June baby born in April. You know what folk will say.'

'Hang on a minute,' Kitty protested. 'What d'you mean, "so-called"? Of course she was due in June. Why else do you think I ended up in hospital? It's because she was so early.'

Naomi's eyes widened. 'There's no need to take that tone. I'm not suggesting you got up to anything you shouldn't have.'

'But you think others will?'

'All I'm saying,' Naomi answered, her calm tone making Kitty's indignation seem unreasonable, even sulky, 'is that when a baby is born sooner than anticipated after a wedding, everyone makes a polite show of pretending to believe in the premature birth. Now, in your case, everybody knows it really was a premature birth, but you can hardly expect them to keep on remembering it for years and years, can you? And when you proudly announce you've been wed for ten years or fifteen or however many, there'll be those who ask, "Didn't Abigail come along the following April?" and they'll do some counting on their fingers and, well, you really will look as if you got up to something you shouldn't have.'

'Naomi, you're being ridiculous,' Kitty exclaimed, but even so her heart beat faster. Was her sister right? Would she really have to let her wedding anniversaries slide by unseen? Even the big ones, like the twentieth, the silver... the ruby?

'I'm just trying to save you some embarrassment, that's all,'

Naomi pointed out. 'I'm your big sister. It's my job to look after you.'

Kitty sighed, feeling better. 'I know.'

Naomi smiled again at the child in her arms. 'And your mummy won't mind keeping her anniversaries quiet, will she? No, she won't, because she's got you and you're worth any amount of trouble.'

Kitty pressed a hand to her heart. Baby Abigail was more than worth it.

'I don't know what to do about the christening robe,' she said.

Naomi frowned. 'What about it?'

'I spent ages embroidering a spray of roses onto each of the corners. Look.'

Kitty lifted the lightly folded cotton shawl from her workbasket and unfolded it to show off her handiwork. Ever since she had known for certain she was expecting a happy event, she had spent many a joyful hour sewing butter-yellow roses and dark-green leaves. Never before had she put so much effort into a piece of needlework.

'It's lovely,' Naomi said as if she hadn't already seen it a hundred times as the sprays of roses grew. 'And you've almost finished it.'

'I expected to have a few weeks more,' Kitty said ruefully. 'But that's not the point. I keep wondering if I ought to unpick it all and begin again, except there isn't time to do all that work.'

Naomi raised her eyebrows. 'Why would you want to do that?'

Kitty held up an embroidered corner. 'Roses for a June baby. It should be daffodils or wallflowers for an April baby.'

To her chagrin, Naomi looked amused. 'Kitty Dunbar, have you lost your mind? You said it yourself: you can't possibly undo everything and start again – and why would you want to? This is exquisite.'

Kitty laughed at herself. 'Thank you. That's what I needed to hear – from somebody other than myself.'

'Abigail Dunbar, what a silly mummy you have – but also a very loving mummy who wants everything to be perfect for you. Just like any first-time mum,' Naomi added, smiling warmly at Kitty. Then she laughed. 'You wait until you've got three, like me. You'll be a lot more casual about it.'

'Much as I love Abigail,' said Kitty, 'I couldn't face a repeat performance of collapsing in the street and then that mad dash to hospital.'

'That was rotten luck,' said Naomi. 'There's nothing to say it'll happen again: isn't that what the doctor told you? Besides,' she added, a suggestion of stiffness entering her tone, 'you need to have several more to get your money's worth out of that posh cradle.'

Kitty shut her eyes for a moment. 'Don't remind me. I swear that all the neighbours who have been trooping in and out supposedly to admire the new baby really came to get an eyeful of the cradle. I made Bill take it upstairs in the end and put it in our bedroom.'

'Didn't you tell him you were having Mavis Carter's cot?'

'Yes. It would have been fine if Abigail had hung on until June, but Mrs Carter's Nellie needs the cot for another month yet, and you know what Bill's like.'

'Yes, I do,' Naomi said in a neutral voice.

'He absolutely adores Abigail,' Kitty said, making an effort not to sound defensive. 'Nobody could fault him on that score.'

'I know, love,' Naomi said gently, 'but you've really got to find a way of reining in the spending.'

'He always says it's because he wants me to have the very best.'

'That's all well and good,' said her sister, 'but—'

'Please don't say anything against my husband,' Kitty cut in swiftly.

'I was only going to say that it grieves me to see you worrying about it,' Naomi said mildly. 'You know I have your best interests at heart.'

Kitty glanced around her parlour, her gaze resting on the pretty china figurine on the mantelpiece that Bill had bought as a surprise after Naomi had been given one that had belonged to her late grandmother-in-law. On the top shelf inside a glazed display cabinet sat a set of six sherry glasses. Kitty knew plenty of families who owned a set of stemmed glasses – but how many of them owned a decanter? A decanter!

As a brand-new bride, she had been thrilled to have such a loving and generous husband. She'd been proud to think he wanted to spoil her. She'd grown up hearing tales of local women whose husbands kept them short, women who were obliged to buy cracked eggs or replace a broken window with paper painted with boiled linseed oil or to use crumbs to bulk out a simple omelette. She knew she would never have to do any of those things. Bill was a good provider. Not only that but he had an open hand and, well... sometimes that could lead to extravagance.

Naomi was the one and only person Kitty had ever breathed a word to about her secret reservations regarding Bill's liberality. There was nobody she trusted more in the world than Naomi, the beloved older sister who had watched over her since she was a baby. Mam and Dad had had three children, Peter and Naomi before the turn of the century and then Kitty some years later. When folk remarked on the age difference, Mam used to say that she'd had two Victorian children and one Edwardian, which used to make Kitty feel special and proud. But then the Great War had come along and taken their Peter from them. The Victorian-Edwardian joke had died with him, leaving Mam simply with two daughters ten years apart.

But those ten years had never stopped them being close. Naomi had always paid Kitty a lot of attention. It was only after she herself had grown up that Kitty had come to appreciate how unusual this was – and how special Naomi was. With a whole decade between them, most older sisters would have regarded the younger as a dratted nuisance.

No matter how deeply Kitty loved and trusted Naomi, there were times when she wished she'd never confided about Bill's spending. After all, it wasn't an everyday occurrence, and no wife should speak against her husband. Naomi's words just now about 'reining in the spending' made Kitty feel guilty for having blabbed.

Even so, she knew Naomi was right.

* * *

Kitty felt happy enough to hug the whole world as Mam cuddled Abigail and cooed over her.

'I can't get over how tiny she is,' Mam said with a chuckle. 'Like a doll. You should have called her Dorothy, then she could be Dolly.' Bending her head, she addressed her granddaughter in a sing-song voice. 'Couldn't you? Couldn't you be little Dolly Dunbar?' Lifting her chin again, she looked at Kitty. Mam had the same blue eyes as Naomi. 'Thank you for having a little girl, Kitty. It's wonderful to have a granddaughter.'

Naomi laughed. 'Steady on, Mam. Yes, Abigail's a little treasure but my boys are special too.'

'Of course they are, love,' Mam agreed. 'All grandchildren are special. You wait until it's your turn and then you'll see what I mean.'

Both Kitty and Naomi exclaimed in astonishment.

'Mam!' said Naomi. 'I'm years off being a grandmother.'

'And Abigail's only just been born,' Kitty added.

'Oh, your faces!' said Mam. 'It'll come round faster than you think.'

'Well, I for one am not going to wish away a single minute,' Kitty declared, her arms suddenly aching with the need to hold her darling child. If it had been anybody but Mam holding Abigail just then, she might have asked to have her back.

'Quite right too, Kitty,' Naomi said. 'You of all people should hang on to every moment.'

'Why me?' Kitty asked, surprised.

'Because it's all happened for you in such a rush,' said Naomi. 'I hope things slow down and happen at a normal pace for you from now on, but let's face it: this time last year, you didn't even know Bill existed and now here you are with a baby.'

Yes, it had happened quickly. Even taking Abigail's early arrival out of the equation, it had still been speedy. It was actually another reason why Kitty had been looking forward to a June birth; she had secretly hoped that her child would arrive on the anniversary of the day when she and Bill had met.

Going to that dance in the church hall on a warm evening last June at the tail end of a gloriously sunny day, Kitty had never imagined her life was about to change for ever. She'd worn a sleeveless cream-coloured dress with a V-neck that had a flesh-coloured infill. With it, she'd worn a short, purple jacket because she thought the colour looked good against her dark hair, but then, at the last minute, she'd taken it off again in case she got too hot.

The church hall windows had been opened in the forlorn hope of encouraging a draught, and the ladies in charge of refreshments, finding that the fruit cordial was in heavy demand, had watered it down until it was all but tasteless. Kitty didn't care. Flushed and happy, not to mention more than a little gratified after being invited to dance by several chaps, all she wanted was something wet and cold to refresh her.

'Who's that?' one of her chums asked, looking over Kitty's shoulder. 'I haven't seen him before.'

Kitty turned round, still holding her beaker to her lips, and looked at a tall, handsome man, some years older than herself, with blue eyes. Even from here, she could see his eyes were blue. Her breath caught in her throat. Fortunately, she wasn't swallowing at that moment or she might have choked. Heat rushed into her cheeks and her pulse did an Irish jig.

Hopelessly self-conscious, she turned away and glugged down her drink, hoping to hide her confusion, though apparently she didn't make a very good job of it, judging by her companions' smirks and giggles. Then someone behind her cleared their throat.

Kitty turned once more and there he was, the good-looking man with the blue eyes.

'Would you like to dance?' he asked.

Unable to utter a sound, Kitty nodded. He had already taken the beaker from her fingers and handed it to one of the others. The next thing Kitty knew, they were waltzing on the church hall's bare floorboards and her skin was tingling beneath the gentle pressure of his hands.

That was how it had started, and it had progressed pretty swiftly. More than once, as she walked along the street, Kitty caught the words 'whirlwind romance' uttered in a low voice by one of the neighbours. Her heart had taken flight each time.

They were talking about her. She was having a whirlwind romance. Her tummy fluttered and her heart raced. She held her head high, proud and excited.

They got engaged in July. Bill took her for a walk in Fog Lane Park and they listened to the town's silver band play 'Goodbye-ee' and 'Take Me Back to Dear Old Blighty' and songs from the music hall. Bill hummed along. He looked smart in a single-breasted three-piece suit and a trilby hat with a dark-blue band around the brim.

Then the band played 'If You Were the Only Girl in the World' and Bill sank down on one knee, right there on the grass in full view of all the people out strolling arm in arm and those relaxing in striped deckchairs in front of the bandstand.

'You're the only girl in the world for me, Kitty,' he said, bringing a ring box out of his pocket. 'Will you marry me?'

Kitty gasped, her palms flying up to cover her mouth. Tears sprang into her eyes, but they were tears of pure joy. A quick glance around told her that everybody was waiting for her reply. She tried to haul Bill to his feet, but he didn't budge.

'I'm not moving until you give me an answer,' he said.

Kitty stopped feeling self-conscious and melted into the delight of the moment. She nodded and managed to say, 'Yes,' on a little splutter of happy tears. For a moment she was aware of applause and smiles all around them, and even a few cheers, but then all that faded away as Bill rose to his feet and slipped the ring on her finger. He took her in his arms and kissed her, and never mind that they were in a public place. It was the most romantic thing that had ever happened, just like at the pictures.

Naomi had surprised Kitty by not being keen on the engagement at the outset.

'He's too old for you. He's older than I am.'

'That's good, surely,' said Kitty. 'It means he's established in his job.'

'You should have someone your own age,' Naomi replied. 'If you're young together, you struggle together as you make your way. That's what binds you as a couple and makes you stronger.'

'Do you want Kitty to struggle?' Mam asked in a reasonable voice.

'No, of course not,' Naomi answered. 'I'm just saying. That's the natural way of things.'

'Was it a struggle for you and Derek?' Kitty asked her sister.

'Yes, since you ask, and it didn't do us any harm.'

'I understand what you're saying,' Kitty replied, 'but it just isn't like that for us.'

Quite the reverse, in fact. 'Struggle' was the very last word Kitty would ever have thought of applying to Bill. His easy generosity made it impossible.

'He's spoiling you,' said Mam. 'Flowers once a week would be a treat – but twice! I never heard the like. Your nana would have said, "I'll go to the foot of our stairs." Do you remember her saying that when she was surprised or taken aback?'

'Do you mean Nana would have been taken aback by Bill bringing me flowers twice a week?' Kitty asked.

Mam relented. 'Of course not, love. She'd have been proper chuffed to know you've got a fine, good-hearted man to take care of you.'

As well as the flowers, Bill brought her chocolate – and not just chocolate as in a bar of Dairy Milk, but chocolates, plural, as in an actual box of Milk Tray. He gave her a fringed scarf that she assumed must be made of rayon because it was so silky, until Bill told her it was real silk.

'Real silk?' Kitty was so surprised that she could hardly

breathe. It wouldn't be polite to say that the gift must have cost a fortune, so she settled for, 'But it's not my birthday.'

That made Bill laugh. 'Just wait until your birthday, Mrs Dunbar-to-be.'

'Of course, it'll only be while we're engaged that he gives me these treats,' Kitty said confidently to Mam and Naomi. 'It's all part of our whirlwind romance. Things will settle down and be normal once we're married.'

Except that it hadn't happened that way.

'You shouldn't be flinging your money around now we're man and wife,' Kitty told Bill after he came home with a new cut-glass fruit bowl. Not just a new-to-Kitty fruit bowl, but a brand-new one.

'I'm not flinging it around,' Bill answered. 'I'm providing a decent, comfortable home for my wife.'

'I know,' said Kitty, 'and it's wonderful of you, but now that we're married, with household bills to pay, we ought to be a bit careful.'

'What sort of a man would I be, what sort of a husband, if I stopped wanting to spoil you the minute we're married?' Bill asked. 'Only a dishonest man would do that. It would be tantamount to tricking you into marrying me. Some men might act like that, but not me. I keep my promises – and that includes providing my wife with only the very best.'

3

After putting on her jacket and hat, Kitty wrapped Abigail in a baby blanket and snuggled her close.

'Let's go to the corner and meet Daddy coming home from work, shall we?'

Bill was a shipping clerk in a warehouse on the banks of the River Irwell, which ran through the middle of Manchester. He had started there as a messenger boy when he left school. Kids left at thirteen back then. Bill was two or three years older than Naomi and he had served his country the same as Peter, except that Bill had come home – and not just come home but returned intact and in fine fettle, unlike many poor blighters, with missing limbs and ruined lungs.

As Kitty hovered at the corner, Bill came along the road. He looked extra handsome in his suit and bowler hat. He had bought the suit for their wedding. It was double-breasted navy wool with wide lapels and flap-pockets, and a matching waistcoat. The trousers had knife-sharp creases and turn-ups.

Kitty's heart expanded with pride. There was no man more handsome than her Bill. Carefully angling the baby, she hooked a gentle finger beneath Abigail's tiny hand and wiggled, making Abigail 'wave' at her father.

Bill's answering smile said how happy he was. Kitty was happy too. They weren't just a couple now. They were a family.

Bill bent his head to brush a kiss against her cheek. He missed and got her nose instead because he was more interested in looking at his daughter. Kitty didn't mind. She loved the way Bill worshipped their baby.

They walked home together. Indoors, Bill unlaced his leather shoes and pushed his feet into the slippers Kitty had left in position beside the doormat, then he went upstairs to change. Around the house he wore flannels and a sleeveless knitted pullover on top of a shirt with an attached collar. Many, if not most, shirts were made with an attached collar these days, but for his wedding-cum-work suit Bill had opted for the traditional kind, with the separate collar that had to be attached with studs.

Kitty prepared their meal. Bill ate his dinner in the warehouse canteen so all that was needed when he came home was high tea – leek pasties or bacon cake or sardine fritters, something of that kind.

Today, Kitty made cheese and parsley soup, which she served with warm oven-bottom muffins. She liked cooking and baking. She'd had two very good teachers in Mam and Naomi and she had been on the receiving end of many a family joke about having a lot to live up to.

Bill enjoyed her cooking. Sometimes, nodding his approval, he would say, 'You're good enough to work in the kitchen at Dunbar's.'

When her husband linked her with Dunbar's, it was a great compliment.

For their pudding Kitty served baked apple stuffed with

dried fruit. Afterwards Bill polished his shoes and had a cigarette while Kitty cleared the table and washed up.

Then it was time to sit down with a cup of tea. Kitty picked up the darning. She'd been brought up not to have idle hands.

'Now then,' said Bill, 'about the christening. I called at Dunbar's today but they haven't got a room free on that particular Sunday, though we could have a room the previous Sunday or the one after.'

Kitty's deft fingers paused. 'Oh, Bill, no. We chose that Sunday specially because it's the closest one to when Abigail would have been born if she hadn't come early.'

'You don't need to explain it to me.'

But evidently she did, if he thought the date could be switched just like that.

'It's important,' Kitty said softly. 'Holding the christening on that day will make it extra special.'

'It'll be a happy occasion whenever we have it,' Bill pointed out.

'Yes, it will,' Kitty agreed, 'but having it on that Sunday will add to the significance. How many babies get christened on the day they should have been born?'

'We don't know the exact day she would have been born,' said Bill.

'You know what I mean,' Kitty replied. 'There are plenty of early babies that don't thrive. We're so lucky to have Abigail, so lucky that, aside from being tiny, there's nothing wrong with her. Holding the christening on that Sunday will make everyone realise.'

Bill nodded. 'We want everyone to understand what a special child she is.' Then he shook his head. 'It's a rotten shame about Dunbar's, though. That would have made the occasion perfect.'

Privately, Kitty thought that the people who were there to share the day with them were far more important than where the celebration took place, but all she said was, 'It would have been very smart.'

Dunbar's was what Bill liked to refer to as 'the family hotel'. It had been established by his grandfather, who had been succeeded at the helm by Uncle Jeremiah, whose son, Bill's cousin Ronald, acted as his father's deputy and would one day take over. Bill had never said it in so many words, but Kitty strongly suspected that her husband envied Ronald.

'I'll make enquiries at the Grove Hotel over the road from Dunbar's,' said Bill, 'and see if they can accommodate a private party that Sunday.'

'We don't need to go somewhere like that,' Kitty protested. 'Think of the cost. I know you don't begrudge it – and before you say it, yes, Abigail would be worth every single penny, but we really don't need to do that. It would be one thing to go to Dunbar's. There are family reasons for that. That's the whole point of a christening, isn't it? Family. Quite honestly, if we aren't going to Dunbar's, I'd be just as happy to throw a party here.'

'Here?' Bill looked round the parlour as if he'd never seen it before. 'We can't hold such a special party here.'

'Why not? This is Abigail's home. It's where we'll bring her up. This is the perfect place for her christening party.'

Bill looked thoughtful, then he nodded. 'Very well then. We'll hold our celebration here. Of course, the house isn't all that big.' He said this as if it might come as news to her.

'Don't be daft. You're talking as if we're going to invite the whole neighbourhood. This house is plenty big enough. It's only going to be family.'

Did Bill have a longer guest list in mind? Who else could he possibly want to invite? Thank goodness Dunbar's was already booked. A small family gathering was much more up Kitty's street.

* * *

Helped by Mam and Naomi, Kitty settled happily into a routine with Abigail. May had brought warm days and Kitty loved taking her little girl out for walks in the pram, a stately coach-built Silver Cross, with larger wheels at the front and a hood that now had a couple of cracks in the folds because of its great age.

'It's not what I envisioned for our daughter,' Bill had said when Mam had pushed it round to their house after Abigail came home.

Mam had chuckled. 'If you envisioned anything at all by way of a pram, Bill Dunbar, you're the first man that ever did. I'll have you know that this here baby carriage has ferried umpteen kiddies about in its time, including my three grandsons. Aye, and it's seen war service an' all. Me and Mrs Welbeck used to work in the soup kitchen during the Great War. We filled cans with soup and took them round to the housebound. Darned heavy they were too, when the pram was full. It took both of us to push it.' More chuckles. 'I'm surprised Silver Cross's famous suspension didn't come to grief.'

Grasping the handle, Bill jiggled the pram as if testing the suspension.

'Don't fret, lad,' said Mam. 'That baby carriage is good for a long time yet.' Her blue eyes twinkled. 'It'll certainly see you and our Kitty through a couple more kiddies.'

'*Mam*,' Kitty had exclaimed.

But Bill had taken the remark in good part. 'I'm not

surprised your mother wants us to have more, now that she's seen what a little angel Abigail is.'

Kitty had rolled her eyes and shaken her head at Mam, but the truth was she was thrilled to have a husband who took such an interest in their baby. Naomi always swore that Derek hadn't looked twice at any of the boys until they were old enough to kick a ball in the park.

Anyway, the pram had stayed and Kitty was glad of it, and not just because it could carry the shopping as well as the baby. It was bad enough having a fairy-tale cradle – wonderful, of course, but also discomforting – without having to push a swanky new pram through the streets. That was probably what Bill had had in mind.

Today, after a morning of shopping and housework, Kitty laid Abigail in the pram and manoeuvred it outside to go to the park. It felt important to walk Abigail among the flowerbeds, to surround her with pretty things. There had been a shower earlier and the grass smelled clean and damp, its aroma mingling with the rich scent of freshly dug-over soil.

Kitty enjoyed the drifts of bright blue forget-me-nots, the dainty white flowers of honesty that almost shimmered in the sunlight, and the graceful hostas, their large leaves edged with gold. Around the edges of the park, creamy-coloured candles of flowers stood erect on the branches of the horse chestnut trees. Kitty had taught her nephews how to play conkers. One day she would teach Abigail. Some folk thought conkers was a boys' game, but Kitty thought it should be for whoever wanted to play it. She smiled to herself. Never mind conkers. She had enough to think about with planning Abigail's christening party.

Abigail chose that moment to screw up her face in the fierce concentration that meant she was filling her nappy. Kitty headed for home. She put on a little spurt as she rounded the final corner. A man stood outside their house. She didn't recognise him. He looked smart but as she drew closer, Kitty spied the faint sheen on his suit that suggested several years of wear. His shoes were polished but there were unmistakable creases in the leather that spoke of age. Kitty might not recognise him personally but she knew his type. She came from a similar background, where you looked after what you had and made the best of it through proper attention and immediate repairs.

'Can I help you?' she asked, coming to a halt.

The man raised his trilby to her, showing oiled-back hair that was already thinning, even though he couldn't be much over thirty.

'Have I the pleasure of addressing Mrs William Dunbar?'

Have I the pleasure, indeed! She would make a joke of that when she told Bill later. She would probably put on a posh voice, even though this fellow's accent was ordinary.

'Permit me to introduce myself. Frank Lever from Flittick & Green's.'

Kitty smiled politely, though at the same time she felt puzzled. Flittick & Green's was one of the department stores in town.

Mr Lever executed a sort of dance-step that brought him to the side of the pram. 'And this must be the lucky recipient of the cradle your husband purchased from us.'

'Oh, that's where it came from, is it?' said Kitty. 'I didn't know. My husband bought it as a surprise.'

'A very pleasing one, I hope?'

'Yes, thank you. What can I do for you, Mr Lever? Is there a problem?' The only problem as far as Kitty was concerned was that Mr Lever might get a whiff of Abigail's nappy.

'No, not at all, Mrs Dunbar. I wonder if I could prevail upon you to pass on this statement of account to your husband, please.' Mr Lever produced an envelope. 'It's a replacement copy. When Mr Dunbar was last in our store, my fountain pen splattered ink all over the original and I had no more account sheets on my pad.'

Kitty nodded. Wasn't he ever going to shut up?

'I asked Mr Dunbar if he could possibly wait while I sent the boy to fetch another one from the storeroom, but he was in a hurry so I promised to deliver the perfect copy myself, since it was my fault that the original was spoiled.' Mr Lever leaned forward as if about to impart a confidence. 'They've let me go early today because I've got raging toothache, so I thought I'd drop this off on my way to the dentist.'

'I see,' Kitty answered briskly. She wanted to get Abigail indoors. 'I'll pass it on to my husband.'

'Thanks most awfully. I do hope Mr Dunbar and your good self will patronise Flittick & Green's again soon.'

With another tip of the trilby, he was on his way.

'Fine-looking man,' remarked Mrs Bulstrode, appearing casually at Kitty's side. 'What did he want?'

'Nothing,' Kitty said breezily. 'Just leaving a message, that's all.'

The last thing she wanted was to stir up interest in the cradle all over again. As much as she loved and appreciated it, it made her feel she must be the talk of the wash house.

Indoors, she took off her jacket and hat and popped Mr Lever's envelope on the mantelpiece. Then she changed Abigail, holding her breath as she dropped the stinky linen into the nappy-bucket and added boiling water.

Soon it was time for Abigail's next feed and Kitty settled in her chair. Afterwards she winded the baby, laughingly praising her for the little splat that landed on the cloth Kitty had strategically placed on her shoulder. Then she sang her daughter to sleep before placing her gently in her cradle and creeping out of the room.

Downstairs, she made herself a cup of tea to sip while she got on with her knitting. She put the cup and saucer on the table beside her chair and was about to sit down when the envelope caught her eye. It wasn't sealed. The flap was simply tucked in. It wasn't addressed to her, but, well, she would like to know how much the cradle had cost. She'd asked Bill but he'd told her not to worry about it.

'Didn't anyone ever tell you it's rude to ask what gifts cost?' he'd asked in a jokey voice.

But the cradle wasn't a gift, was it? Not really. You couldn't call it that when the father provided something for the baby and the mother wanted to know the price.

Even so, she shouldn't look. She shouldn't open something addressed to Bill. Oh, who was she trying to kid? Of course she was going to look. It wasn't as though she would have to steam the envelope open and paste it down again. That really would be unacceptable.

With gentle fingers, she eased out the flap and removed the piece of high-quality paper from within. It was folded in half. She unfolded it – frowned – and then gasped.

'Ohmygoodness,' she whispered as if it was one word. 'Ohmygoodness, ohmygoodness.'

How could he—?

She'd had no idea—

How *could* he—?

Ohmygoodness, ohmygoodness.

* * *

Kitty spent the rest of the afternoon in a state of agitation. She would have to have a baby every year for the next fifteen years to make the expense of the fairy-tale cradle worthwhile. She had assumed Bill had plundered his savings, but no, he hadn't paid for the cradle outright. He'd bought it on the never. Oh, the shame. Kitty had been brought up to believe that debt was shameful. Mam had never once asked for tick at the corner shop.

'You can always hold your head high if you don't owe anything,' she maintained. 'No matter how hard up you are, you must never spend what you haven't got. Being hard up is a worry, but being in debt is worse. It's a trap.'

And Bill was in debt. Call it buying on the never-never. Call it hire purchase. Call it what you flaming well liked. It was debt, plain and simple.

Mr Lever's words fell into place now. Kitty hadn't paid that much attention at the time. The state of Abigail's nappy had seemed far more compelling. But now she recalled the words 'statement of account'. Not 'the bill' or 'the receipt'. The statement of account.

Call it what you wanted. Make it sound as posh as you liked. It was still buying on the never.

Kitty went cold inside. She sucked in a deep breath to steady herself, trying to make this feel less of a catastrophe. After all, plenty of folk had domestic debts. It wasn't as though Bill had gambled the money away or poured it down his neck in the George and Dragon. He was a respectable man with a responsible job. Just look at how he had risen through the ranks at Congreve's Shipping, from messenger boy to office boy to trainee clerk to junior clerk to clerk, and all by the age of thirty, and that was despite being absent for four years to fight for king and country. The position of senior clerk beckoned, though he would have to wait a few years yet for that.

Kitty loved Bill. He was the father of her child. That made her think again of the cradle, the blasted fairy-tale cradle with its fancy basketwork, its ruffles and bows. Yes, it was beautiful and the quality was undoubtedly top-notch, but even so, talk about costly! And it wasn't as though Abigail was going to sleep in it for more than a few months at best.

Kitty thought of Bill's other extravagances – how insignificant they seemed now. Had she really fretted over the probable cost of the figurine on the mantelpiece? That was small fry compared to this. The way Bill had brought her and Abigail home from the hospital by taxi instead of on the tram or the bus had felt unnecessary and wasteful, but also generous, exciting and loving... and understandable.

Had she really whispered her concern to Naomi last autumn when Bill proudly produced a brand-new photograph frame for their wedding picture?

'It feels... excessive,' she had confided to her sister. 'You can get perfectly nice frames second-hand.'

'You can,' Naomi had answered, 'but he's bought new because your wedding photograph is special.'

Back then, Naomi had wanted to offer comfort, but had she secretly harboured the same thought as Kitty? That it was the photograph that mattered, not the quality of the frame around it?

Then there was the picnic hamper, complete with crockery, cutlery and provisions boxes with lids.

'A picnic hamper?' Naomi had exclaimed. 'What's wrong with your wicker basket?'

'He says he wants me to have the very best,' Kitty had told

her. She felt guilty for spilling the beans but she'd badly needed to say something.

Naomi, bless her, had overcome her shock sufficiently to offer support. 'It's wonderful that he wants to spoil you, Kitty. Nobody can fault him for that. What does he earn? As a commercial shipping clerk, he gets – what? I don't suppose it's as much as four pounds a week.'

'Three pounds ten shillings,' said Kitty.

'Which is a reasonable sum, but only if you live within your means,' said Naomi.

'You sounded just like Mam then,' said Kitty. 'You won't tell her, will you?'

'I won't breathe a word to anybody, not even Derek,' Naomi promised. 'It's going to be up to you, Kitty. You have to dissuade Bill from this sort of thing. A picnic hamper! I ask you!'

Suddenly they were both laughing like drains. Kitty felt better afterwards, but it didn't solve the problem. She decided to have a go at admiring the items for sale in the window of the second-hand shop and remarking to Bill on how good they looked, just to make her point. She'd felt rather self-conscious when she did it, but afterwards her spirits had lifted and she'd even had a little laugh about it when she was alone.

But she hadn't felt like laughing when the sherry decanter had appeared.

'Isn't it a beauty?' Bill had asked.

'Yes, but...' Kitty had been puzzled.

'But what?'

'I don't recall it being this shape.'

'Oh, this isn't the one from the second-hand place,' Bill said airily. 'This is new. How could you think otherwise? Only the best for Mrs William Dunbar.'

So much for admiring second-hand goods.

Now Kitty returned to the mantelpiece. When she had first set eyes on the statement of account and understood what it was, she'd re-folded it and slid it back into the envelope with fumbling fingers that had lost their feeling.

Once more she took it out. She'd little more than glanced over it the first time. Now she made herself read it properly.

Ohmygoodness, ohmygoodness.

The sum at the foot of the statement wasn't the price of the cradle. Did it make it better or worse to know that the cradle wasn't as violently expensive as she had first assumed? The statement contained a three-piece suit as well, with two shirts, a tie and two collars; also a pair of studs. That was Bill's wedding suit, which he now wore for work.

But they'd got wed last September, and now it was May, so why was he still forking out for the suit? Surely he should have paid it off by now? Kitty frowned over the statement. It didn't make sense. It was a while before the truth penetrated her mind. The statement made perfect sense – once she stopped trying to deny what it was telling her.

Bill had paid off very little towards the suit. Some months he'd paid back nothing at all, just the interest on the credit.

And now he'd purchased the cradle as well, adding it to his account. Panic speared Kitty. Could they return the cradle? No, it was way too late for that. They'd have to keep it and pay for it.

And if Bill's payments towards his suit were anything to go by, little Abigail would have outgrown her fairy-tale cradle long before it had been paid for.

4

Kitty was perched on the edge of her armchair when the front door opened. She shot to her feet, then sank down again. The urge to dash out of the parlour and confront Bill in the hallway was strong, but she had to do this calmly.

The door opened and Bill appeared, handsome as ever in the suit he hadn't paid for.

'Well!' he said jovially. 'My girls didn't come to meet me at the corner today. Is Abigail all right?'

'She's fine.' Kitty felt wrong-footed. How was she meant to get from Abigail's health to Bill's debts?

'And are you all right?' he asked. 'My slippers weren't by the front door.'

Kitty blinked. 'They're... they must be upstairs.'

'I'll go up and change. Don't worry. I shan't disturb Abigail. What's for tea?'

'Never mind tea. There's something we need to talk about.'

'Can't it wait?' Bill asked. 'I've had a long day.'

Kitty plucked the envelope from the mantelpiece. 'This came for you from Flittick & Green's. It was delivered by hand.'

'Thanks.' Bill took it from her and put it in his pocket.

'I opened it,' Kitty said quickly. Her heart thumped.

What had she expected? A slumping of the broad shoulders? A telltale flush? But Bill displayed no sign whatsoever of guilt. On the contrary, it was annoyance that flickered in his eyes.

'You shouldn't open letters that come for me,' he said.

'I know, but it wasn't sealed – and I wanted to see what the cradle cost.'

'You opened my post.'

'I'm sorry about that,' said Kitty, 'but that's not the point just now.'

'I would say it's exactly the point.'

Kitty pressed on. 'What matters is... Oh, Bill, it's a statement of account. It's things you've bought and are paying off.'

'What's wrong with that?' he asked.

For a moment she was too taken aback to reply. 'If you want something, you should save up for it, not get it on tick.'

'It isn't tick. Don't be so old-fashioned. It's a proper account with a respected shopping emporium.'

'It's a *debt*,' Kitty said, desperate for him to understand.

'It's a responsible way of buying things,' Bill replied, 'and the fact that Westall's were happy to let me purchase on account shows the kind of man I am. They don't hand out accounts to any old Tom, Dick or Harry. Having an account is the way people of substance shop.'

'Wait a minute,' Kitty put in. 'This is from Flittick & Green's. You just said Westall's.'

'No, I didn't.'

'Yes, you did. I heard you.'

Bill shrugged. 'Slip of the tongue.'

A New Home at the Wartime Hotel 35

Kitty's flesh suddenly felt clammy. 'Have you got an account at Westall's as well? Please, Bill, have you?'

'No,' he said. 'Listen, Kitty. Your job is to look after the house and the baby and manage the housekeeping. Do I tell you how to do that? No, I don't. My job is to provide for my wife and family. I consider I do it jolly well and I don't appreciate your criticism. I wouldn't have been allowed to have credit if there had been any question of my ability to pay for what I bought.'

'But you haven't paid,' Kitty said. 'Sometimes all you do is pay the interest.'

Bill scowled. 'I manage my money as I see fit. If that means spreading out the credit, then that's what I'll do – and I don't require permission from you.'

Kitty stared at him. She didn't know what to say that would get through to him. How could he possibly see the statement of account as anything other than a debt? A chill hit her right in the centre of her being as shock set in. They had different ideas about money. Not just different but opposing. She'd never seen it that way before. Maybe she should have. The picnic hamper and the decanter should have told her.

But she knew now. Oh, she knew now.

She knew something else too. Bill had lied to her about not having an account at Westall's. It was another blow on top of the first.

But she wasn't going to get any further by criticising, as Bill had called it. Pinning on a smile, she tried again.

'You're a good provider, Bill. There's no question about that. I know how lucky I am to be married to a man who wants to give me the best of everything.'

'I'm glad to hear you say so.' Bill's tone was stiff. 'I was beginning to wonder.'

'You've got a generous heart,' Kitty went on, 'but I don't want you to feel you have to spoil me and Abigail like this. We don't need you to spend a fortune on us. Can't we... I mean, can't you stop buying brand new?'

'Brand new is best,' said Bill.

'Something given with love is best,' answered Kitty.

'That goes without saying.'

Was he starting to come round? Kitty felt a surge of hope.

'Bill, it worries me to think of what is owed. Paying back over time means the interest adds up and you end up forking out more than the thing was worth in the first place.'

'Since when did you become a wizard of finance?'

'Can't we please pay it off in full? I know it'll take time. I thought that maybe I could get a job, maybe in a shop—'

'I'm not having my wife going out to work,' Bill declared.

'Only until the statement is paid off.' Kitty couldn't give up now. 'Please, Bill. Then we could start again from fresh with no debts hanging over us. That would mean the world to me.'

'It's your husband and child that should mean the world to you,' said Bill.

'And you do!' Kitty exclaimed. 'How could you suggest otherwise? You and Abigail are my world and I want everything to be perfect for you – for us. Paying off the debt, and then saving up for what we need: that's what I want. And I'm offering to help make it happen by earning money myself. I'm not expecting you to pay the money back.'

'I've already said,' Bill replied stonily. 'My wife is not going out to work. That's all there is to it. How could you even suggest it?' His lips twisted in disgust. 'It would look like I can't afford to keep my own family. I'm not having that. It would bring shame on me – *you* would bring shame on me. You stand there, looking all righteous, and you want to bring shame on your husband.' He held up a hand when she would have spoken.

'Not flaming likely, Kitty. And that's my last word on the subject.'

* * *

That evening and the following morning, Kitty made an effort to appear as normal, though she knew that the moment she had finished waving Bill off on his way to work, she would start turning the house upside down in search of the statements of account from Westall's that she was positive were here somewhere. A voice in her head asked what good it would do to find them, but if she did find them, then at least she would know how bad the situation really was. And how was that going to help her, if she wasn't permitted to do anything about it? Maybe it wouldn't help, but at least she'd know.

When Bill was ready to leave, the last thing Kitty did every morning before he put on his bowler was brush his jacket. The clothes brush had been among their wedding presents, so at least she needn't expect to find it on a statement of account. Standing behind Bill, she brushed first his shoulders and then the back of the jacket. After that she moved around, brushing his right sleeve and the right-front followed by the left-front. He didn't turn in a circle. It was her job to walk around him. Funny: she'd never realised that before.

As she brushed the left-front with swift strokes, the brush passed over a slight bulge in the pocket. Kitty didn't pause even for a second, nor did she lift her eyes. She just brushed Bill's left sleeve.

But she knew – she *knew* – that there was nothing to be gained by looking for the Westall's statements, because Bill was taking them to the office with him.

Kitty placed the clothes brush on the shelf beside the coat

pegs and opened the front door. She looked back with the usual smile as Bill positioned his bowler. She even raised her face for his kiss. Same as normal. Same as every other day.

She stepped aside for him to go past, then followed him outside to watch him walk up the road. At the corner he turned to wave and she waved back. Then he was gone and her heart thumped as she went indoors. She shut the door and leaned against it, needing the support as the tension that had held her upright evaporated from her muscles.

'Bugger that for a game of dominoes.'

Dear Grandpa had uttered those very words in a tone of exasperation years ago when she was a little girl. Nana and Mam had both exclaimed in horror and Mam had darted across the parlour and clapped her hands over Kitty's ears, as if she could cross the room faster than that shocking word 'bugger' could. For years afterwards, Kitty had believed that 'Bugger that for a game of dominoes' was the worst thing that anybody could say.

Bugger that for a game of dominoes.

She did everything as normal. She might feel like climbing up the ladder to the attic and out of the skylight onto the roof and screaming, but she didn't. She couldn't do what she intended until later. For now, she had her routine.

She cleared away the breakfast and swept up the crumbs; made the bed and tidied the bedroom; then took the china bowl from the washstand and emptied it into the bucket, which she carried downstairs and emptied down the drain outside the kitchen door. Returning to the bedroom, she fetched the bowl and matching ewer, bringing them downstairs to be rinsed. After that it was time to sweep the hallway, stairs and landing. Then, this being Friday, she ought to give the parlour its weekly turning out, which meant shifting all the furniture and lifting the rugs to sweep underneath. Friday was also her morning for cleaning all the windows on the inside with vinegar water and buffing up the glass with screwed-up newspaper, but, as sure as eggs were eggs, she wasn't going to go anywhere carrying the faint whiff of vinegar on her hands.

Not today.

It would soon be time for Abigail's next feed. After that Kitty would change her and have a cuddle before taking her round to Mam's. She hadn't been apart from her daughter before this, but she couldn't take Abigail with her on this errand. She wanted her precious child to be kept well away from such unpleasantness.

* * *

The clock high up on the outside wall of Congreve's warehouse, where Bill was a clerk, was about to strike the half hour when Kitty arrived at the gates. She wasn't sure what to do, where to go, but she couldn't afford to be bashful. There was a booth beside the gate, with a man inside it. Bill had mentioned him on various occasions and Kitty knew he was Mr Exham. He had apparently once been very clever and capable but he had left his nerves behind in Flanders and manning the booth was all he was good for these days. He was lucky to have a job.

Inside the gates was a wide cobbled yard with tall buildings on three sides. Over on the other side of the building facing her must be the River Irwell.

On the far side of the yard, a couple of women hovered outside a closed door. One woman was older, her thin shoulders rounded beneath her shawl. Did she come here every week? Was that what had given her the stoop? The shame, the worry? The other woman was younger, in a coat and hat. Kitty knew the type: desperately trying not to look shabby, wanting to maintain appearances, fooling nobody.

As the clock finished striking the half, the two women shifted position, apparently ready for something. More women entered through the gates, passing Kitty, and headed across the yard. Kitty drew in a breath and followed. This was what she had come for. A line had formed along the wall. As Kitty peeled off to join the end, the door opened at the front.

Standing at the end of the queue, Kitty glanced up at the banks of overlooking windows. Was Bill in one of those offices? What if he looked out and saw her, saw his wife in the line of shame?

If anybody had suggested to her at any point since she and Bill had started courting that one day she would be queuing up to beg for some of her husband's wages before his weekly pay packet was sealed, she would have had a job to know whether to laugh out loud or feel deeply offended.

Yet here she was now. The queue shuffled forwards. The woman in front of Kitty bobbed in through the door and a minute later emerged, stuffing something into her pocket. Each woman who had come out had shut the door behind her, and the next woman had knocked before entering. Kitty knocked and went inside, finding a small, dark office, if you could call it that when it was big enough for nothing more than a tall cupboard and a desk of the variety the teachers had had at school, set on tall legs, with a sloping front.

Oh crikey. Kitty recognised the fellow sitting at the desk. Would he remember her too?

'Good morning.' She spoke in her clearest voice. 'I'd like as much of my husband's wages as you can give me. William Dunbar. Please,' she added.

The clerk frowned. 'I dunno about that. You're not one of the reg'lars. Can you prove who you are?'

'Come off it, Joe McManus. You know fine well who I am. You were in the class above me at St Cuthbert's. My mam fed you bread and dripping often enough when your mam was laid low.' Drunk out of her brain, more like.

'Aye, I know that, but—'

'But nothing,' said Kitty. 'Can I have half Bill's money or can't I? Or preferably more than half.'

'You can't have more than half—'

'But I can have half.' She didn't make a question out of it. 'Good. Where do I sign?'

* * *

Should she walk to the corner with Abigail to meet Bill coming home or, now that he had received his depleted wage packet, would that look like an act of defiance? But if she didn't go to meet him, and the neighbours noticed – and they noticed everything – then there might be whispers that the Dunbars had fallen out. Bill wouldn't like that and neither would she.

Seeing raindrops on the window, Kitty went to look out. A downpour would let her off the hook, but it was only a shower and was soon over.

She went up to the corner as usual and engineered Abigail's little wave. Then she walked home by Bill's side. He tipped his bowler to a couple of housewives they passed. To anybody else, they must look like a happy little family.

Once they were indoors, it was different. Kitty wasn't one to use her baby as a shield to ward off unpleasantness. She took Abigail straight upstairs and settled her in the cradle. Abigail was surprised and not pleased.

'Sorry, little one.' Kitty brushed the baby's smooth pink cheek with her finger. 'I have to sort something out with your father.'

Until now she had called herself 'Mummy' when she spoke to her daughter. 'Mummy's taking you to the grocer's now... Mummy will rock you to sleep.' But not any more. From now on she had to be more than Abigail's mummy and Bill's wife. She had to find new inner strength, a fresh identity. That word 'I' was part of it.

Downstairs, Bill was waiting for her. The moment she opened the parlour door, he started on at her, not even waiting for her to get inside the room.

'You made a holy show of me at the office. McManus couldn't wait to spread the word about you turning up.'

'I wanted—'

'Do you know the type of females that join the line of shame every Friday? The wives of the drunks, that's who. The wives of men who, at clocking-off time, head straight down the pub. Then there are the wives whose only hope of getting their hands on any money at all is to get it before it can go into their husbands' pay packets, because their husbands keep every last penny that they can for themselves and begrudge everything they have to dole out. And today you joined the line and you made me look like one of those men. Proud of yourself, are you?'

'I did what needed doing,' Kitty flared. 'You're the one who's brought debt on this house—'

'Give me strength!' Bill exclaimed. 'I've told you before to leave the finances to me. I know what I'm doing.'

'Oh aye? Still forking out for your suit and your collars eight months after you bought them: that's you knowing what you're doing, is it? Paying the interest and nowt else; that's high finance, is it?'

'Don't take that tone with me. I'm your husband and I'm entitled to your respect.'

'And I'm your wife,' cried Kitty, emotion rising. 'You're supposed to take care of me, not run up debts and hide them from me.'

'And you're not supposed to go poking your nose into my private business.'

Kitty hauled her temper back under control. 'Bill, I only—'

'What did you do with the money?' he demanded. 'Aside from make a monkey out of me, of course.'

'I got thirty-five shillings – half your wages. One pound five of it is up there.' She nodded at the mantelpiece. 'I haven't forgotten what things cost or what we need for the rent and the rates and the insurance. I reckoned I could afford – *we* could afford to pay off ten bob on the debts.'

'Ten shillings!' Bill exclaimed. 'Ten whole shillings – gone, just like that.'

'It's money you *owe*,' Kitty insisted.

'I'd pay it back in my own good time.'

'And how much interest would you pay on top? I've reduced the debts by ten shillings today.'

'I've a good mind to go round to Flittick & Green's and say you made a mistake and ask for it back.'

'Bill, *no*,' Kitty begged.

'I'm not having you do this to me.'

'It's already done. I paid off five bob at Flittick & Green's. Oh yes, and you know that account you *don't* have at Westall's? I paid off five bob there too. You lied to me, Bill. You stood there in that very spot this time yesterday and swore you weren't in hock to Westall's.'

'You—' Bill broke off. He jutted out his chin and jerked it to one side, his mouth turning down at the edges. 'You've had your fun and games and it won't happen again. D'you hear me?'

'It won't need to happen again,' Kitty said quietly. 'I'll set aside money each week out of the housekeeping.' She chewed the inside of her cheek. 'About me turning up at the warehouse today. I'm sorry it had to come to that. I'm sorry if it made you look bad in front of your colleagues.'

To her astonishment, Bill thrust out his chest and tilted his head with a smirk.

'I told everyone you had my permission to fetch the money. There's Abigail's christening party to sort out, isn't there?'

'We're having it here in our house,' said Kitty, baffled by this change of direction.

'No, we aren't,' Bill replied smoothly. 'We're holding it at the Grove Hotel. We're hiring a room, having the catering done. They're going to bake a special cake with sugar roses on it. I asked for golden roses to match the christening gown. I told everyone in the office that the Grove wanted the deposit and the quickest thing was for you to take the money round in person.'

Dread rolled in Kitty's stomach. 'Please tell me you said all that just to save face. Please say it isn't really happening.'

'Of course it's happening,' said Bill. 'I called at the Grove after I left the office. It's all arranged. Our little girl is going to have a splendid christening party – and it's all thanks to you.'

5

THIRTEEN YEARS LATER: JANUARY 1941

As Kitty set off with her wicker shopping basket over one arm and her gas-mask box dangling from her other shoulder, the brisk morning breeze carried the distinct smells of soot, smoke and cordite from last night's air raids. There had been several, the warning sirens and the all-clear sounding alternately from late in the evening right through until the early hours. Kitty had bundled Abbie down to the Anderson shelter in the back garden at the sound of the first warning, then woken her a couple of hours later and encouraged her to climb out of her narrow bunk to return to the house, only to shepherd her back to the shelter less than an hour later.

After that they had stayed in the Anderson, not because Kitty possessed a crystal ball that told her it wouldn't be worth going back indoors, but simply because Abbie was fast asleep and she couldn't bear to disturb her yet again. Kitty had barely snatched any sleep herself. As was normal for her when they spent the night in the shelter, she lay awake in the bottom bunk, worrying as to the wisdom of allowing her precious daughter to have the top bunk. Shouldn't she have insisted upon taking the top? That way, if the worst happened and an incendiary came crashing through the galvanised corrugated steel roof, it might kill Kitty outright but Abbie, below, might have a chance. Sometimes Kitty felt like the worst mother in the world for letting Abbie sleep up top. On the other hand, she acknowledged with a private smile, Abbie would consider her the worst mother in the world if she hadn't.

Kitty came to the heap of rubble on the corner, which up until just days ago had been the Rigbys' house. Among the shattered bricks, broken roof tiles, shards of glass and slivers of wood, some piano keys were scattered. Kitty noticed them each time she went by. Most of the heap, though, seemed to be made up of bits and pieces so small that you couldn't tell what they had started off as.

'They're smithereens,' Abbie had said knowledgeably. 'You know, as in "blown to smithereens". I never really understood what smithereens were before I saw my first bombed-out house.'

That had been another moment when Kitty had felt like the worst mother in the world. But if she was, then plenty of others were too. It was the fault of that damn phoney war. When war had been declared, Abbie, along with thousands upon thousands of children in cities and towns all over the country, had been evacuated to the safety of the countryside. The only thing that had stopped Kitty's heart from cracking straight down the middle had been the thought of keeping Abbie safe from the bombs that everyone had expected to start falling at any moment.

But they hadn't fallen. All through that first autumn, winter and springtime of the war, they hadn't fallen. Kitty and Bill had been only too glad to fetch Abbie home. Many other parents did the same, some as early as straight after that first Christmas.

The bombings had started in the summer of 1940 and hadn't stopped since. For Manchester and Salford, the worst had come just a few short weeks ago. During the two nights before Christmas, the Luftwaffe inflicted the two heaviest raids the two neighbouring cities had endured. So many fires had burned, with such intensity they had been visible from more than twenty miles away. What had made it even worse was that at the end of the second raid, when the Luftwaffe had departed, strong winds had got up, which had sent the fires in new directions, increasing the danger and destruction.

Kitty shut her eyes for a moment against the memory of the guilt and worry of having Abbie at home, but she couldn't bear the thought of sending her away again, any more than Bill could. Kitty hated Jerry for giving her innocent daughter firsthand knowledge of war. Why, only yesterday the child had explained to her astonished parents how to tell the difference between an incendiary and a high explosive just by looking at the curtains.

'When incendiaries land, the curtains don't move, but when there's an HE, the windows rattle and the curtains waft inwards.'

Kitty and Bill had stared at her.

Then Bill said, 'If incendiaries and HEs are raining down, I sincerely hope you'll be inside the Anderson shelter and not in any position to see what the curtains are or aren't doing.'

'Oh, *Daddy*.' Although Abbie put on a groan, her eyes held that special sparkle. She adored Bill and he adored her.

Thinking of that now, Kitty acknowledged that there were good moments even in the darkest times.

Take Christmas Eve. Late on Christmas Eve, after two solid nights of what was now being called 'the Christmas Blitz', Kitty had been one of many hundreds of volunteers in and around Manchester who had worked all through the night in order to ensure there would be Christmas dinners for those who had lost their homes in the bombing. Kitty had taken Abbie with her to work in the kitchen of the local school.

'This is to make something good come out of the blitz, isn't it, Mummy?' Abbie had asked.

Her daughter's simple goodness had brought a lump the size of a golf ball to Kitty's throat.

'Yes,' she'd managed to say. 'All those people need help and we're going to help them.'

She had wanted Abbie to be a part of this. It was something she would remember long after she'd grown up, something she would look back on for the rest of her life, the occasion when, after two terrible nights of destruction, the ordinary folk of Manchester had got together to make festive meals for those who had lost their homes.

Kitty had much preferred Abbie to focus on that than on the long lists of fatalities, both the identified and the unidentified, and those seriously injured in hospital, though it was impossible for anyone to be unaware of the scale of what had taken place.

Now, Kitty realised she had come to a standstill beside the remains of the Rigbys' house.

'Morning, Mrs Dunbar.' Mrs Bulstrode appeared by her side. She too looked at the rubble. 'Tragic, isn't it? Difficult to tear your eyes away.'

Heat rose in Kitty's cheeks. Had she really been so lost in thought that she had stood here gawping?

'The Rigbys are all safe and well,' she said. 'That's what counts.'

'Oh aye,' Mrs Bulstrode agreed. 'They've moved in with Mrs Rigby's sister over in Fallowfield.'

'What, all of them?' Kitty asked. The Rigbys had five youngsters still at school.

'It'll be a squeeze,' said Mrs Bulstrode, 'and heaven alone knows how long they'll be there. Certainly until the end of the war, and probably for some time after that an' all.'

'It makes you grateful your own house is still standing.' A tiny shiver rippled through Kitty. If that bomb had fallen just a hundred yards in the other direction...

The two of them walked to the shops together. Mrs Bulstrode peeled off to join the queue outside the fishmonger's while Kitty made for the butcher's, where two headscarfed women at the end of the queue were talking about the imminent reduction in the meat ration.

'Instead of being allowed one and tenpence worth a week, it's going to be one and six.'

Kitty tagged on behind them. She didn't know them but the three of them exchanged good mornings and the two friends automatically included Kitty in their chat. It was like that in queues. Apart from the occasional grump, folk were friendly. Well, you needed to be, didn't you? It made the time pass quicker and goodness knew, they all spent considerable portions of their days queuing up.

Mrs Harding and Mrs Finley from Kitty's road also joined the queue, immediately inserting themselves into the conversation, which quickly turned to the Christmas Blitz.

'It's difficult to believe it happened only last week,' said Mrs Harding. She was a skinny woman whose tobacco-stained teeth always reminded Kitty to take particular care of her own oral hygiene. 'So much has happened since.'

'Everyone has mucked in with the clearing-up,' agreed rosy-cheeked Mrs Finley. 'So much damage.'

'The Free Trade Hall has gone,' said one of the housewives

who had been here when Kitty arrived. Her coat had seen better days and she had sewn corduroy patches over the elbows. She'd also added a narrow piece of the same corduroy to the edge of the collar, which made the elbow patches look less of a mend and more of a fashion detail. What a good idea. Kitty stored it away for future reference.

'The Free Trade Hall?' said Mrs Harding. 'That's a rotten shame. I went there once for a school speech day.'

'You never went to a posh school that had speech days, Gladys Harding,' Mrs Finley challenged her at once.

'Not me, you idiot,' Mrs Harding said good-naturedly. 'It was our Irma's boy. He passed the eleven-plus exam and Irma and her husband scraped together every penny they could to send him to grammar school.'

'It's summat special being able to send a child to grammar school,' said the woman with the elbow patches.

'It kept 'em poor for years,' Mrs Harding replied. 'They make you sign a form, you know, to promise you'll keep your kid there until they're fifteen. If you try to take 'em out at fourteen, you get fined.'

'How did we get started on grammar schools?' asked the friend of the woman with the elbow patches. She had keen blue eyes and a bit of an overbite. 'Oh aye: the Free Trade Hall.'

Kitty hesitated before saying, 'I don't want to sound ghoulish, but my sister and I went into town at the end of last week. We wanted to see for ourselves what's become of the city centre. There had been such stories.' She glanced at her listeners, willing them to understand.

'It's all right, love,' said the woman with the elbow patches. 'It's a natural thing to do, not morbid at all. Manchester's where you belong and you wanted to know what's happened to it.'

'That's it exactly.' Gratitude at not being condemned added emotion to Kitty's voice.

'What was it like?' asked Mrs Finley and all four women leaned closer to Kitty, not being nosy parkers, just needing to know, the same way Kitty and Naomi had needed to know.

Oh my, what a morning that had been.

'I gather the buses can't get into town because of all the damage,' said Mrs Harding, 'and everyone gets chucked off along Oxford Road.'

Kitty nodded. 'We had to be careful where we put our feet because of all the debris and glass everywhere. All those shops and offices with their windows blown out or their fronts blown off. Vast heaps of rubble that used to be enormous buildings; you know the size of some of those places in town.'

'It said in the *Evening News* that some of the worst fires were around Piccadilly,' said Mrs Finley.

The keen-eyed woman nodded. 'All those textile warehouses. They'll have gone up like fireworks.'

'We walked down that way,' said Kitty, 'but we didn't get very far. An ARP warden stopped us, said it wasn't safe. Even though it looked like the fires were out, some of the ruins were still smouldering inside. He said they were going to blow up some of the buildings that were still standing, to create fire breaks, just in case.'

'If I could get my hands on that Herr Hitler...' said the lady with the elbow patches.

'But there is some good news,' Kitty said. 'The Town Hall is still there and so are Central Library and the Midland Hotel.'

'Aye, and you know why that is, don't you? The Midland, I mean,' said Mrs Finley. 'Rumour has it that Adolf wants to use the Midland as his Manchester headquarters after the war.'

'He won't win,' Kitty replied immediately.

'Of course he won't,' Mrs Harding agreed. 'The Christmas Blitz has made us all the more determined about that.'

'Speaking of hotels,' said Mrs Finley, and Kitty winced inwardly, 'did you go and see Dunbar's? Is it all right?'

'There was no need to.' Kitty kept her tone as light as she could. 'My husband had already been, and it survived intact, thanks for asking. It's just far enough away from the city centre to have escaped unscathed.'

'That's good,' said Mrs Finley.

Kitty was about to move the conversation along but she wasn't quick enough. The keen-eyed woman got in first.

'Dunbar's? I've heard of that. What's it to you?'

Mrs Finley instantly stuck her oar in. 'This is Mrs Dunbar and her husband is the heir.'

'Really?' the lady with the elbow patches asked in a tone of great interest.

Once again Kitty wasn't fast enough.

'Oh aye,' said Mrs Harding. 'The real heir copped it early on in the war.'

Mrs Elbow Patches gave Kitty a look of sympathy. 'I'm sorry to hear that.'

'It wasn't what you're thinking,' Kitty felt obliged to explain. 'My husband's cousin didn't fall in combat. He was run over in the blackout when it was new and before we all got used to it. It came as a dreadful shock.'

'You don't think of folk dying in road accidents in wartime,' said Mrs Finley. 'You think of bombs falling and buildings collapsing or Jerry flying low and strafing the ground.'

'The last thing you think of,' added Mrs Harding, 'is stupid drivers going too fast when they can't see a blessed thing in the pitch dark.'

That was quite enough of that topic. Kitty asked Mrs

A New Home at the Wartime Hotel

Harding if she had heard from either of her sons in the army recently and successfully changed the subject.

She had never felt comfortable talking about Dunbar's. It felt showy-offy. It hadn't been so bad when Cousin Ronald was still alive and had helped Uncle Jeremiah run the place, knowing it would one day be his.

But once Ronald was gone, things had changed.

'Poor Uncle Jeremiah,' Bill had said when the news of Ronald's death had started to sink in. 'He hasn't just lost his son. He's lost the next owner of Dunbar's as well.'

That had made Kitty look at him sharply. She knew what he was thinking, though he didn't put it into words.

Not yet.

It hadn't been long before Uncle Jeremiah had told Bill that one day Dunbar's would come to him.

Bill had immediately offered to pack in his job at Congreve's so he could learn the ropes.

'Under normal circumstances, I'd say yes,' Uncle Jeremiah had replied, 'but we're at the beginning of a war and you're doing your bit in a reserved occupation. If you were to leave Congreve's, you'd automatically be called up – supposing you were permitted to leave, of course.'

'True,' said Bill.

Since then, he had made sure that he, Kitty and Abbie visited Dunbar's regularly. It was a handsome building in a discreet sort of way, not at all showy, situated in a quiet backwater a short distance from the middle of town on Lily Street, which was off Oxford Road and within easy reach of the Palace Theatre. Lily Street was also not far from – or, rather, used to be not far from – the Free Trade Hall, which had been the home of the Hallé Orchestra.

Dunbar's clientele was divided between well-to-do permanent residents who had lived there for years, and visitors to Manchester who wanted somewhere smart and conveniently situated, but who couldn't afford outright luxury.

Since Bill had become Uncle Jeremiah's official heir, there had been a change in his manner when he took his little family to Dunbar's. Previously they had been visitors – welcome visitors, but visitors all the same. Now, when Bill entered Dunbar's, he threw back his shoulders and puffed out his chest. His voice was louder, his manner all bonhomie when he spoke to the resident guests. It was clear to Kitty, if to nobody else, that he was only too aware that one day they would be *his* resident guests.

It made Kitty cringe inwardly but it didn't seem to put any noses out of joint, so maybe it was just her being oversensitive. She was, after all, constantly alert to Bill's moods and behaviour, as she had been ever since she had learned of his attitude towards money. It was something she had kept secret from everybody aside from Naomi. Sometimes she wished she hadn't confided in her sister, but she would have exploded if she'd had to keep it entirely to herself, and Naomi had always encouraged her and made her feel better about things.

In spite of the arguments over money, Kitty loved Bill – oh, not in the all-consuming, desperately-in-love way she had right at the start. She didn't think he loved her in that way any more either. There was nothing like diametrically opposing views about money to bring you down to earth and knock the romance out of you, but that didn't mean you stopped caring. Kitty consciously looked for things to like and respect in Bill. He was hard-working and good at his job. Those things mattered. It was something for a wife to be proud of. And he did little things to help her, like fetching in the coal, polishing the shoes and cleaning the fire irons. Plenty of husbands left those jobs to their wives.

Above all else, there was Abbie. Whenever Kitty became annoyed or frustrated with Bill, she only had to picture his great love for their daughter. Whatever Bill's faults, his devotion to Abbie was his greatest strength as far as Kitty was concerned.

She might not have the marriage of her dreams, but she could never regret it, not while she and Bill had their darling Abbie.

6

February brought a bitter chill but at least it was dry, which made cycling easier. Beatrice set off on her usual route but a DANGER UNEXPLODED BOMB notice in the middle of the road meant she had to double back. She hoped it wouldn't make her late. Everyone understood about craters in the road and suchlike, but Beatrice knew the pressure her ladies were under. That was what she called them to herself, 'her ladies' – and they were all ladies, not a single man among them. That wasn't what the Corporation called them. Come to think of it, Manchester Corporation, which provided and ran all the local services, such as transport, education and council housing, didn't call them anything. They were just women whose domestic and family responsibilities were taken utterly for granted.

But to Beatrice, they were her ladies and she tried to bring a note of civility, good nature and understanding into their tired lives. Understanding: that was the most important thing. These women's lives had been hard enough before the war, but now, with shopping queues lengthening their days and air raids disturbing their nights, some of them were worn to a frazzle.

Beatrice was the inco lady – the incontinence lady. Every Monday to Friday, and again on Saturday until two o'clock, she cycled round from one house to the next where a woman, most often a grown-up daughter or a daughter-in-law, looked after an infirm relative who... well, who was in need of adult nappies. It was a service they could sign up for – aye, and make a contribution towards. The Welfare Department of the Corporation picked up the rest of the bill but you had to be able to stump up your share or the Corporation wouldn't want to know.

Beatrice negotiated her way carefully round the corner. Attached to her bicycle's saddlepost was a long tube of metal, which was attached at the other end to a small two-wheeled trailer. It wasn't heavy but it meant that going round corners could be a bit hairy. She couldn't afford to misjudge.

Drawing in towards the kerb, Beatrice slowed her old boneshaker. Lifting herself from the seat, she stood on the pedals, then placed one foot on the ground, holding the handlebar as she brought her other foot across. She used her foot to flick the stand into position, making sure the bicycle was stable before letting go.

This was a nice street, its houses all with small front gardens behind low curtain-walls of red brick, out of the top of which sprouted matching sets of railings. A woman in a wraparound pinny was up a stepladder, cleaning her windows of the dust from last night's raid. *'She should have done that this morning,'* said Beatrice's late mother's voice inside her head, but Beatrice was more tolerant. A couple of women were nattering and another pair walked along together with their shopping baskets over their arms.

Beatrice tried the front door. There was no answer. She stepped back and glanced up the road. Sure enough, here came Mrs Holland running along, her shopping bag banging against her leg, her headscarf askew over the mousy hair. She was the daughter of an elderly lady who was set upon dying in her own bed, like her husband before her.

Mrs Holland's face was flushed as she scrabbled in her handbag for her key. 'I'm sorry, miss,' she said to Beatrice. Opening the door, she called, 'It's only me,' and wiped her feet before going inside.

Following her in, Beatrice fixed a smile in position. She mustn't show that she could detect the sour smell of incontinence that no amount of disinfectant or talcum powder could smother. Talcum powder: there was precious little of that around these days. Like so many ordinary everyday items, it had become as scarce as hens' teeth, thanks to the war. When Beatrice had handed in her last batch of signed sheets, the Corporation clerk had informed her that paperclips were all but impossible to find. He had made this sound like the most appalling calamity and Beatrice had wanted to tell him he must lead a very cushy life if this was the worst inconvenience he could imagine, but of course she hadn't uttered a word.

Mrs Holland's mother, Mrs Preston, lived in the downstairs front. Once, it would have been the sitting room, kept for high days and holidays. Now it was Mrs Preston's whole world, with her bed against the back wall, a commode beside it, and a chest of drawers covered with the clutter of being a looked-after person in wartime – cloths from cut-up old clothes instead of cotton wool; home-made cucumber lotion instead of skin cream; herb salve made from lard, elderflowers and groundsel instead of bedsore liniment. Towels and sheets formed toppling piles on a low table and there were pills on the mantelpiece. The armchair by the window had a telltale rubber pad on the seat.

Mrs Preston lay in the bed. The pillows that had propped

her up were still in position, but she had slipped down. The face she turned towards them drooped on one side. Her spectacles were skew-whiff; Mrs Holland stepped forward and righted them.

Strictly speaking, Beatrice wasn't allowed to know anything about the people who needed the inco service, but the ladies who did the looking after were usually glad of the chance to talk – let off steam, more like – and so Beatrice knew from Mrs Holland that her mother was paralysed down one side following a severe stroke that had also left her incontinent.

'Shall I pop the kettle on?' Beatrice offered.

She headed down the tiled passage to the kitchen at the back of the house. Damp nighties hung from the high ceiling on a pulley-airer. Bedding was draped over the clothes horse crammed into the scullery. Through the back window, Beatrice saw yet more bedding hanging from the line in front of the mound formed by the Anderson shelter. Poor Mrs Holland.

She made tea and took it through to the front room, walking in upon the sight of Mrs Holland positioning herself to heave her mother up the bed. Beatrice immediately plonked the tray down on a wooden chair.

'Here, let me help.'

She wasn't supposed to. She was only meant to deliver the consignment of nappies, ask for a signature and then get back on her bike and head for her next address. But Mrs Holland was a skinny wisp of a thing and her mother, virtually immobile these past five years, had put on a considerable amount of weight. But that was one of the features of being a looker-after in the home. You had to be strong or you'd never manage, as Beatrice herself had learned a long time ago.

Feeling under the bedclothes, she located the draw-sheet. Taking a firm hold, she caught Mrs Holland's eye and nodded.

Between them, they dragged the draw-sheet upwards towards the head of the bed, bringing Mrs Preston with it.

'Ups-a-daisy,' said Beatrice, lifting the invalid's head and shoulders so Mrs Holland could rearrange the pillows. 'There you go, love.' She lowered Mrs Preston.

Although she habitually used words like 'love' and 'ups-a-daisy', she never spoke in a baby voice or a jolly voice to the invalids, but used a brisk, no-nonsense approach. She didn't want them thinking she felt sorry for them, even though her heart sometimes bled. In any case, the ones she really felt sorry for were her ladies – the looker-afters.

No sooner was Mrs Preston settled than a pungent aroma invaded the air. Mrs Holland started to groan, but cut it off.

'I'm sorry, miss,' she began.

'No need.' Beatrice wiped her features clean of any reaction. Sometimes someone would remark that she must be immune to the smell by now, but, honest to God, it clobbered her every time. 'It'll be twice as quick if we do it together.'

'Oh, I couldn't impose,' said Mrs Holland, but it was only a token protest. It wasn't the first time this had happened when Beatrice was here.

Together they changed the bed, turning Mrs Preston as they eased the sopping sheets away. Holding her breath, Beatrice carried them to the scullery and dumped them in the copper.

Back in the front room, she cocked her head on one side, wordlessly asking the question, though she already knew the answer.

'No, thanks.' Mrs Holland's words said one thing, though her eyes said something different. 'She wouldn't like it. It wouldn't be respectful.'

Removing Mrs Preston's voluminous nightgown, washing and creaming her, then dressing her again would be a darned sight easier with two of them, but if Beatrice's help wasn't wanted, there was nothing she could do about it.

'It'd be different if you were the district nurse,' Mrs Holland said apologetically, 'but it isn't your job.'

Personally, Beatrice thought this ought to make her offer of assistance all the more acceptable. The fact that it wasn't her job surely showed that the offer came from her heart. Not that she was some sort of Good Samaritan. Far from it. She was just someone who knew what it was like.

Beatrice fetched in the nappies and got Mrs Holland to sign for them. She would keep them washed and dried, then once a week she had to bundle them up and suffer the indignity of leaving the sack on the front step to be collected. She was responsible for her mother's clothes, bedding and towels, but once a week the nappies were taken away to be washed in an industrial machine at a temperature a domestic copper couldn't achieve.

Beatrice made several more calls before she cycled home, late as usual after the extra time she had taken at each of her calls. Well, late by anyone else's standards, late by the Corporation's standards, but if you didn't have a family at home waiting for you, how could you be late?

She trundled around the final corner and her heart sank at the sight of the children playing in the road. Oh no, not again. Lifting her chin, she steeled herself.

It started the moment the kids saw her.

Inky Stinky Inkerman
Inky Stinky Inkerman
In-KY Stin-KY
Inky Stinky STINKERMAN!

Would it never end, the name-calling? She had been called Beatrice Stinkerman at school by lads who had thought themselves the greatest wits on earth.

'It's only teasing, miss,' the lads had said, all innocence, when the teacher had heard them.

And somehow the fact that she couldn't take a bit of teasing had reflected badly on Beatrice, not on her tormentors.

'What you have to do,' Beatrice's mother had told her, 'is say, "Sticks and stones may break my bones, but names will never hurt me." That'll show them. Anyroad,' she'd added, 'it's only teasing.'

Only it hadn't been teasing. It was bullying – although Beatrice had been grown up before she'd realised that.

The boys she'd gone to school with had grown up and had sons of their own, and now this new generation was teasing her. It had been all right at the start of the war, because they'd all been evacuated, but then the phoney war had dragged on and their mums had fetched them home. When the raids had started – and by crikey, things had been bad ever since last summer – Beatrice had hoped the kids would be dispatched again, but that hadn't happened.

At some point in recent months, the song had started.

Beatrice had tried knocking on doors and complaining to the mothers.

Mrs Abbott had heaved a sigh. 'Our Tommy needs a firm hand. He needs his dad here to give him a thick ear.'

Mrs Simpson had looked defensive. 'It isn't our Joseph's fault. He's easily led.'

Mrs Langton had rolled her eyes. 'Here's me working ten-hour shifts at the munitions and then coming home to cook and clean and heaven knows what besides, and what do you do all day, Beatrice Inkerman? Sail around on your bicycle, that's what. Some of us do real war work.'

Even so, the singing had stopped, but only for a while.

Beatrice cycled along the road, wishing she could go faster, but pulling the trolley slowed her progress. She felt like chasing the boys down the street with a rolling pin, but that would only make it worse. She kept her eyes to the fore.

In-KY Stin-KY
Inky Stinky STINKERMAN!

7

The chilly air in the dark bedroom nipped at Lily's face as she opened her eyes. It was another cold day – her last one working at Dunbar's. Should she be excited or scared? Everything had happened so quickly – marriage, the baby – though not in that order.

Pushing herself upright, she pressed a gentle hand to her swollen belly for a few moments, then shoved her hand beneath the bedclothes, feeling about for her dressing gown, which she had tucked inside the bed last night so it would be warm to put on this morning.

Swinging her legs out of bed, she pulled on her dressing gown at the same time as her toes scrabbled about to find the slippers she had left on the mat. The mat was thin and worn, not a bit like the luxurious Axminster she would have benefited from had she carried on living with Daniel's mother. But all that was behind her now. What mattered was looking ahead.

In the meantime, there was today to get through. When she'd first worked at Dunbar's, she had lived in. Second time around, things were different. Dunbar's had provided her with a safe refuge when she'd needed it, but the happy feeling of her first stint here hadn't returned. Well, that was understandable.

She'd started here the day after she left school, aged fourteen. She had found the job for herself. The school did its best to channel girls into shop or factory work and Lily would probably have let herself be sent down one of those routes too, but earlier in the year she and her chums had gone on the bus into town for a Saturday afternoon of window shopping. They hadn't had enough coppers to cover the full fare, so they had got off halfway up Oxford Road. It was then, as they'd walked along, chatting and laughing, that they had noticed the sign saying LILY STREET.

The others had thought it hilarious.

'Lily Street! That's your road, that is, Lily, your own private road.'

Giggling, they'd darted into Lily Street to take a look, but the others had lost interest almost at once because there weren't any shops. Lily was interested, though, because that was when she spied Dunbar's, a handsome building with long sash windows that sparkled in the sunshine.

Just before her friends turned to retrace their steps, a taxi had pulled up and a couple emerged and stood for a moment on the pavement. The lady wore a charcoal-grey belted coat with large black fur cuffs and revers. She carried a black leather clutch bag in one of her gloved hands, and a shallow-crowned hat with a small brim showed off her elegantly shingled hair. Leather high heels emphasised how tall and slim she was.

Accompanied by her equally well-dressed husband, she went up the steps. At the top, a uniformed doorman with more braid than a field marshal opened the doors to admit them into the hotel. That was the moment when Lily had known what she wanted to do. Not shop work or factory work, but hotel work – and not just at any hotel, either, but at Dunbar's on Lily Street.

The school had written to Dunbar's for her and, heart pounding, she'd survived an interview with Mr Dunbar himself, a sharp-eyed gentleman in an old-fashioned frock-coat, together with his son, young Mr Dunbar, who was amazingly old to be called young, and the housekeeper, Mrs Swanson, a buxom, double-chinned lady with surprisingly dainty ankles. She had a quiet, respectful manner, but at the same time there was a glint in her eyes that reminded Lily of school.

A fortnight later, the school received a letter offering Lily a live-in position as chambermaid, subject to parental permission. Lily's parents were dead and she lived with her aunt and uncle, who had five nippers under ten, all squashed into a in a two-up two-down, so sending her off to a live-in post suited everyone.

'You won't be living with us,' said Uncle Irwin, 'so we shan't expect you to hand over any of your wages.'

'Thanks,' Lily had said. She had known, even though it wasn't said in so many words, that her not being expected to contribute to the household meant that her uncle and aunt's duty to her was done and she couldn't ever go back to live there.

Since she had already had her fourteenth birthday, she was allowed to finish school at Easter instead of waiting for the summer.

Chambermaiding was jolly hard work, but Lily was a grafter and she loved the well-appointed rooms with their beautiful furniture and high-quality fabrics. She was taught to do everything 'the Dunbar way', which soon became second nature. If she lived to be a hundred, she would still be sweeping the fireback clear of soot every morning instead of a couple of times a week like Auntie Nettie, and she would always have separate brushes for the banisters and the upholstery.

When her first Christmas came around, the resident guests each gave her a card with a coin or two inside the envelope, as a thank-you for taking care of their rooms for them. The major gave her a whole half-crown. Lily put together all her extra money to buy presents for her young cousins, a box of Rowntree's Pastilles for Auntie Nettie and a packet of Capstan cigarettes for Uncle Irwin. She had been to see them several times and always enjoyed it, but best of all she liked returning to Dunbar's where, for the first time in her life, she had her very own room.

Strictly speaking, a chambermaid only worked upstairs and if Dunbar's had been a massive place like the Midland Hotel, that would have applied to Lily. But, Dunbar's being smaller, there were times when she worked downstairs, cleaning the silver, polishing the hall floor or dusting the dining room.

She had even been called upon to work as a waitress on occasion. Oh, she had never waited at tables or anything like that, but sometimes when Dunbar's was hosting a large gathering, she had the job of standing inside the doorway with a tray of sherry or wine for the guests to help themselves from as they arrived.

Which was how she had met Daniel.

* * *

Lily had her breakfast in the staff dining room off the kitchen, then she made herself useful creating a new batch of homemade polish from turps, vinegar and linseed oil, since it was becoming increasingly difficult to find furniture polish in the shops, not to mention Silvo, Duraglit and Bluebell Metal Polish.

Presently it was time to start on the bedrooms, making beds as precisely as you'd find in any hospital ward, dusting and tidying dressing tables, going over the rugs with the carpet sweeper, polishing mirrors and cleaning the communal bathrooms. Lily had always enjoyed good health, and never more so than during this pregnancy, but even so, her chambermaiding had become physically more taxing in the past week or two.

Nevertheless, being here was better than being in Daniel's family home with his mother. The mere thought of that was enough to send a little shiver cascading through her. The baby shifted as if he or she could feel it too.

Lily worked her way steadily from room to room, leaving Miss Rivers until last because, even though she had resided here for years – the long-term guests didn't live here; they 'resided' – and knew perfectly well that she was supposed to vacate her room each morning by ten so it could be cleaned, she never did.

The rooms took longer to do these days as there weren't as many chambermaids. One had gone off to join the land army and two had gone into a munitions factory, crowing about how good the money was going to be. They had tried to persuade Lily to go with them, but nothing would have made her leave Dunbar's. To her, this was more than a job. It was her home and she felt a deep sense of loyalty to it. She'd known that when she was a little older, she would be called upon to do war work, but until then she intended to stay put and devote her energy to Dunbar's.

And then she had met Daniel.

Their eyes had met across the room, just like in the romantic stories Lily enjoyed. It had never occurred to her that such a thing could happen in real life. In any case, it shouldn't have happened at all, for all sorts of reasons. Class, for one. Work, for another.

It had happened last June. Lily remembered the British withdrawing from Norway in May; she remembered Belgium,

A New Home at the Wartime Hotel 69

Luxembourg and the Netherlands being invaded. She remembered Mr Chamberlain resigning and Mr Churchill becoming prime minister and offering his 'blood, toil, tears and sweat'. She remembered Dunkirk vividly at the end of May, and the way, in early June, Mr Churchill's 'We shall fight them on the beaches' speech had made her skin tingle all over.

But after that it was a bit of a blur, because all she could focus on was Daniel. Dunbar's had held a wedding reception. Not a big sit-down meal like it would have been before the war, but an altogether more casual affair.

'No, Lily, it is not casual.' Mrs Swanson had raised her drawn-on eyebrows at Lily. Her voice was stern but, all the same, the twinkle in her eyes declared her fondness for her. 'Nothing that Dunbar's does is ever casual. The correct term is "less formal", and I'll thank you to remember that.'

Less formal it might have been, but it was still exciting because it wasn't just a wedding but a double wedding – two brothers who had both survived Dunkirk, tying the knot side by side. Because of staff shortages, Lily had been called upon to stand inside the doorway with a tray of glasses of sherry, port and gin. Alcohol was scarce but the father of one of the brides had apparently spent the summer of '39 stocking his drinks cupboard.

Lily had been enchanted. She missed the long white gowns of the pre-war weddings, but everyone said that simpler clothes were patriotic and the two girls were both in floral dresses with linen jackets and pretty hats. They might not look like Lily's idea of the perfect bride, but their radiant faces made her realise there was more to weddings than a fancy frock.

She had stood in her allotted position, holding the tray steady and murmuring, 'Sherry, port or gin' over and over. The moment the tray emptied, it was whisked away and replaced by another one without her being required to budge an inch. She was under strict orders to keep her eyes on the tray or on the person she was about to serve, but when the tray emptied for the second time, which meant everyone had arrived, she dared to look around at the happy, chattering group before she left the room.

And that was when her eyes had met Daniel's.

* * *

Although Lily had been dazzled, she had somehow, despite her wildly beating heart, carried on performing her duties. Later on, after the speeches, Daniel – though, of course, at that point, he had simply been the handsome young man with the hazel eyes and the lean, athletic frame – had intercepted her as she crossed the foyer.

'Excuse me, miss, but I've spilled some port on the carpet. I wonder, could you possibly...?'

'Of course, sir,' Lily said, or at least she hoped she'd said it. It was entirely possible that she'd opened her mouth and a string of babble had come out. She made herself take a breath. 'All it'll take is some soda-water. I'll fetch some from the kitchen.' She stopped. Now she really was babbling. This chap was a toff and toffs didn't care how things got cleaned. They just knew that it happened.

Lily flew down the basement stairs to the kitchen.

'Where are you going in such a hurry?' asked Cook, raising her eyebrows.

'Spillage,' said Lily. 'Port.'

'On the carpet?' Cook asked. 'You'll need soda-water – and have some salt handy as well, just in case.'

Lily was already running back up the stairs, half-panicked,

half-thrilled. Would he be waiting for her in the foyer? Please let him be there. She would die if he wasn't.

He was there. He took a step towards her as if he might reach for her hand, but then he turned and led the way into the room where the wedding reception was in full swing. Indicating a small table in the corner, he led the way as if she couldn't have found it without his help.

'On the floor on the far side.'

He looked at her and Lily's knees turned to jelly. It was a good job the spill was on the carpet, because she wasn't sure she could have stayed standing if it had been on the tablecloth. As she bobbed down between the table and the wall, the young man sat on one of the chairs, lifting the long tablecloth out of the way. Not that it really needed moving, but he did it all the same.

Lily's senses were alert as never before, yet she managed to say in a calm voice, 'This will be easy to clear up. There's barely a mark.'

The young man leaned down a little. Lily didn't dare look at him.

'I spilt my drink on purpose so I could speak to you.'

Now she did look at him, just the briefest glance, her eyes meeting his and bouncing away again immediately. She couldn't look, she mustn't. She would drown in his gaze if she did.

'I wanted to meet you,' he said. 'You're the prettiest girl I've ever come across. I thought my heart was about to leap out of my chest when I saw you.'

Lily had been warned about this, about men who tried it on with the staff, men who wanted a bit of slap and tickle and no questions asked; men who might well have a wife or a sweetheart elsewhere, men who thought maids were fair game.

If any other man had spoken to her like this, she'd have run a mile, but with this young man – and with her feeling as she did, responding to him as she had, and with her knowing, somehow just *knowing* that she could trust him – when he said, 'Please may I see you again?' she answered, 'Yes,' without hesitation.

* * *

Lily had never been happier. She only had to think of Daniel and her face broke into smiles. That was his name: Daniel – Daniel Chadwick. He took her to the Worker Bee, a café on Deansgate. He would gladly have taken her to the Midland Hotel or the Claremont for afternoon tea on her day off, but Lily asked to go somewhere simpler, so they went to the Worker Bee, where they had scones that were probably very nice but Lily could never remember how they tasted afterwards. Pouring the tea, she felt special and grown-up, as well as proud and amazed to be keeping company with such a handsome man, who had held her chair for her as she sat down and who was polite to the staff. Good manners counted for a lot. Auntie Nettie had told her that.

When they left the Worker Bee, they walked for ages, hours possibly, though, however long it was, it didn't feel like long enough. Lily let her hand brush against his accidentally on purpose and he took her fingers in his and nestled them in the crook of his arm, like they were a real couple. Well, they were a real couple. She already knew it. She'd never been more certain of anything in her life.

They couldn't stop talking, each of them eager to learn all about the other.

Daniel was the youngest of four brothers. The older three

had joined the RAF, the army and the Royal Navy respectively. As for Daniel, he had signed up with the merchant navy.

'It was the only one left,' he said with a boyish grin that made Lily's heart turn over. 'On top of which, my grandfather, my mother's father, has a farm, so he's helping to feed the nation. By being in the merchant navy, I'm doing the same.'

Lily told him about being orphaned, which made him raise her hand to his lips to kiss her palm.

'Oh, but it turned out happily,' she was quick to assure him, 'because I was taken in by Uncle Irwin and Auntie Nettie. They couldn't have been kinder.'

'They took you in?' Daniel smiled. 'That makes you sound like a stray kitten. Do you still live with them?'

'I live in at Dunbar's. I've got my own bedroom on the third floor. That's where the staff sleep. I've worked there since I was fourteen.' After a moment, Lily said, 'I bet you didn't leave school at fourteen.' She said it in a teasing voice, but there was another meaning underneath and Daniel didn't pretend not to understand.

'You're right. I didn't.' He cupped her chin in his hand and looked into her eyes. 'We're from different stations in life, you and I, Lily, but we're the same as one another in every way that counts. Never forget that. We're meant to be together.'

* * *

Lily and Daniel had made love only once. Afterwards Lily knew she ought to be ashamed, but how could she when she was so gloriously happy and Daniel was the man of her dreams?

'The last thing I intended was to take advantage,' Daniel had murmured, holding her close and murmuring in her ear.

'It wasn't just you,' Lily had assured him. 'I wanted to every bit as much, but we mustn't do it again. It's not respectable.'

How could something so shameful feel so right? But it had. Joy and desire radiated through Lily's body. She would have given anything to sleep with Daniel again, but nice girls didn't behave like that, only she'd been bowled over by the warmth in his hazel eyes and the intriguing touch of vulnerability about his mouth when he smiled at her in that special way.

In spite of all the hours of talking, all the meetings, the snatched moments, the plain fact was that Lily and Daniel had known one another for hardly any time at all before she found out she was in the family way. She felt dizzy and her heart pounded as fear streamed through her. Even though she was scared of telling Daniel, she knew he would stand by her because they were perfect for one another. Marriage hadn't actually been mentioned yet but Lily had known, and sensed that Daniel knew too, that they were going to spend the rest of their lives together.

After his initial shock, Daniel had been thrilled about the baby. He caught Lily in his arms and kissed her. Lily felt sure she must be glowing with joy as she gazed into his face. His eyes were bright and full with happiness.

The next thing she knew, he was down on one knee in front of her, holding her hand in both of his.

'Lily, I know we've done everything the wrong way round and I'm sorry that I... except that I'm not sorry because I'm going to be a father. You're the prettiest, kindest girl in the whole world and I want to look after you for the rest of our lives. Will you marry me, Lily? Please?'

* * *

'When Daniel told me your eyes had met across a crowded room,' said Mrs Chadwick, 'I immediately envisaged a ballroom. Then he said he met you at a wedding and I naturally assumed you must be one of the guests. It never occurred to me for a single moment that you might be... a member of staff.'

Mrs Chadwick pressed the flat of her hand to her bosom as she uttered the final words. Lily was ready to sink through the floor. Daniel had tried to warn her, but all the same this was far worse than her direst imaginings.

Daniel's mother was a well-built woman with perfectly coiffed salt-and-pepper hair. She was expensively dressed – expensively corseted too. Her lightweight wool dress didn't betray a single lump or bump. Lily reckoned she was the sort of lady who would wear pearls even if she was gutting a fish or digging shrapnel out of the vegetable patch.

Daniel's home was every bit as grand as his mother. It was a large Victorian villa on Edge Lane in Chorlton. On either side of the front door was a bay window, each with another one above. Over the front door was a tall window with stained glass, the colours as rich as jewels. Lily hadn't known you could have stained glass in a house. She'd thought it was a church thing.

When she arrived for her first visit, anxious to make a good impression, one of the first things she said was, 'What a lovely parlour, Mrs Chadwick,' though the words seemed inadequate as she took in the wine-red carpet, the marble chimneypiece and the velvet curtains. Even the piano was a grand instead of an upright.

Mrs Chadwick had shot a glance at Daniel before assuming an artificial smile. 'We refer to it as the drawing room.' She didn't actually add the words *in our rank of life*, but she didn't need to, because Lily heard them loud and clear.

Everything had gone downhill from there... and that was

before they'd told Mrs Chadwick that Lily was in the family way.

* * *

It was a good thing Lily had never doubted Daniel's love for her. It was her belief in him that saw her through.

Mrs Chadwick had been relentless in her determination to prevent the wedding. She tried to buy Lily off to make her disappear from Daniel's life. When that failed, she changed tactics. Seeing as Lily needed a letter of parental consent to get married, as she was only eighteen, Mrs Chadwick transferred her attention to Uncle Irwin, offering him an eye-watering sum to refuse to give Lily the letter the registrar required. Uncle Irwin wouldn't have told Lily about that. It had been a furious Auntie Nettie who'd spilled the beans under the guise of warning Lily about the kind of woman she was up against, though Lily had sensed that, while Auntie Nettie was desperate for her to be respectably married, she also needed to punish her for bringing shame on the family by getting herself in the family way.

Lily and Daniel married on three days' notice using a special licence because Daniel was due to return to sea. Lily didn't tell him how his mother had tried to bribe her. Even though she was angry about it, Lily also felt ashamed.

'You're a gold-digger,' Mrs Chadwick had informed her coldly. 'How long was it after meeting my son that you dropped your drawers for him?'

Lily resented the attitude but she couldn't deny that Mrs Chadwick had a point. Judgemental she might be, but she had good cause. Lily and Daniel had indeed got carried away very quickly.

Daniel talked Lily into moving in with his mother while he

was away. His father spent most of his time in London these days because of working at the War Office, so it would be just Lily and Mrs Chadwick.

'Where else would you live? That's my home and it's where you ought to be. There isn't time for me to sort out a place for the two of us before I go back to sea.'

In any case, the nightly air raids had started by then and houses were being blown up or irretrievably damaged. People who had lost their homes took priority when it came to finding somewhere new. A young bride whose mother-in-law could put her up didn't stand a chance.

'I know it's going to be difficult at first for you to be with her,' Daniel had acknowledged to Lily, 'but you'll soon settle down together. Everything has happened so fast, that's the trouble. While I'm away, I'll like thinking of you living in the home I grew up in.'

Lily missed Daniel dreadfully when he left. She worried desperately, too, and followed the news as never before. While the Battle of Britain raged in the skies, Lily longed for, and in equal measure dreaded, word of what was happening in the Atlantic. Although the danger to merchant shipping had her in a state of constant fear, she was proud of Daniel for doing his part to keep the country fed.

But when Lily mentioned to Mrs Chadwick what Daniel had told her about doing the seafaring equivalent of the work done by his grandfather on the land, Mrs Chadwick stared at her in disbelief.

'My father is not a *farmer*,' she declared. 'He is a landowner. Yes, he oversees the home farm, but the estate also includes other farms that are run by tenants. My father resides in a manor house with a substantial stable-block.'

That was just one of many occasions when Mrs Chadwick

put Lily well and truly in her place after Lily moved in with her. Lily had done her best to please her mother-in-law but it hadn't worked and, during the two months Daniel was away, Lily had crept back to Dunbar's and asked for her old job, complete with her bedroom. Mrs Chadwick didn't exactly come rushing after her to beg her to return to the family home.

When he returned, Daniel was surprised and disappointed, but Lily wouldn't give in. She was careful to smile her way through the discussion.

'It suits me and it suits Dunbar's. They lost another of the chambermaids to the munitions so they're glad to have me back because I know how to do things the Dunbar way. Mrs Swanson won't let me overdo it, so you needn't worry about that. I owe Dunbar's a lot, you know. They didn't just give me a job when I left school. They gave me a roof over my head.'

During Daniel's brief leave, he arranged at short notice to borrow a friend's flat while he was away. It was bliss for the pair of them, like having their own home.

'That's what I'd love more than anything,' Lily said with a sigh, 'somewhere of our own.'

'That won't happen any time soon,' said Daniel. 'My address of record is my parents' house and there's space for us there, so we haven't a hope of getting anywhere else. Anyway, once the baby comes, that's where you'll be, the two of you.' He laughed. 'The three of us.' He drew Lily close. 'In a few months, the two of us will be the three of us.'

'You aren't sorry?' Lily asked.

'Not one bit,' Daniel declared. 'Well, I'm sorry that everything happened in such a rush and I didn't get the chance to court you properly, the way you deserve.' After a moment he added, 'Things would probably be more straightforward now if I'd been the perfect gentleman I ought to have been.'

Lily snatched his hands and held them tight against her. 'Don't be sorry for that. I know we shouldn't have done what we did, but it was because of how much we loved one another.'

When Daniel had returned to duty and Lily was back at Dunbar's once more, in her small room in the attic, she imagined the way things might have been, the excitement of being courted. But... if there hadn't been a baby so quickly, if everything had happened the way it should have, would Mrs Chadwick have persuaded Daniel not to pursue this ridiculous romance with the little chambermaid?

Of course not. Nothing could ever have come between them. Look at how determined Daniel had been to marry her. And not just determined to, but happy to.

* * *

Now it was February and Lily was going to leave Dunbar's tomorrow to go to a maternity home until her baby was born. To a girl of her background, the idea of eight weeks of being cosseted in a private home was utterly unheard of. In fact, for a girl like Lily, even a fortnight in a smart place like that was out of the question. That was something for the well-to-do wives of educated, professional gentlemen belonging to the middle class. Lily was working class. In her world, you had your baby at home and the local women made sure you got one good night's sleep afterwards, then it was back to everyday life and all it entailed.

'Don't argue.' Daniel had placed a gentle finger on her lips when she had tried to object. 'You're my wife and I want to know you're being taken care of while I'm away.'

'But it will cost a fortune,' Lily had protested. 'Eight guineas a week!'

'I've saved the money my godmother left me,' Daniel reassured her. 'My lovely Lily, if I'd had to sell everything I possessed, I'd have done it to give you this.'

Tears had sprung to Lily's eyes. This was more than generosity on Daniel's part. It was recognition of her unwillingness to move back in with his mother, and she couldn't stay at Dunbar's until the birth.

'They'll take great care of you at Rookery House,' said Daniel, 'and you can stay there for three weeks after you have the baby. When you leave there,' he added, his voice gentle, 'it will be to return to my parents' house. That's the right place for my wife and child to be. You understand that, don't you, Lily?'

8

Beatrice stood stock-still, her mouth dropping open at the sight of a house cut clean in two. The right-hand side was still intact and upright, not a brick or a roof tile out of place. The left hand side – well, there wasn't a left-hand side. Simple as that. Instead of half a house, there were stony-faced men digging for bodies.

Dust blew into Beatrice's mouth. She stepped back, screwing up her face and trying to puff the powder out again. 'Dust' sounded so tiny, just a gossamer layer of minute particles, but there was nothing insubstantial about the dust conjured up by a high explosive. What had thrust itself into Beatrice's mouth was nothing short of a wodge. When she wasn't trying to spit it out, she was coughing, each brief struggle for breath sucking yet more of the stuff into her throat.

Someone thumped her on the back, then someone else pulled her away. She stumbled against the kerb but managed to right herself. Her breathing coming under control, Beatrice glared at the ARP warden who had dragged her aside. He pointed at a large patch of black on the road. It gleamed in the light from the burning houses.

'Oil,' he warned. He was an old boy with a lined face. 'You were about to step backwards into it and it's a devil to get off your shoes.'

Damn these oil bombs. Beatrice was grateful to have been saved from stepping into the oil, though at the same time, with the half-house in front of her and burning houses behind, it wasn't as though shoes mattered – except that they did. Everything mattered when it was in short supply.

She turned to look at the houses that were ablaze. The Auxiliary Fire Service people were doing their best but it wouldn't be long before there was nothing left, not with oil all over everything inside. The hedges in front were coated in oil too, and the pillar-box on the pavement was black instead of red.

Beatrice ran her dust-thickened tongue around the inside of her mouth, which felt as if it was coated in sand. Then she got back to work. She was with the Women's Voluntary Service and they were a familiar sight during air raids. Sometimes Beatrice worked in one of the mobile canteens, doling out tea, cigarettes and sandwiches to people who had just lost their homes and to the men of the civil defence services who were searching for bodies, battling fires, restoring electricity and gas, and using all their skills and strength to perform rescues.

At other times, Beatrice would be on duty in the local rest centre, the place where the bombed-out were sent. Here, she and her colleagues took care of people who were glassy-eyed with shock, most of whom arrived with no more to their names than the clothes they stood up in. Some didn't even have that dignity, their clothes having been torn from their bodies by the force of the blast. Beatrice had spent many a shift handing out cups of tea or wrapping people suffering from shock in blankets and settling them on thin palliasses or writing down their personal details. The most heartrending job – though, of course, you mustn't let it show – was getting the names of the missing from them.

'Whatever you do,' Mrs Dempsey, who ran the WVS branch, had said to Beatrice when she was a new recruit, 'when someone says, "Our Nancy is missing," don't say, "I'm sure she'll be all right." We mustn't dole out false hope. Be honest about the situation. Tell people the best they can do is give us as much information as they can so we can find out what has happened to their loved ones.'

Tonight, Beatrice was out with the mobile canteen, which had been a furniture removal van before the war and was now equipped with a water tank, a counter, cupboards and shelves. She had left the van with a tray of mugs of tea for the ARP bods and the rescuers, which was when she had nearly stood in the oil on the road. Now she quickly went around gathering the empty mugs and loading up her tray.

'Thanks, love,' said one of the men, wiping his mouth on his sleeve.

'I needed that,' said another. He rolled his shoulders. 'Back to it.'

A shout went up from the heap of rubble that had previously been half a house.

'Can we have some hush, please?'

Everyone went silent. This was a regular occurrence during a rescue, when the men on the spot crouched low or lay down, pressing their ears to the remains of the building, straining to hear any sound beneath. Everyone quietened and stood still. Overhead, the drone of Luftwaffe engines mixed with the clatter of the ack-ack guns, but the folk on the ground stayed as still as statues, as if their silence would enable the tiniest sound to be heard through the layers of destruction.

After a minute, the man in charge of the rescue team gave the signal and work commenced again. Holding the tray steady, Beatrice picked her way across ground strewn with bricks and roof tiles. Shattered glass crunched underfoot and she was glad of her stout leather shoes. She had never had a lot of money but she'd always seen shoes as an investment. Plenty of folk were obliged to line their inadequate footwear with old newspaper, and what protection was that against rain or snow?

Beatrice's shift ended at six in the morning but she stayed on longer to help soothe an old lady who had lost the house she had entered as a bride sixty years ago and whose principal concern now was that she must write a note to the newsagent to cancel her daily paper.

'Eh, love, you don't need to fret about that,' said the woman sitting beside her. She was a little dumpling of a creature with a mackintosh fastened tightly over her nightclothes, her hair in rollers under a hairnet. 'That's the least of your worries.'

'That's exactly why she needs to think about it,' Beatrice explained quietly to the well-meaning woman. 'It saves her thinking about her house.' In a louder voice, she said to the old lady, 'I'll find a piece of paper and we can get your note written, then we can think about what to do next. One thing at a time. That's how to get through.'

One thing at a time. It was a basic principle that had served Beatrice well ever since she was a little girl with adult responsibilities. Back then, 'one thing at a time' had soothed her when she panicked and steadied her when she felt overwhelmed.

Her Women's Voluntary Service work finished, Beatrice walked home. March had come and, although the air was distinctly cool, the bite of winter had gone. Beatrice knew that when she cycled around, she would have the pleasure of glimpsing the pom-pom blooms of drumstick primulas and cheerful yellow daffodil trumpets in the corners of gardens that had otherwise been turned into vegetable patches.

She had lived in the same house all her life – although if she had to say it out loud, she was careful to say that she'd lodged in the same house. A few years ago, she had told another of the inco ladies that she had lived in the same house all her life and the response had been a wide-eyed, 'Oh, you lucky thing. Did your parents leave it to you?' Ever since then, Beatrice had been careful to be accurate.

Even so, her accuracy didn't extend as far as describing how her lodgings had shrunk, even though she knew it wasn't something to be ashamed of.

'It's patriotic, you see,' Mrs Thornton, her landlady, had said when war was declared. 'Manchester is an important place and people will have to come here to work, so I have to make space to take in more lodgers. Only these won't be lodgings. They'll be billets for war workers.' She gave Beatrice a wide smile. 'So you shan't mind, Miss Inkerman, shall you?'

'Of course not,' Beatrice had replied willingly.

But when it happened, when she'd seen for real what it meant, she had minded dreadfully. Honestly, she was as patriotic as the next person, but this new arrangement was hard to swallow.

Mrs Thornton had got her brother to slice Beatrice's bedroom in half by inserting a plywood wall down the centre. It wasn't just the room that was divided. The window was too, which led to arguments about when and how much to open the sash.

Beatrice made her way upstairs. It had been a terrific squeeze to get the little washstand into her reduced bedroom but she had never regretted it. Getting in after a night shift and being able to wash at once, without having to hover outside the shared bathroom, was more than worth it.

After she'd washed, Beatrice had a go at combing the dust from her hair, all the while knowing it would take a thorough wash to achieve that; then she dressed and had a quick breakfast.

Instead of starting her inco round, this was a morning when she had to go to the office in the Town Hall to hand in all the signed sheets that showed she had made her deliveries.

On the bus she sat behind a pair of women in overcoats and felt hats, who were talking about the jobs women were doing as part of the war effort – not the voluntary work like Beatrice did with the WVS, but paid jobs.

'Our Elsie has got a job as a postman, though she doesn't get paid as much as a man.'

'That's not exactly fair, is it?' said her companion.

'Well, I don't know,' said the first woman. 'Women have never earned as much as men. It's because men are breadwinners. Anyroad, our Elsie loves the work. She says it's far more interesting than the charring she was doing before.'

'That's good. Mrs Heywood-over-the-road's daughter – not Clodagh, the other one – she's in the land army up in Cumberland somewhere. Mrs Heywood says it took her a while to settle in, but now she loves it and there are other girls to be pally with.'

'Janet,' said the first woman.

'What?'

'Janet. The one that isn't Clodagh. I'm glad she's doing well. Our Maggie is starting in the munitions next week. The pay's good there.'

'Long hours, though,' commented her friend.

The first woman made a 'huh' sound. 'It's long hours everywhere these days, no matter what you do, but the choice of jobs is like nothing we've ever seen before.'

Sitting in the seat behind, Beatrice listened avidly. It was all she could do not to lean forward, stick her head in between the other two and join in. There were so many opportunities for women these days. It had never occurred to her before that she would ever, could ever, be anything other than an inco lady. If she could get a wartime job, the experience could stand her in good stead after the war.

Maybe she didn't have to be the inco lady all her life.

* * *

Beatrice was permitted thirty minutes for her dinner, but she seldom took the whole time as she was so often running behind because of staying to lend a hand. But the one time each week when she made sure to take her allotted time was after she'd delivered a consignment of nappies to Mrs Blacker in Fig Street for her mother-in-law. The Blackers lived downstairs and afterwards Beatrice would go upstairs to see old Mrs Gates, a bedbound lady who loved company. Physically frail she might be, but she was as sharp as a tack and she and Beatrice were true friends. Mrs Gates didn't require the inco service. If she had, Beatrice wouldn't have been allowed to make friends with her. There were strict rules about that.

The two of them ate their midday meal together. For Beatrice it was a meat-paste sandwich. Mrs Gates nibbled at a piece of bread thinly spread with butter.

Once or twice Beatrice had tried urging her to have something more, but Mrs Gates was nothing if not strong-willed.

'If I wanted to be nagged, I'd get my daughters round here.'

And that was that.

Today, once Beatrice was settled at the bedside, Mrs Gates asked, 'How are you, Miss Inkerman, dear? Tell me about the world outside these four walls.'

Beatrice couldn't hold it in any longer. 'I've started to wonder if there's a war job I could do.'

'So that you can do your bit.'

'Yes, but also to give me another string to my bow,' said Beatrice, 'so I might possibly have the chance of a better job after the war.' Heat flooded her face. 'I don't mean to make the war sound like an opportunity, but it would be nice to have a better job than delivering nappies.'

'Don't underestimate the value of what you do,' Mrs Gates advised.

'I know it's an important service,' said Beatrice, 'and I just wish more folk could afford to pay for it, for their sakes. But...' Her voice faded away. She wasn't used to putting herself first and she didn't want to be disloyal to the people she helped.

'But you want a better job,' Mrs Gates said bluntly. 'Something more interesting.'

'Well – yes.'

'There's no shame in that, my dear,' said Mrs Gates, 'especially not for a spinster like you.'

Beatrice hoped her smile looked natural. She hadn't grown up expecting to be a spinster, but then, who did?

'I wish you luck,' said Mrs Gates. 'I also wish you...'

'Yes?' Beatrice prompted when her friend's voice trailed away.

'I wish you to accept a little gift from me.'

Embarrassed, Beatrice said quickly, 'Inco ladies aren't allowed to accept gifts.'

'Need I remind you that I don't use the inco service?'

'But I met you because you live upstairs from someone who does, so I'm sure it wouldn't be allowed.'

'Before you say no, take a look at it.'

Mrs Gates picked up something from the top of the cupboard on the other side of the bed, switching it to the hand closest to Beatrice. In her wavering palm lay a brooch. It was in the shape of a wing and was set with red stones.

'It's lovely,' Beatrice said truthfully. 'But you really ought not to offer it to me. I'm sure I'm not allowed to take it and, anyway, wouldn't you like to give it to one of your daughters?'

'If I wished to give it to Olive or Renee, I wouldn't be offering it to you,' Mrs Gates answered tartly.

'I appreciate your kindness, but I really can't accept it.' Beatrice held her breath, willing her friend not to press the point.

Mrs Gates huffed a brisk sigh, looking vexed. Then she smiled. 'You know best, I suppose – and that isn't something I often say, so make the most of it.'

When she left Mrs Gates, Beatrice climbed onto her boneshaker and set off for her next delivery, towing her trolley behind her. She had a new looker-after to go to, a Mrs Williams whose father, Mr Trent, was incapacitated. His inco service was being paid for from a fund for old soldiers.

Beatrice handed Mrs Williams a sack. 'You must wash the nappies as you use them, of course, then once a week put them in this sack to be taken away for an industrial wash and you'll be given a sack for the following week.'

She didn't add that Mrs Williams's sack was dark blue, which marked out her father as a charity case. With luck, if none of the neighbours knew the significance of the colour, Mrs Williams would never find out.

'Have you lived here long?' Beatrice asked. She liked making conversation. She wanted her looker-afters to feel comfortable with her so that it would be easier for them to accept her help when she offered it.

'Just a few weeks,' said Mrs Williams. 'The Chapmans upstairs used to rent the whole house, but Mrs Chapman fell on hard times when her husband got killed in an accident. She gets by on subletting the downstairs to us. The last lot of downstairs people did a moonlight flit and after that, we moved in.'

Beatrice gave her the form to sign. 'This says I've made the delivery.'

There was the softest of taps on the door. If Beatrice hadn't been so close, she wouldn't have heard it.

'Shall I?' she offered and opened the door.

A scrawny scrap of a lass stood on one foot, chewing half of her lower lip. Her face was pinched, eyes anxious.

'Mam says, can she have the rent, please?'

'Shouldn't you be at school?' Beatrice asked.

The girl transferred her meagre weight to the other foot.

It was Mrs Williams who answered. 'Her mam's poorly – isn't she, Dora? And Dora is stopping at home to look after her.'

Alarm bells rang in Beatrice's head. It really was none of her business but she waded in.

'Give us your rent book, Mrs Williams, and I'll nip up and get Dora's mum to initial it for you.'

Armed with the money and the rent book, Beatrice went upstairs, with little Dora scurrying behind. She was approximately eight-year-old sized, which, given the obvious poverty, meant she might be ten. That was one good thing about the war. With the state taking control of every aspect of life, school dinners had improved no end – so why hadn't young Dora grown and filled out like so many poor children had?

The child had left the door open when she'd ventured downstairs. Beatrice knocked and walked in at the same time.

The room was both parlour and bedroom. Mrs Chapman, thin as a stick, with sunken cheeks and grey skin, lay in the bed.

'Afternoon,' said Beatrice. 'I've got the rent from downstairs. Let me count it out for you and then you can initial the book.' Once this had been achieved, she added, 'I gather your Dora is at home helping you.'

'Are you from the truancy?' was the immediate reply.

'No, but she should be at school, you know. It'll make a real difference to her life later if she doesn't miss school now.'

'I need her here.' Mrs Chapman's voice was a thin wheeze. 'I send her to school when I can.'

Beatrice felt pretty sure that wasn't all that often. Little Dora was a looker-after. Beatrice's heart gave a tug inside her chest. It wouldn't make any odds what she said. Mrs Chapman wouldn't magically start sending Dora to school every day.

Beatrice smothered a sigh. Looking at Dora was like looking at herself all those years ago.

9

Bill was out with the Auxiliary Fire Service that night. Kitty did as many WVS shifts as she was allowed during the day so as to be at home with Abbie overnight. The nights when both Bill and Kitty were on duty, Abbie stayed with Naomi unless she too was on duty, in which case Abbie went to Bill's mother, Kitty's own dear mam having died suddenly three years ago. Although Abbie obeyed without a murmur, she had recently started dropping the messenger service into the conversation, making Kitty's blood run cold.

'You're far too young,' Bill had said repressively. 'You're only twelve.'

'I'm thirteen next month,' Abbie had replied. 'Lots of boys are allowed to be messengers when they're thirteen.'

Kitty closed her eyes. The messengers cycled through air raids from ARP post to first-aid post to rest centre, delivering information, and never mind that HEs and strings of incendiaries were pouring from the skies. The thought of Abbie— No, Kitty refused to allow the thoughts into her mind.

Now, as she and Abbie returned to the house as the all-clear sounded, Kitty switched the gas, electricity and water back on while Abbie raced upstairs and climbed the ladder to the attic. Moments later, she came running back down.

'The attic's clear,' she reported.

'Good,' said Kitty.

She hated letting her beloved daughter check whether an incendiary had penetrated the roof, but children were growing up faster than ever and responsibility was good for them. They all wanted to be part of the war effort.

The government had instructed everyone to empty their loft space and put down two inches of sand. That had been the point when Abbie's fairy-tale cradle had finally been passed to another family. Kitty and Bill had kept it and kept it... but there had never been another baby to occupy it.

Kitty had endured three miscarriages. They had been secret losses that had happened early on each time, before the magic three-month date had been achieved. There was an unwritten rule that stated you weren't allowed to announce a pregnancy until you'd made it safely to three months. Kitty had no idea how she'd come to know this rule, but she did know it and also knew – though again without knowing how – that all other women were aware of it too.

Bill had known about her pregnancies, of course. He had been bitterly disappointed about the first miscarriage and they had clung together in their grief. But then he'd said, 'Still, the doctors did warn you after Abbie came so early...' as if that made it possible for him to accept it. Should she have accepted it too? Just like that? But how could she, when she had pictured their new future, seen them as the parents of two children? How was any mother supposed to accept having her newly imagined future ripped from her?

That had happened to her three times, in all. She had

learned to cope by focusing on her beloved Abbie, who had brought such joy and meaning to her life and her marriage. She and Bill both adored her.

The tiny doll-like baby with wisps of hair the colour of vanilla ice cream had grown into a slim, energetic child with blue eyes and hair of a richer blonde. As a young child she had always been smaller than her peers but, with her thirteenth birthday on the horizon, she had more or less caught up.

Now, with the house restored to post-air raid normal, it was so near to getting-up time that it wasn't worthwhile going to bed, so Kitty and Abbie made an early start. Just as they sat down at the table to have breakfast, the front door opened. Abbie immediately bounced up from her seat without asking for permission and dashed to meet her father.

Kitty moved her own untouched breakfast across the table to Bill's place and got up to prepare more for herself.

'Was it a bad night, Daddy?' Abbie asked.

Bill gave a huff of mock-exasperation. 'I could see a fire inside one house. I got in and the curtains were ablaze. Of course, the water was switched off, but there was a bowl of eggs on the sideboard so I chucked them at the flames.'

'You never!' cried Abbie, lapping up the story.

'Did so,' answered her father. 'It took nineteen eggs to put it out.'

As Abbie hooted with delight, Kitty silently blessed Bill for picking an anecdote designed to entertain.

'Abbie.' Kitty nodded at the clock. They had a clock in each room, thanks to Bill's 'generosity'.

'Please may I leave the table?' Abbie asked.

Kitty nodded permission and Abbie disappeared to prepare for school. When she was ready, she called goodbye to Bill, who was washing and changing, then she kissed Kitty goodbye at the front door.

Kitty stood on the step, watching her on her way. The morning air smelled smoky but alongside that, Kitty detected the bright tang of springtime in the air.

As soon as she had seen Bill off to work, Kitty donned her apron and started on the housework. Wet-dusting was always the first job of the day after an air raid. Presently it was time to go to the rest centre to do a short shift, so she put on her WVS uniform. Unlike many members, who only had whatever pieces they could afford, Kitty had the full shebang. She would have been happy with just the jacket or even just the hat, but that would never have been good enough for Bill. Even though Kitty had taken the precaution of telling him not to shell out for the whole uniform, he had done so. Of course. When did Bill ever turn down the chance to spend money?

That morning Kitty was on letter duty, encouraging newly homeless women to write cheerful letters to their husbands in the services.

'You don't want him worrying about you, Mrs Beamish,' Kitty advised. 'He'll want to know you and the children are fine.'

Mrs Beamish looked at her as if she was mad. *Still in shock*, thought Kitty. It would take a while for her to perk up and take her new situation on the chin.

Kitty leaned towards her. 'Concentrate on *now*.' She had perfected the art of mingling sympathy with straightforwardness. 'The children have gone to school, haven't they? Tell him that. Tell him about the help you're receiving with the compensation paperwork and clothes and new ration books.'

A glint of something that might be humour appeared in Mrs Beamish's eyes. 'In other words, sing the praises of the WVS.'

'Not at all. I'm just suggesting you reassure your husband. Show him you're managing, and that will give him a boost.'

That afternoon, Kitty was sent out on the mobile laundry, going to places where the water supply had yet to be restored, so that the housewives could do at least some of their washing. They had to keep life as close as possible to normal. That was what it was all about.

On her way home, Kitty did her shopping. The queues weren't so bad at this time of day. On the other hand, you took the chance that the shopkeepers would have run out. Jam, marmalade, syrup and treacle were all on ration now. Bill's mother said it wouldn't be long before they were making carrot jam and carrot marmalade.

No sooner had Kitty arrived home and put the potatoes and baking apples in the vegetable rack and the tin of tuna – the last one in the shop! – in the cupboard than there was a knock on the front door and she found her mother-in-law on the step. Ivy Dunbar's face was all points – sharp cheekbones, sharp chin. Sharp eyes too, and a thin-lipped mouth that could shower you in criticism without a single word being uttered.

Although they greeted one another with smiles, there wasn't much love lost between them. Mrs Dunbar had been against her son marrying someone more than ten years younger than himself.

'You're little more than a girl,' she had said to Kitty at the time. 'No offence intended.'

'None taken,' Kitty had replied, taking loads.

Afterwards, Bill had given Kitty a hug. She'd snuggled close, expecting him to say, 'Don't mind my mother. She's a bit surprised by the age difference, that's all, but she'll soon come round and love you as much as I do.'

A New Home at the Wartime Hotel 97

Instead he'd said, 'She's always got a bee in her bonnet about something or other.'

'And I'm currently the bee?'

She still expected Bill to reassure her that his mother would come round, but he said, and he laughed as he said it, 'Once a bee, always a bee, as far as she's concerned. If you pressed your ear to the side of her head, that's what you'd hear: buzz, buzz, buzz. A bee in her bonnet and a grudge in her heart; that's my mother for you.'

Now, Mrs Dunbar asked, 'Are you going to let me in?' as if Kitty had kept her waiting on the step for ages.

As Kitty stood back to admit her, a movement along the road caught her eye. The telegram boy on his bicycle. Kitty's expression must have changed because Mrs Dunbar turned to look as well.

'Ah,' she said and heaved a sigh. 'Still, at least you know he's not going to stop outside your house.'

But he did.

* * *

Unless she had to go to the Town Hall to hand in her signed sheets, Beatrice started every working day at the district nurses' station, where she collected her allocation of nappies. Miss Todd, another inco lady, was there at the same time. There was a bit of a hold-up because Miss Fletcher, who counted out the nappies as carefully as if she personally paid for them, was on the telephone.

Beatrice and Miss Todd chatted while they waited. Miss Todd was a wiry little woman with a no-nonsense manner, which made Beatrice secretly feel sorry for the people she dealt with. Their lives were enough of a strain without being treated brusquely. But then, Miss Todd probably felt sorry for Beatrice's ladies for having to put up with someone who oozed syrup.

'My niece is about to join the Wrens,' said Miss Todd.

'Her parents must be proud,' Beatrice said politely. Then the thoughts that had been bubbling away since she'd earwigged on that conversation on the bus couldn't be contained any longer. 'It makes you think, doesn't it?'

Miss Todd looked at her. 'Think what?'

'All those young girls going off to do their bit,' said Beatrice. 'Such opportunities.'

'I would hardly describe the war as an opportunity,' Miss Todd replied with a touch of self-righteousness.

Beatrice refused to be quelled. 'Wouldn't you? I'm not so sure. Women of all ages and backgrounds are doing all kinds of different jobs these days. The war won't last for ever. A good job now, new experiences, new responsibilities… who knows what it might lead to afterwards.'

'Miss Inkerman, are you thinking of leaving the inco service?'

As exhilarating as the idea was, it was scary too. Beatrice backpedalled. 'For all I know, inco could be a reserved occupation. I mean, when you consider what we do and how people rely on us. Maybe it counts as an essential service. I suppose it has to, really.'

Was she right? A reserved occupation meant that the job you did was essential and so you couldn't be called up to join the services or be put into war work. You had to stay put and carry on doing what you were doing. Was the inco service one of those jobs?

'Maybe you should ask Sister District,' said Miss Todd. 'Then at least you'd know for definite.'

A New Home at the Wartime Hotel

Little pulses beat at top speed in Beatrice's wrists and at her throat. 'No time like the present.'

Of course she should have known better. Sister District wasn't available, and certainly not without an appointment. Feeling very daring, Beatrice made an appointment for later that day. It would mean keeping strictly to her proper times and not lending her ladies a hand, which would surprise them, but she must put herself first for once. That in itself would be a novel experience and enough to make her senses spike and become more alert.

Later that day, Beatrice stood in front of Sister's desk. Sister was a slim woman with an upright posture, a straight nose and intelligent eyes. She had a way of turning her head to look directly at something rather than just glancing. Her surname was Evans but because she ran a district nurses' station, she was known as Sister District. Her full title was Sister District South Central, there also being a Sister District South West and Sister District South East, and, of course, there were various Sister District Norths covering the north side of Manchester as well. It must be quite a mouthful when all the Sister Districts got together and had to use their full titles.

'Good afternoon, Miss Inkerman,' said Sister. 'What can I do for you?'

Beatrice had had all day to prepare what to say. 'I don't mean to suggest I'm unhappy in my work, Sister, but please can you tell me if the inco service is a reserved occupation?'

Sister District gave her an assessing look. 'I've never been asked that before and the honest answer is that I don't know. Does this mean you're considering...?'

'Thinking of it, yes, Sister, but only thinking.' Beatrice felt flustered. The last thing she wanted was to appear disloyal.

'Leave it with me and I'll find out for you.'

'Yes, Sister. Thank you, Sister.'

As Beatrice left the office, shutting the door softly behind her, hope bloomed inside her, causing a flutter in her belly. Did she really dare to dream?

* * *

Lily started to get out of the taxi, then remembered to wait for Daniel to walk around from his side of the motor to help her. She stood looking up at Rookery House, the maternity home in Sale, while Daniel paid the driver.

'It was originally built as a grand family home years ago, I believe,' Daniel remarked, coming to stand beside her.

'It must have been a jolly big family to need somewhere so huge,' Lily replied with a smile.

Turning around, she viewed the gardens. Within a wall of red brick were deep beds of trees and glossy-leaved shrubs. What must once have been a sweep of lawn was now a vast vegetable bed, some of which was under glass, but Lily was more interested in the one remaining flowerbed, at the back of which arched a forsythia, its graceful stems glowing with yellow flowers. In front were the soft colours of hellebores, the jolly hues of bachelor's buttons, together with clusters of pretty primulas and dainty violas.

Catching Daniel looking at her with a tender smile, Lily said, 'I love flowers. We didn't have a garden, of course, so I went to the park a lot and got the gardener to tell me all the names.'

'I'm sure my mother would be happy to let you have your own little flowerbed,' Daniel murmured, then picked up her suitcase before she could reply.

Lily didn't want to reply, anyway. Glancing along the drive, she saw a girl of probably the same age as herself walking along carrying a cardboard case. Lily's case, courtesy of Daniel, was made of leather and had a lock. The other girl's shoulders were rigid, giving her a strained look.

'Lily,' Daniel said behind her and, turning, Lily saw the door had been opened by a maid.

Feeling fluttery inside, she walked indoors, followed by Daniel. Lily looked back, expecting the maid to hold the door open for the other girl, but she didn't.

In answer to Lily's soft exclamation, the maid said, 'She's a greenie, madam. They go round the back. This way, if you please.'

The superintendent of the home was a middle-aged lady, very well groomed, called Mrs Walters, who met Daniel and Lily in a pretty parlour to welcome them over tea and home-made ginger biscuits.

'It is a pleasure to have you here, Mrs Chadwick,' she said. To Daniel, she added, 'I understand that you will be away at sea for some time. I assure you we will take the greatest care of your wife.'

'Thank you,' said Daniel.

Lily simply had to ask. 'When we arrived, there was another girl—'

'So I understand,' said Mrs Walters. 'Very unfortunate. She wasn't supposed to arrive until later on.'

'The maid said she was a... greenie.' Lily brought the word out hesitantly in case she hadn't heard it properly.

'Most of the patients we take care of here in Rookery House are respectable married ladies,' said Mrs Walters, 'but we also have a scheme for looking after...' She coughed delicately. 'We have a benefactor, you see, who set up a special scheme so we could take in unmarried mothers. I must explain,' she added quickly, 'that these are girls for whom this is their first fall from grace. I wouldn't want you to think that we would ever take a young woman for whom it was her second offence against decency. They live separately from our ladies until it is time for them to deliver.' Another glance at Daniel. 'I apologise for the direction the conversation has taken.'

The direction Lily had instigated. She oughtn't to press the point, but she had to know. 'And the reason for calling them greenies?'

The only explanation she could think of was that they were so green and unsophisticated that they had fallen for the silver-tongued promises of some rogue who had left them high and dry.

'We provide them with dark-green wraparound pinnies to wear while they do the housework,' said Mrs Walters. 'It is perfectly normal to expect girls in their situation to contribute in this way. You would find it wherever you went. And now, perhaps you would like to see your room?'

* * *

Lily felt sorry for the greenies but when she tried to befriend one of them, Mrs Walters put her foot down. Gently and politely, but nevertheless in no uncertain terms.

'It won't do, Mrs Chadwick,' she explained. 'What would your husband think if I let you keep company with a girl of that type?'

Lily wasn't entirely sure what Daniel would think, but she was in no doubt as to what Mrs Chadwick's opinion would be.

It was best to let the matter drop. She was one of the respectable mothers-to-be and she was proud of it. She loved being Daniel's wife and being called 'Mrs' was a joy she was sure she would never take for granted.

She had been shy of the other mothers-to-be to start with because they were older than she was and also she was aware of her humble beginnings. But they were kind to her and, since Lily had come to Rookery House earlier in her pregnancy than they had, they were happy to share their experiences so she knew what lay ahead.

They all knitted for their coming babies. One lady was busy hemming a series of little white garments, made of what appeared to be linen.

'My husband is an architect,' she explained. 'Drawings used to be made on fabric. He dug out some old ones for me and I bleached out the markings.'

The women also made rattles out of matchboxes covered in scraps of material and filled with buttons.

'When Baby grows out of the rattle,' said Mrs Walters, 'don't forget to put the buttons in your button-box.'

Lily soon began to feel like an old hand. Being here for so much longer than anybody else meant she saw others come and go, and it was rather a thrill when Mrs Walters said to a new patient, 'This is Mrs Chadwick. If there's anything you need to know, ask her. She's our resident expert.'

Before he had gone back to sea, Daniel had taken Lily to a draper's so she could choose lengths of fabric to be made into maternity dresses. She had spent ages lingering over the choices. Not that the selection was anything like it would have been before the war.

'What about this one?' Daniel had suggested.

Lily took a look. 'Apple-green. I like it.'

'It'd look lovely against your fair colouring,' said Daniel – which was all it took to make up Lily's mind.

She enjoyed wearing the dress all the more because of Daniel's compliment – until the day Mrs Spencer arrived. She was the latest mother-to-be and Mrs Walters had mentioned her name in advance. That afternoon when Lily walked into the sitting room, the new lady waved her over. Thinking Mrs Spencer wished to introduce herself, Lily gladly complied, smiling as she crossed the room.

'Hello,' she said cheerfully. 'Welcome to Rookery House.'

'Thank goodness you walked in when you did,' said Mrs Spencer. 'I've spilt my tea on the carpet. Would you clean it up for me?'

Lily was always happy to help anyone, but this lady's tone wasn't an appeal for assistance. It was nothing less than a demand that Lily would do as she was bade.

She stared. The other mothers-to-be glanced at one another, looking uncomfortable.

'This is Mrs Chadwick,' Mrs Atkins said to the new lady, 'and she's a resident here, the same as the rest of us.'

'I know,' said Mrs Spencer. 'Mrs Walters told me about the greenies – although,' she added with a tinkling laugh, 'I don't think I'd have called them the same as us.'

'I'm not a greenie!' Lily exclaimed. Her face felt hot. Even her eyes felt hot.

'They wear dark green,' said Mrs Atkins, 'not this pretty green.'

'Oh, but – oh my goodness.' The new arrival pressed her palm to her cheek. 'I'm sorry, my dear. My mistake.'

'That's all right,' Lily answered in a hollow voice, though it felt as if nothing had ever been less all right.

'It wasn't just the dress, you see,' Mrs Spencer continued. 'It's your voice. You sound like... well, like—'

'Like the sort of girl who gets herself in the pudding club without being respectably married,' Lily flared. Then she realised that this was precisely what she had done, which left her feeling even more ashamed. A burst of anger made her prop her fists on her hips. 'Just because I don't talk posh doesn't mean I'm not respectable. My husband's in the merchant navy, I'll have you know.'

Later, Mrs Walters smoothed things over and Mrs Spencer apologised again, this time without putting her foot in it, though Lily would have much preferred that no more had been said. Had she been fooling herself by settling in at Rookery House? What did the other ladies really think of her? Shame thickened inside her throat.

Daniel was an absolute darling to send her here. It was kind and generous and protective of him. But did the other mothers-to-be see her as a fraud?

10

It was April now. At the end of March, the meat ration had been reduced to the value of one shilling per week – one shilling! – and the War Budget early in April put up income tax. But there was Abbie's birthday to look forward to and the sun was bright. The trees filled out with fresh leaves and the sweet fragrance of blossom mingled with the clean, earthy smell of newly turned soil. Ever since the telegram had come in March to announce Uncle Jeremiah's sudden death, Kitty had had a devil of a job keeping Bill in his post in the shipping warehouse. He couldn't wait to get his hands on Dunbar's.

Kitty had to remind him more than once of Uncle Jeremiah's instructions.

'After Ronald died, Uncle Jeremiah said you need to stay put at Congreve's. You're in a reserved occupation there. If you leave, they'll have you in the army before you can say Jack Robinson.'

Bill pressed his lips together in frustration, though he had no choice but to agree.

'But telling him once wasn't enough,' Kitty lamented to Naomi. 'It's as if he's so eager that he keeps forgetting.'

'As long as he doesn't forget when he's at Congreve's and ends up handing in his notice,' Naomi said with a smile.

Kitty smiled back. Naomi always knew when to sympathise, when to make a light-hearted remark and when to jolly Kitty along. Kitty appreciated her sister's unfailing support all the more because all three of Naomi's boys were serving their country.

'Who was the queen who said that when she died, they'd find "Calais" engraved on her heart?' Kitty asked. 'I swear I've got "Don't resign" written on mine.'

A few days after that, Bill came home with news.

'More soldiers are needed, so the bosses of places where the men are in reserved occupations are under orders to reallocate responsibilities and generally juggle things around so that they can provide men for the call-up.'

'Who's going from Congreve's?' Kitty asked.

'Don't know yet. They're working it out, then there'll be a list. They've asked for volunteers, though volunteering doesn't mean you'll definitely be allowed to go. It's up to the senior clerks in charge of the various offices to sort out the duties and the workload. It'll take time to get it sorted out.'

The past month had seen all the formalities regarding Uncle Jeremiah's death taken care of. The will had gone through probate and ownership had been transferred. Bill was embarrassingly pleased by the healthy state of Uncle Jeremiah's bank balance... until the solicitor used the lot to clear up the death duties.

'It's good in a way,' said Kitty. 'It shows the value of Dunbar's. That's something to be pleased about, surely.'

'That's a cock-eyed way of looking at it,' said Bill.

Kitty strongly suspected he wasn't going to be pleased about anything until he could take over the hotel properly. She pictured herself jollying him along.

Bill announced that they were going to move into Dunbar's and live in the family flat.

'It'll mean Abbie will have to change schools,' he said, 'but it'll be worth it for us to live in Dunbar's.'

'Won't the new manager need the flat?' Kitty asked.

'What new manager?' Bill's mouth set in a stubborn line.

'You're staying at Congreve's, so you'll need to employ a manager.'

'Certainly not. I'm not putting my inheritance in someone else's hands. The staff are experienced. They can manage on a day-to-day basis, and I'll be there when I'm not at Congreve's.'

'Oh.' Kitty couldn't think what else to say.

'And I suppose,' Bill added grudgingly, 'that you'll need to learn the ropes.'

'Me?'

'It's not as though you've got work responsibilities like I have.'

It would take a man to say something like that, wouldn't it? Kitty pictured the hours she spent on WVS business, not to mention all the hours standing outside shops in long queues, but then those thoughts were swept aside on a wave of excitement.

'Am I really going to help run Dunbar's?' she asked.

'I've no option, have I?' Bill replied ungraciously.

His attitude hurt, but Kitty clung to the excitement. So what if Bill had made the offer because of not having a choice? The result was the same. What an opportunity!

* * *

Pulling her unwieldy load, Beatrice cycled past Alexandra Park. Last year there had been a terrible incident when the park keeper's house, which had been turned into a first-aid post for the duration of the war, had taken a direct hit and the young girl who'd been manning the telephone had lost her life.

Not so long ago, the flowerbeds would have been filled with tulips and daffodils at this time of year, but the park was now being used for allotments. Even so, the trees remained. A wonderful magnolia was in bloom and an ornamental cherry was smothered in pink blossom. A memory popped into Beatrice's mind. A wedding – herself as the bride. No, not a real memory, but the memory of an expectation. Other girls had dreamed of being June brides, but she had set her heart on being a springtime bride, visualising herself and her new husband posing for a photograph beneath a tree laden with fragrant blossom.

She shoved the picture to the back of her mind. It did no good to think of it. If she'd known then that she was going to spend her life as the inco lady...

But maybe she wasn't. Maybe she was going to get a new job that would lead on to something better after the war. Her face broke into a smile. She'd been told to report to the district nurses' station that afternoon as Sister wished to speak to her. Had she found out if Beatrice would be allowed to seek alternative work?

Mr Trent was next on Beatrice's list. She drew her bicycle into the kerb outside the shabby house, hoping Mr Trent's daughter, Mrs Williams, was already here. Sometimes the woman doing the looking after ran late because of all her responsibilities. It was understandable, but it made things awkward for Beatrice.

Mrs Williams answered the door, looking flustered. 'Oh, it's you. Sorry, miss. I don't mean to be rude. I only got here two minutes ago.'

'Sort yourself out while I nip upstairs and say hello to Mrs Chapman.'

'Oh aye? On your inco list, is she?'

'No,' Beatrice said firmly. 'But she might be glad of a little chat, if she's housebound.'

'Don't fret about her,' said Mrs Williams. 'She's got company. Dora's there.'

Beatrice felt a little internal sag of disappointment. She had hoped Dora would be in school. You only got one chance at education, as Beatrice knew to her cost.

'I'll pop up just for a minute,' she said.

Upstairs, she knocked and went in.

'Only me,' she called cheerfully as if Mrs Chapman and Dora were some distance away instead of right in front of her. Then she caught her breath before saying, 'Dora – my dear,' concern ringing in her voice.

Poor Dora was in floods of tears, eyes puffy. Her mother looked even more pinch-faced than she had last time.

'Has something happened?' Beatrice asked.

'Don't you fret about us, miss.' Mrs Chapman's voice was raspy. 'We'll be all right.'

'But we *won't*,' Dora exclaimed. 'The rent man is due later and what am I to say to him?'

'It shouldn't be you dealing with him,' said Beatrice. 'You're a child.' She raised her eyebrows at Mrs Chapman.

It was Dora who answered. 'The rent man can't come up here, not with Mam in bed. It wouldn't be respectable.'

Beatrice huffed a sigh. 'I can see that.' Then, even though she knew she shouldn't say it, the words popped out of her mouth. 'If he's due here soon, perhaps I could have a word with him for you.'

The Chapmans stared at her.

'Oh, miss, would you do that?' Mrs Chapman whispered. 'You don't know us.'

But I do, Beatrice thought. *I know you better than you imagine.* Aloud, she said, 'What do you want me to say to him?' She went cold inside. It was bound to be lack of money.

'It's him downstairs, miss,' said Mrs Chapman. 'He's always behind with his rent. Well, it's not his fault. He's bedbound. It's his daughter, the one that comes here to look after him. I know things must be hard for her, with everything she has to do, but you'd think she would make a point of paying her dad's rent on time. You'd think it was coming out of her own pocket, the way she hangs on to it. It's because our Dora has to go down and fetch it.'

Dora's chin wobbled and she fastened her lips tightly together.

'It's not your fault, chick,' Beatrice assured her. 'It's difficult for a child to ask a grown-up for something.'

'That Mrs Whatsit takes advantage,' said Mrs Chapman. 'She knows I can't get down them stairs, so she fobs Dora off.'

'Does she indeed?' Beatrice replied grimly.

Mrs Chapman took a couple of shallow, shaky breaths. 'But the rent man doesn't care about that. It's me that'll get it in the neck if the rent isn't paid in full.'

'I'll be back in a minute,' said Beatrice.

At the door, she hesitated. Should she take young Dora with her? No, that wouldn't be appropriate. Mrs Williams might deserve to be shown up, but it wouldn't help matters.

As Beatrice went downstairs, Mrs Williams emerged from the front room, pulling the door shut behind her, but not before the pungent smell of urine had wafted into the hallway. Mrs Williams looked both frazzled and embarrassed.

'I'll lend a hand if you like,' Beatrice offered.

'Oh, would you? That would be such a help. Are you allowed to?'

'It isn't the role of an inco lady,' said Beatrice, 'but I help folk if I can. It makes a difference, doesn't it?'

'It certainly does. My sister does bugger all, I don't mind telling you. Leaves it all to me.'

'Tell you what,' said Beatrice. 'You get the lid off the copper ready for the soiled sheets and while you're doing that, I'll take the rent up for you.' She looked straight at the woman.

Mrs Williams shifted from one foot to the other. 'Has that girl been telling tales on me?'

'Is that your way of asking if she's in floods of tears because you didn't hand over your father's rent?'

'Now steady on,' Mrs Williams began indignantly, but she wasn't in any position to be vexed and she knew it.

'I understand how hard you have to work.' Beatrice spoke matter-of-factly. 'You've your own home to take care of and you've everything to do for your father. How many times a day are you here? Three? Four?'

'Sometimes I'm that tired I don't know which way is up.'

'That's understandable, but you can't brush off things that need doing,' said Beatrice. 'It isn't fair on Mrs Chapman if you're late with the rent. Has Mr Trent got the wherewithal?'

'Oh aye. He's got his pension, and that old soldiers' fund chips in by paying for the inco service, so the rent isn't a problem.'

'Then why didn't you just pay it when you were asked?' Beatrice posed the question in a gentle voice.

Mrs Williams shook her head. Her face sagged with exhaustion. 'I have so much to do every day and the way I cope is by making a list in my head. As long as nowt else comes along, I can manage.'

'And your dad's rent wasn't on today's list?'

'No, it wasn't.'

'Well, it should have been,' Beatrice said bluntly.

'You don't understand. It's such a faff. Dad insists on keeping his money box under the floorboards. Not that he can get down on his hands and knees and fetch it out, mind you. That's all down to me. And when that little lass came knocking earlier, wanting the rent, it was one thing too many.'

'So you sent her away with a flea in her ear.'

'I know I shouldn't take it out on her, but... Anyroad, I'll pay her tomorrow.'

'You'll pay her today,' Beatrice said firmly. 'You'll pay her right now and I'll watch you do it. I'll tell you something else too. I'm going to keep an eye on this situation. You aren't the only one who has things tough. Try thinking what it's like for Dora.'

Mrs Williams rolled her eyes. 'You're not afraid to stick your nose in, are you?'

'No, I'm not,' Beatrice shot back at once, though the truth was she'd never done anything like this before. In a kinder tone she added, 'Come on, love. Let's get the rent paid and get your dad sorted out.' Risking a smile, she asked, 'You wouldn't want to fall out with the person who's offered to help you change that stinky bed, would you?'

* * *

Beatrice perched on the edge of the wooden chair in front of Sister District's desk, hands clasped in her lap. She was here to find out about the possibility of a future outside the inco service, but right now little Dora was uppermost in her mind.

She poured out the story to Sister District, ending with, 'Is there anything that can be done to help, Sister?'

'Sadly, no,' said Sister District. 'Does Mrs Chapman not have a relative who can help?'

'I don't know,' said Beatrice. Should she have asked? 'But presumably not, or else why keep Dora off school? There must be something we can do.'

'We?' Sister District raised a single eyebrow. 'If Mrs Chapman's doctor requests it, I can send a nurse to see her, but something tells me that wouldn't solve the problem.'

'No, it wouldn't,' said Beatrice. 'I don't know what ails Mrs Chapman, but I do know that Dora doesn't spend all her time on nursing duty. She does the shopping and the cooking, keeps the flat clean, does the washing and the ironing...'

'Girls do when there's a need at home,' Sister District pointed out.

Beatrice shook her head sadly. 'I left school before the Great War. You left at thirteen in those days, not fourteen.'

'There's talk of the school leaving age going up to fifteen,' Sister District remarked.

'You're kidding,' said Beatrice. 'I'm sorry, Sister. I didn't mean to sound flippant – but, honestly, what would they do in the classroom until that age?' After a moment she added, 'How lucky to have all that extra education. What a privilege.'

But education shouldn't be a privilege, should it? It was supposed to be a right, which meant everyone should have access to it, including children like Dora.

'When I was at school,' Beatrice recalled, 'when you'd had your twelfth birthday, you could go half-time and only attend school in the mornings, as long as you had a job the headmaster approved of in the afternoons. It was a way of earning a bit extra for the family.'

'Is that what you did?' Sister District asked.

'Me? No. I needed all the school time I could get. I was a looker-after.'

'Like Dora Chapman.' Sister District nodded. 'That's why you're interested in her. I'll give you the same advice I give to my nurses, Miss Inkerman. Do your job to the best of your ability but do not allow yourself to become emotionally involved. It never helps in the long run. Do I make myself clear?'

Beatrice sat up straighter. 'Yes, Sister District.'

Sister District gave her a smile, but it wasn't a real one, just a brief professional curving of the lips. 'We've spent enough time on that. Let's move on to the real reason for this interview. I have made enquiries about whether you might be permitted to leave the inco service in order to undertake war work.'

'Thank you, Sister.' Beatrice's heart thumped in anticipation. Was this the moment when her life took a fresh turn?

'As you know,' said Sister District, 'each inco lady has her own area to cover. I've been told that one lady may leave, and her area will then be divided up to make the surrounding areas larger.'

'Yes, Sister.' Beatrice blinked away a happy tear.

'You shall have to be interviewed by outsiders – someone from the Labour Exchange and someone from the Town Hall. That is the fairest way to treat the pair of you.'

Beatrice frowned. 'The pair of us?'

'Yes, indeed,' said Sister District. 'Two of you have sought permission to leave. The other is Miss Todd. She said you were the one who gave her the idea.'

11

Bill wanted them to take Abbie to see the family flat in Dunbar's before they moved in.

'Why?' Kitty asked. 'It's not as though she's never seen it before.'

'I know.' Bill's eyes crinkled as he smiled. 'But it's different this time. She won't be there as a visitor on her best behaviour. It's about to become her home. You too, Kitty. I want you to see it through new eyes.'

Kitty softened. This meant so much to Bill. To her as well, of course, and all the more so now she was anticipating having a hand in running the business.

'You're right,' she said. 'It's a good idea.'

'We're going to make a success of this,' Bill said, looking serious and determined. 'We owe it to Uncle Jeremiah and Cousin Ronald. Dunbar's should never have come to me, but it has, and we have a tradition to maintain.'

Kitty squeezed his hand. 'Yes, we do.' Inheriting Dunbar's was going to be the making of Bill. It was going to be the making of them both.

'Bring Abbie into town on Saturday,' said Bill, 'and I'll meet you outside Congreve's after I finish work at one o'clock.'

Kitty shook her head. 'Abbie's been invited to go to the children's matinee at the flicks with Martha. It's Martha's birthday treat.'

'You meet me at one,' said Bill, 'and my mother can bring Abbie along later. Then Mum can see the flat too. She's another one who never thought we'd be in this position.'

Bill's mother was only too pleased to fall in with the plan, so on Saturday, Kitty made her way into town, heading for the long line of warehouses. If she'd had Abbie with her, she wouldn't have been allowed inside, but because she was on her own, Bill had sought permission for her to come to the office where he worked.

'Mr Congreve wants to congratulate you,' he had told her.

'What for?' asked Kitty.

'On my inheriting Dunbar's, of course.'

Kitty reported to Mr Exham in the booth by the front gates and he waved her inside. Did he remember that occasion years ago when she had come here to cadge some of Bill's wages? It was no good telling herself that everybody else would have long forgotten it. She would never forget as long as she lived.

As she walked across the yard, she spied Miss Patten, the personal clerk to Mr Congreve himself. She had worked here for years and Bill said there was nothing she didn't know about the business.

She was carrying two stout cardboard boxes, one stacked on top of the other. Papers were visible in the upper box.

'Good afternoon, Miss Patten,' said Kitty. They knew one another slightly, having met before the war, in the days when Congreve's gave an annual dance for the office staff. 'May I help you with the boxes? It's no trouble.'

Settling the string bearing her gas-mask box securely on her shoulder and pushing her handbag up her forearm, Kitty took the top box and accompanied Miss Patten inside and up a couple of flights to her office.

'Come in, Mrs Dunbar,' said Miss Patten when Kitty hesitated politely in the doorway.

Kitty stepped inside and was impressed. Fancy a woman being given a large office like this. Mind you, all those filing cabinets needed plenty of space.

'Put it here.' Miss Patten placed her box on a table and moved aside so Kitty could do likewise. 'Thank you, Mrs Dunbar.'

'You're welcome.'

There was a tap on the door and Kitty looked around to see a freckled office boy whose twinkling eyes and quick smile belied his starched collar and buttoned waistcoat.

'What do you want, Howard?' Miss Patten asked.

Howard held up a big envelope, and not just an ordinary envelope but one made from thickened paper. It was fastened by a loop on the flap that wound around a button on the body of the envelope.

'Mr Johnson said to say he's added his names, Miss Patten,' said Howard.

Miss Patten took the piece of stationery from him and placed it on the blotter on her desk. She nodded to the lad. 'You may go.'

'Thank you, Miss Patten.'

When Howard had disappeared, Miss Patten gave Kitty a rueful look. 'I take it Mr Dunbar has told you that Congreve's, along with all the other shipping warehouses, has been ordered to provide army recruits if possible?'

'Yes,' said Kitty. 'It must be unsettling for all the young men.'

Miss Patten glanced her way. 'And not just the young ones. It isn't just that more lads are needed for the battlefield. More mature men also have something to offer the services. All our clerks here are skilled at organising the transportation of goods, not to mention keeping on top of what goods are being stored in which of our warehouses. Our clerks are highly trained and experienced.'

'I never thought of it that way,' said Kitty.

Miss Patten glanced at the sturdy envelope. 'The list is going around the offices in turn and the senior clerks are adding their nominations. I'll type up the full list on Thursday and the names will be announced on Friday. Not the happiest way to end the week. Oh, I do apologise, Mrs Dunbar. There's a smudge on your blouse. It must have come from the box you carried.'

Kitty looked down. Above the fastened buttons of her jacket was a grey mark on her white blouse.

'Let me fetch a damp cloth and you can clean it off,' said Miss Patten.

She hurried away before Kitty could protest, returning a minute later with the promised cloth. Kitty took off her jacket and dabbed at the stain.

'That should be fine when it dries.' She gave the cloth back. 'Thank you.'

'That's a nice cardigan,' said Miss Patten. 'I like the fern lace stitch. Did you knit it yourself?'

'Yes. I've still got the pattern somewhere.'

Kitty put her jacket back on and Miss Patten came to the door with her.

'Thank you again for your assistance with the box,' said Miss Patten. She snapped her fingers and Howard practically leapt out of a doorway further along, looking guilty. 'Ah,

Howard, please will you escort Mrs Dunbar to Mr Dunbar's office.'

It wasn't long before Bill escorted Kitty to Mr Congreve's office and she was having her hand shaken by Mr Congreve himself and accepting his good wishes, while Bill stood by looking pleased with himself.

After that, she and Bill walked to Lily Street and entered Dunbar's. Bill seemed taller and Kitty felt herself to be taller too, now that she was going to be instrumental in running the business. She squeezed Bill's hand, grateful for the opportunity he was giving her, even if he hadn't exactly been gracious about it.

Some of the permanent residents were in the sitting room and Bill and Kitty went in to have a chat before Bill collected the key to the flat from Mrs Swanson.

When they reached the door to their new private quarters, Bill inserted the key in the lock but didn't open the door.

'Close your eyes,' he instructed.

'Bill, I know perfectly well what the flat looks like.'

'Close your eyes,' he repeated.

Kitty did. She heard the door open, then Bill took her right hand in his right hand and placed his left at the back of her waist. Kitty tried not to hesitate as he guided her inside.

Bill stopped. 'Here we are. You can open your eyes now.'

Kitty did so – and sucked in an enormous gasp of shock, unable to believe what she was seeing. Then she found she could believe it. This was Bill, up to his old tricks.

'Why?' she demanded. 'We've got a perfectly good three-piece suite of our own – and it isn't that old.'

Kitty had secretly shed many tears of fury and despair over that wretched suite. It had been yet another of Bill's showy brand-new purchases that had brought the entire neighbourhood traipsing through their front door to have a good old gawp followed, no doubt, by some serious criticism of the Dunbars once they were back in the street.

And now – and now—

Tears rose behind Kitty's eyes, blurring the sight of the new furniture.

'You always said Uncle Jeremiah's furniture made this sitting room look dark,' said Bill.

'I know I did, but even so—'

'And you said that the leather chairs having metal studs gave the place a medieval look.'

'I was joking, and even if I wasn't, I would still never have wanted this.' Kitty rounded on her husband. 'How could you, Bill? There was no need for this, no need at all. Please tell me it isn't brand new.' But even as she said it, she knew it was. 'Oh, Bill, why? And don't say you did it for me because I didn't care for Uncle Jeremiah's taste.'

A stubborn look settled on Bill's face. 'It's part of our new start. I want to give my family the best. That's all I've ever wanted – for you and Abbie to have the best.'

The same tired old reason. Kitty was sick to death of hearing it. The days were long gone when her husband's generosity had touched her heart and gone some way to making his extravagance acceptable.

'I should have known you'd spoil things,' said Bill.

'*Me* spoil things?' Kitty exclaimed. 'That's rich!' Clawing back her self-control, she lowered her voice. 'There was no need for this, Bill. It was an unnecessary expense.'

'That's your opinion,' said Bill. 'I happen to think it was worth it. I happen to think that the Dunbars of Dunbar's Hotel are worth it. If we live well, it's a sign that the hotel is doing a good trade.'

'We haven't even moved in yet,' Kitty said in despair. 'And

how are people meant to know we live well? Are you going to bring all the guests up here and show them our new furniture?'

Bill gave her a look of contempt. 'You should be proud and grateful. This was the very last new suite in the showroom because the place that makes the furniture has run out of materials – which incidentally is another reason for purchasing this.'

Kitty threw up her hands in frustration, but she held her tongue. What was the point of saying anything? It had never worked before. Why should this be any different?

Bill looked anxious. 'You won't spoil it for Abbie, will you?'

Kitty closed her eyes for a moment. 'Of course I won't. I'd never do that.'

And indeed when Abbie and Mrs Dunbar arrived, Kitty plastered a smile on her face and played her part to perfection.

'Shut your eyes, Abbie,' said Bill. He gave a throaty chuckle. 'You too, Mum.'

'You're a silly,' Mrs Dunbar said with the affection that always warmed her voice when she spoke to or about her son. She held her hands over her eyes.

'*Daddy*,' said Abbie, pretending to groan. 'I'm too old to close my eyes like this.'

'If your gran isn't too old, then you definitely aren't,' Bill answered. He guided the two of them inside. 'You can look now.'

'The furniture's changed,' said Abbie.

'Goodness me, so it has,' said Mrs Dunbar.

Kitty had never discussed Bill's spending habits with her mother-in-law, but the glance Mrs Dunbar sent her now made her wonder if she too disapproved.

'What do you think, Abbie?' Kitty asked. 'Do you like it?'

Abbie sat down, running a hand along the fabric. 'It's nicer than what was here before.'

Kitty smiled, hiding her wretchedness. 'It's to celebrate our new home – isn't it, Daddy? Our new home and our new lives.'

* * *

As her family walked downstairs after visiting the flat, Kitty kept a smile on her face but inside, her heart was aching. Nothing had changed. Inheriting Dunbar's hadn't made Bill examine his ways. He was still extravagant, still a spendthrift, still happy to part with money he didn't have. Kitty had never understood it. Her parents had saved up for things they wanted. Debt was something to be ashamed of. It was something to fear.

But that wasn't the way Bill saw it. To him, buying on the never was in itself a kind of money. If a shop was prepared to let him spend a pound on tick, then to him that was the same as having that pound. Kitty had been forced to harden herself since she got married. Otherwise, she would have died of shame. She had always made sure that Abbie had no idea about her father's spending habits, impressing upon the child from a young age the importance of saving up.

Now, heading downstairs in Dunbar's, Kitty felt tears rise and she blinked them back. How differently she felt now from the way she'd felt when she had walked up these stairs earlier on.

It wasn't possible simply to leave the building. As the new owners, they had to pop into the residents' sitting room and have a word with whichever guests were in there.

Bill turned on the charm, introducing himself to a Mr and Mrs Appleby who were in Manchester for a week, and chatting with the resident guests, exchanging a few words about the latest news with the major and flirting decorously with Miss Winspear, who was eighty if she was a day. He introduced his mother and stood with a loving hand on Abbie's shoulder while she was asked questions about school.

It ought to have been the perfect moment – but it wasn't because Bill had splashed out on that dratted furniture, blast his eyes. Kitty wanted him to put his arms around her and promise never to overspend again, but mainly she wanted to throttle him.

'Since there's a good little crowd of us here,' said Bill, 'I think we should drink a toast to the new Dunbars who are moving in. What d'you say, Miss Winspear? It's not too early for a glass of sherry, is it? I know alcohol isn't easy to obtain these days, but my uncle kept a good cellar and I expect there are still one or two bottles.' He beamed around the room. 'You'll all join me in a toast, I hope? On the house, of course.'

'Oh, Mr Dunbar!' Miss Winspear trilled.

'How generous,' said Mr Appleby.

'I don't mind if I do,' said the major.

'I expect you'd rather not have a sherry, though, Major,' said Bill, all bonhomie. 'How about a drop of the hard stuff?'

'Bill.' Kitty tugged his arm while flashing a dazzling smile at the guests. 'We can't. The cost…'

'It's a special occasion,' he replied quietly. 'Don't spoil it.'

She tried again. 'You can't give away drink.'

'I have to be a good host,' Bill answered before shaking her off and ringing the bell for a member of staff.

Kitty felt like pounding her fist on the sideboard, but she had to keep smiling. Her mind churned. Then all at once it settled. She knew exactly what she had to do.

No, she couldn't do it. She couldn't. It wouldn't be right. Only, if she didn't do it, what sort of future lay ahead for her family?

Bill would end up bankrupting them if he carried on like

this. Kitty had spent all those years worrying about their family finances, and that had been bad enough, but at least it had only been on a domestic level. Now matters were on a business footing and if Bill wasn't careful, he would ruin them. He would end up in the bankruptcy court, and she and Abbie would be dragged down with him.

She wasn't going to let that happen. She had to prevent it. The palms of her hands turned clammy with fear – and the fear was just as much for what she must face if she was to prevent the bankruptcy as it was for the prospect of the bankruptcy itself.

* * *

As she went into town on the bus on Thursday, Kitty sat beside the window and probably seemed to be gazing out, but, truth be told, she wasn't seeing anything. Her brain was a mush of worries and fears. This had to work. It *had* to. Part of her still didn't believe she was really going to go through with it. What, throw herself on Miss Patten's mercy and beg her to add Bill's name to the call-up list? It was an appalling thing to do – but less appalling than letting Bill stay here and run Dunbar's into the ground, which Kitty didn't have any doubt was what would happen. Tears rose behind her eyes and she blinked rapidly to clear them. Abbie would be heartbroken if Bill went away.

You have to do this, Kitty told herself fiercely. *Dunbar's is our future, our livelihood. This is the only way to get Bill off the scene.*

But what if he was sent to the front line? She would never forgive herself. She clung to the thought of what Miss Patten had said about experienced shipping clerks. Perhaps Bill would end up working in stores, responsible for the safekeeping of equipment of all kinds, and then for its transportation to wherever it was required. Kitty couldn't let herself picture any other outcome to what she intended to do.

When she approached Congreve's gates, she had to force herself not to slow down. Pinning a smile in place, she went to Mr Exham's booth.

'Morning, Mr Exham. When I was here last Saturday, I offered to lend a knitting pattern to Miss Patten.'

'A pattern for Miss Patten, eh?' Coming from the nervy Mr Exham, this was a great witticism and Kitty smiled dutifully.

'I promised to pop it in.'

'You can leave it with me,' said Mr Exham.

'That's kind of you, but would you mind if I dropped it off in the post room? That's what Miss Patten asked me to do.'

'Of course. In you go.'

Kitty hurried across the yard. Inside, she went upstairs, heading for Miss Patten's office. Having never confided in anyone except Naomi, she was about to spill some highly personal beans and beg Miss Patten to help her by adding Bill's name to the call-up list.

Miss Patten's door was open and the office was empty. Drat. How long before Miss Patten came back? Then Kitty saw the document envelope with the loop-and-button fastening on the blotter.

Not allowing herself time to consider what she was doing, she slid inside, shutting the door softly behind her. She darted across to the desk, opened the envelope and removed the sheet of paper.

There were two columns of names, written in various hands and with different pens. Miss Patten's fountain pen lay on the blotter. Kitty removed the top, sucked in a deep breath and added Bill's name to the list, slipping it into the middle of the second column. She blew on the ink to dry it, then replaced the cap on the pen. After blowing gently on the ink once more, she slid the paper back into its envelope and fiddled with the fastening.

With her head almost spinning at her own audacity, she opened the office door and peeped out. No one was in the corridor, so she slipped outside and stood beside the doorway. Her heart banged like a big bass drum and she longed to lean against the wall for support, but if she did, she might never find the strength to stand up on her own two feet again.

Hearing footsteps, she turned. It was Miss Patten.

'Mrs Dunbar, what a surprise. What can I do for you?'

A feeling of calm descended on Kitty, as if she was an observer watching herself doing this.

'Good morning, Miss Patten. You were kind enough to admire my cardigan last week, so I've brought in the pattern for you.'

Miss Patten's expression changed from formal and serious to one of pleased surprise. 'How very kind of you.'

'It's my pleasure.' Kitty handed it over. 'I mustn't keep you from your duties. Good morning.'

12

Beatrice had to go to the Labour Exchange in town for her interview. Evidence of the Christmas Blitz was everywhere and would be for a long time to come. Further raids had added to the damage. The raids weren't taking place every single night now, like they had last year, but there were still several each week. The road sweepers were out, energetically brushing smashed glass into the gutter to make the pavements safer for pedestrians. It was a bright morning and the shattered fragments caught the sun's rays and sparkled among the debris.

Beatrice pushed open the door and entered a cool, dim foyer. There was no reception desk, but other people were making for a pair of double doors straight ahead, so she followed. Through here she found a large room in which desks were arranged, each one with a filing cabinet and a set of shelves. Smartly dressed clerks sat behind the desks and people queued up to speak to them. The clerks looked highly efficient, seeming to know exactly which drawer to open or which tray to riffle through.

Beatrice's gaze landed on Miss Todd, who was seated in front of a desk over to one side. Beatrice's heart dipped. Were the interviews to be held here in this public room where anyone close by might listen in?

Behind the desk was a trim lady in her fifties, with a prissy mouth. Her hair, flattened on top, was worn in neat curls at the sides. When Miss Todd indicated Beatrice, the look on the lady's face suggested Beatrice was late, which she most certainly wasn't.

As she made her way self-consciously across the busy room, another woman got up and headed towards her. She was younger, late twenties or maybe thirty, and strikingly good-looking, with a fine-boned face and hair of the most gorgeous deep red. She wore an olive-green jacket and a hat with a jaunty feather. She smiled and Beatrice felt grateful. That hat, though – this young woman couldn't work here or she would have taken it off when she clocked in.

The redhead held out her right hand. 'Miss Inkerman? Good morning. You found us all right, then?'

'Yes, thank you. I was given the new address.'

'So many offices and shops have had to up sticks and find new accommodation,' said the redhead. 'I'm Fay Brewer and I'm one of the interviewers. The other is Mrs Quinlan, whom you can see over there with Miss Todd. She works here and I'm from the Town Hall. Come and say how do.'

Miss Brewer almost made it sound like a social occasion, but Beatrice wasn't deceived by the friendly charm. Miss Brewer's hazel eyes were intelligent and Beatrice was sure she was one of those folk who missed nothing.

At the desk, Miss Brewer performed the introductions. Mrs Quinlan reached across to shake hands.

'I had intended to hold the interviews here at my desk as I am very busy,' she said, 'but somewhere private might be more suitable.' A glance in Miss Brewer's direction showed whose idea this had been.

'This way, ladies,' said Miss Brewer. 'Through that door and along the passage.'

As they approached the room, Mrs Quinlan put on a spurt and bustled in first. Miss Brewer followed, emerging a moment later with a wooden chair, which she set down.

'Would you care to take a pew, Miss Todd?' she offered. 'Miss Inkerman, we'll see you first.'

Beatrice walked in and Miss Brewer shut the door behind her. Mrs Quinlan was already ensconced behind the desk. There was another chair to one side, where Miss Brewer sat. Beatrice took the chair facing them both. She was wearing her best coat – more accurately, her only coat – a double-breasted gabardine with a buckled belt. It was decidedly pre-war. A few years back, when hemlines had begun to rise, Beatrice had started to take up the hem, then chickened out in case she spoiled it. She also wore her good hat and sturdy brogues.

Miss Todd, she had been dismayed to see, was decked out in her Sunday best, including a dinky pillbox hat with a net-snood attached to it, with her salt-and-pepper hair neatly tucked away. Beatrice had felt smart when she'd left home, but now she wasn't so sure. Next to Miss Todd, did she look like she hadn't made an effort?

Mrs Quinlan tilted her chin in a self-important way. 'My task today—' She looked at Miss Brewer and corrected herself. 'Our task is to decide between you and Miss Todd as to which of you is best suited to leave her current role and do war work. The two of you do the same job and I've been furnished with a list of the duties. Miss Inkerman, please could you explain your approach to your work.'

Beatrice started to talk about her job but Mrs Quinlan interrupted her.

'Pardon me. Perhaps I didn't make myself clear. I don't require you to explain your duties. I – we wish to know about your attitude.'

'Sorry.' Beatrice cleared her throat. 'I take my job seriously. There are plenty who wouldn't wish to do it but I'm proud to be part of a service that helps people.'

Miss Brewer leaned forward. 'I imagine it's a service where people are always pleased to see you.'

'Definitely,' Beatrice agreed.

'Pleased?' said Mrs Quinlan. 'I would have expected them to be embarrassed. After all, the service is to do with... bodily functions.'

'I don't want people to feel awkward,' said Beatrice. 'I'm always cheerful and practical. I think that helps.'

'Do you keep to time?' Mrs Quinlan asked.

'I never miss a call,' said Beatrice, 'and my ladies know they can rely on me. They understand that if I'm a little late, it's because I'm helping someone change the sheets or I've put the kettle on because a lady is particularly tired.'

'A mixture of initiative and kindness,' Miss Brewer commented.

'I don't call it initiative,' said Mrs Quinlan. 'I call it playing fast and loose with the rules. Is it your job to change the beds and make the tea?'

'No,' Beatrice admitted.

Mrs Quinlan made a show of rolling her eyes. 'And what about your qualifications, Miss Inkerman? I don't imagine you attended grammar school and took your School Certificate.'

'No, I didn't. I went to elementary school and left at thirteen.'

'So you have an elementary leaving certificate.' Mrs Quinlan stretched out a hand. 'May I see it, please?'

Beatrice froze.

'You have brought it with you?' Mrs Quinlan asked.

'No,' said Beatrice.

'For heaven's sake,' Mrs Quinlan muttered.

'Do we really need to see the certificate?' Miss Brewer asked. 'Both ladies left school a long time ago. Do we need evidence of their proficiency in the three Rs?'

Mrs Quinlan was clearly about to disagree but Beatrice forestalled her.

'I haven't got a certificate.'

Mrs Quinlan's eyes popped open wide. 'Are you saying your reading, writing and arithmetic aren't up to scratch?'

Although Beatrice's insides seemed to collapse under the humiliation, she lifted her chin. 'I don't know about now, but in those days elementary school certificates weren't just to say you had the three Rs. They were about behaviour as well, and attendance. That's why I didn't get mine. I didn't have the attendance record. My mum kept me at home a lot of the time because she wasn't well. The headmaster let it happen, but then he refused to give me my leaving certificate. But I got the three Rs,' she added. 'When I was in my twenties, I paid a retired teacher to give me lessons to make sure of it.'

'That's very commendable,' Miss Brewer murmured.

But Mrs Quinlan didn't look impressed. 'Thank you, Miss Inkerman. If you'll wait outside, we'll see Miss Todd now.'

Feeling disheartened, Beatrice took the seat vacated by Miss Todd. The door clicked shut, signalling the start of the next interview. Beatrice could have wept. If only she had never talked to Miss Todd about war work!

A short while later Miss Todd emerged.

'I think that went quite well,' she remarked. 'How was yours?'

'Difficult to tell,' Beatrice lied gamely.

It felt wrong to remain seated while Miss Todd was on her feet, so she stood up too.

The door opened again and Miss Brewer looked out.

'Miss Todd, would you come back in, please?' Instead of following Miss Todd, Mrs Brewer slipped outside, closing the door behind her. She gave Beatrice a sympathetic look. 'I'm afraid you won't have the chance to apply for war work.'

'Oh well, at least I tried.' Beatrice tried to sound sensible, as if she had no trouble accepting the decision, but really her disappointment was such that her ribs seemed to tighten, making it hard to breathe.

'It was the lack of the certificate that did it,' said Miss Brewer. 'We had to decide between you, and that was the difference.'

'Not me changing beds or making tea?' Beatrice asked.

'No,' answered Miss Brewer. 'If that had been the sole disparity, I'd have defended you to the death.'

'Really?' Beatrice asked, surprised.

'Definitely,' said Miss Brewer. 'I think it's splendid that you're so devoted to your ladies. You strike me as a highly capable person, Miss Inkerman. This particular opportunity might have passed you by, but I'm sure you'll find something you can do to assist others.'

* * *

'Here we go again,' said the midwife and Lily stared at her blankly. Having just fought her way through the latest powerful contraction, she knew there wouldn't be another immediately. Catching her looking, the midwife pointed to the ceiling, or rather she pointed through the ceiling and the roof to the sky. 'Air raid siren.'

Blood and sand, that's all I need. Had she just said that out loud – sworn out loud? Auntie Nettie had always said that 'blood and sand' was swearing because everyone knew it was really a way of saying 'bloody hell'. Anyway, Lily didn't care if she had sworn. She'd known childbirth was going to be painful but she was appalled that it was as bad as this. The mothers-to-be for whom this was the second or third time said you forgot the pain afterwards. They even laughed when they said it, adding, 'Just as well!' But Lily was certain she would never forget.

Matron held Lily's hand. 'Never mind what's happening out there,' she said encouragingly, as if Lily had been clamouring to be taken to the safety of the cellars. 'You just concentrate on what's going on here. Let's bring Baby Chadwick into the world.'

Lily gasped as another contraction started.

'Breathe, breathe,' said the midwife.

Lily obeyed all the instructions. She pushed and strained and breathed and—

'One more push should do it. One more push.'

Did she have another push left in her? Lily heaved with all the strength she had left.

'Come on, little one, out you come,' said the midwife. 'It's a boy.' She held him upside down by his ankles and slapped his bottom, causing him to take a huge breath and start to cry.

'Congratulations, Mrs Chadwick,' said Matron. 'Nurse will give him a wash and weigh him. Then you can hold him for a minute while we wait for the afterbirth.'

For a short while, Lily drifted in a mixture of exhilaration and exhaustion, longing to see her baby, her son. Honestly, how long did it take to wash and weigh a baby?

The midwife manipulated her stomach. 'This will bring the afterbirth.'

'I thought I was going to hold my baby first,' said Lily. *My baby!* She was a mother. Tears of joy spilled over and dampened her cheeks.

'Have you chosen a name?' the midwife asked.

'Toby – Tobias. Tobias Irwin. Me and my husband both like Toby and Irwin is after my uncle who brought me up.' Lily pushed herself up on her elbows. 'Where is he? Where's Toby?' Lily looked from side to side – he wasn't here. She thought she was going to ask about Toby, but the question that came out was, 'Where's Matron?'

'She had to pop out for a minute,' said the midwife. 'She's got Baby Toby with her. They'll be back soon. Here comes the afterbirth.'

A different nurse gave Lily a wash. Another plumped her pillows. Someone else brought her a cup of tea. She kept asking for her baby and each time a soothing voice said, 'He'll be here soon,' but Lily didn't feel soothed.

Finally, Toby was brought back and placed in her arms. She gazed at him, emotion radiating throughout her body. It was a moment of perfect love.

'Make the most of him while he's still here,' said Matron.

'You mean before you take him to the nursery,' said Lily.

But Matron didn't mean that at all.

13

After she had sneaked Bill's name onto the call-up list, Kitty had walked on eggshells. Would the addition be spotted? Would she be revealed as a treacherous wife? Indeed, did she deserve to be revealed as such after what she'd done? How could she ever justify it? Yet, if she hadn't done it, she would have existed in a state of perpetual dread for their future.

Then Bill had come home from work, his features set like granite, his eyes dark with shock, and she had known she'd got away with it. Her muscles went weak with relief. She felt ashamed too. What sort of wife was she? But then she reminded herself why she'd acted as she had and her resolve stiffened all over again. She was doing this for the good of her family. She recalled for the hundredth time what Miss Patten had said about the skills a shipping clerk had, and crossed her fingers that Bill's knowledge and experience would be put to good use by his country.

'At least you'll have the chance to live in Dunbar's for a few days before you go,' Abbie told her father consolingly.

Abbie – Kitty felt yet another stab of guilt. The child adored

A New Home at the Wartime Hotel 137

her father. She had been his precious little girl ever since he'd chosen her name. She would miss him dreadfully.

'I wish I could be here for your birthday, Abbie,' Bill said.

The move from Withington to Lily Street was completed, though without Bill being cock-a-hoop. It was a relief each morning to see him off on his way to work. Kitty was still fearful that the truth would somehow come out. She wouldn't feel safe until he'd gone.

Meanwhile she immersed herself in her new world.

'I've so much to learn,' she admitted to Mrs Swanson as the two of them stood in the small office behind the reception desk. 'I have *every*thing to learn and I hope you'll be happy to teach me.'

The housekeeper looked pleased. Buxom and double-chinned but with dainty ankles, she had worked at Dunbar's for a long time and was well into her fifties. 'I'll give you every support, Mrs Dunbar. Shall you be responsible for your family's meals or do you wish the kitchen to provide them?'

Did she dare ask for the kitchen to cook her family's meals? What sort of housewife handed over that kind of responsibility?

Maybe the internal war showed in her face because Mrs Swanson said, 'If you have the same meals as the residents, it shows your confidence in the kitchen staff.'

Kitty grabbed this with both hands. 'Then that's what we'll do. Thank you, Mrs Swanson.'

'You'll need to give me your ration books. The wartime rule for dinner is to restrict yourself to two courses, either a starter and a main course or a main and a pudding. Visiting guests may choose which to have but the arrangement we have with the resident guests is starter and main course one day and main course and pudding the next.'

'My family will do the same as the resident guests,' said Kitty, for which she received a nod of approval.

'I suggest you spend your time with me and I'll show you the ropes,' said the housekeeper. 'Excuse me,' she added as the post-lady appeared.

The two of them exchanged a few words about last night's raid, then the post-lady went on her way.

Mrs Swanson sifted through the letters. 'Some are for the residents. Anything for the hotel must be dealt with at once.' She stopped sorting and smiled. 'Here's one from Lily. I know her handwriting. She used to be one of our maids. She went off to have a baby, so I expect she's sending news of her happy event.' Her expression clouded. 'She's addressed this to Mr Jeremiah Dunbar. Of course. She left just before he passed away, so she doesn't know. I suppose this letter ought to be given to your husband.'

Kitty smiled. 'If it's about a baby, I think we should open it ourselves, don't you?'

Mrs Swanson smiled too. 'I must admit I'm dying to know.' She held out the envelope.

'No, you open it,' said Kitty. 'She knows you.'

There was a letter opener on the desk. Mrs Swanson carefully slit open the envelope so it could be used again in accordance with wartime etiquette.

'Is it a boy or a girl?' Kitty asked.

'Oh my goodness.' Tears sprang to Mrs Swanson's eyes and her mouth twisted in distress.

'What's happened?'

'The baby... oh, Mrs Dunbar. Lily had a little boy... and he died. Oh my goodness.'

Even though she had gone cold with shock, Kitty rose to the occasion. 'Come and sit in the office and I'll make us some tea.'

'I have to tell the staff – and the residents. Everyone will be so upset.'

'That can wait,' Kitty said firmly. 'You've had a shock. I can see how much you care for this Lily. Give yourself a bit of time, then we'll worry about telling other people.'

Kitty quickly made tea and took it to the office, shutting the door for privacy. Both the door and the wooden wall had windows so she would see if she was needed.

Mrs Swanson took a gulp of tea. 'Poor Lily, poor child. She was a little lass of fourteen when she came here. She had to live in because she was an orphan.'

'You must know her very well, then,' said Kitty.

'A hard-working girl, very willing,' said Mrs Swanson. 'I've never had any maid learn the Dunbar way quicker than Lily did. Then she got married.' She looked around as if an eavesdropper might leap out from behind the cupboard, then she dropped her voice to a whisper complete with exaggerated lip-movements. '*Shotgun wedding.*' Mrs Swanson gave a nod of great significance.

'Many a successful marriage has started that way,' said Kitty.

'Let's hope so,' said Mrs Swanson. 'Her husband's with the merchant navy and he sent her to live with his mother, but they didn't get along and Lily fetched up back here, poor love.'

'And now she's lost her baby,' Kitty whispered, her heart aching for the unknown Lily.

'You ought to read the letter, Mrs Dunbar. She didn't write just to say about the baby. She's asking for help too.'

'What sort of help?'

'She needs money. She has to pay for the funeral. She says the undertaker doesn't charge for a baby's funeral, but there are other expenses – cemetery fees and so on. She doesn't feel able to approach her mother-in-law, and her uncle and auntie are lovely people but they haven't got sixpence to scratch themselves with. So Lily's hoping for a loan. Of course, she thinks she's asking Mr Jeremiah Dunbar. What do you think your husband will say?'

'He'll agree with me,' Kitty stated firmly. 'We must send Lily a postal order immediately. Will you see to that, please – and would you write to her as well? But don't tell her about Uncle Jeremiah. She's got enough to worry about without that.'

'Of course, Mrs Dunbar – and thank you.'

Kitty sighed softly. Poor Lily. Kitty felt herself slip back in time to the day she had collapsed in the street and been rushed to hospital, where Abbie had been born two months early. She thought too of her miscarriages, the appalling pain that had shot through her belly, sending her plunging to the floor.

She closed her eyes. When she opened them again, they were moist and the office was out of focus. She drew in a breath. This wasn't the time to think of her own losses.

'Mrs Swanson,' she said, 'do you feel ready to tell the staff and the residents? I think we ought to do that now.'

* * *

Bill said his goodbyes the evening before he left. He put on a good show, shaking hands with the male guests and instructing the staff to work hard in his absence.

Abbie was upset. She had been assured all along that her father was in a reserved occupation, and now here he was answering the call. Kitty felt wretched for her daughter.

'Children are adaptable,' said Mrs Swanson, 'and she'll still be here with you, not like all those poor little mites who've been sent off goodness knows where for the duration.'

Kitty hugged Abbie. 'You have to be brave for Daddy's sake. You don't want his last sight of you to be a long face.'

Abbie's slender frame straightened at once. 'It's patriotic to be cheerful when a soldier has to leave.'

'Good girl.' Emotion swelled inside Kitty and she had to force a swallow past a constriction in her throat. In that moment, she hated herself for getting rid of Bill, not just for Abbie's sake, but for her own sake. Whatever their differences, she had never stopped loving him.

He had to be up at five on the morning he was due to leave. Kitty had imagined waving him off from the front steps on her own, but Abbie got up too. So did the live-in staff, which touched Kitty deeply.

'I remember watching young Mr Ronald marching off to war back in 1914,' Mrs Swanson said tearfully. 'He wasn't much more than a boy.'

That made Kitty feel even worse about what she'd done. She had to keep reminding herself why she'd done it. Bill would have ruined them, she was sure of it. He loved spending money, felt entitled to spend it, even when it meant asking for credit that he never actually paid off. If, on top of that, he had acquired a taste for playing the genial and open-handed host – Kitty shuddered as she pictured the occasion when he had poured sherry with a generous hand, proudly letting Dunbar's bear the cost. And it wouldn't have ended there. Bill would have found other ways to pour money down the drain.

Now that he was gone, she had to take a deep breath and look to the future. She needed to get to grips with running the hotel and earning money. She knew without anything having been said that Bill would have arranged for her to have the smallest possible allotment of his wages. The sight of the pounds sign on the piece of paper would have been too much for him to resist. She was certain he would have instructed the army payroll people to give him the lion's share of his wages and her the minimum sum he was permitted to give her. Even if he didn't have the chance to spend his share, he would still want to receive it.

Should she feel angry? Let down? What she actually felt was excitement. Determination. She was going to make a success of this venture. No matter how many hours a day she had to work, no matter how challenging it was to learn the ropes, she, Kitty Dunbar, was going to carry the quaint old hotel through its wartime years and she was darned well going to do it successfully.

She wasn't going to be the domesticated female any longer. She was going to work at what before the war would have been seen as a man's job. It was always the men who were in charge. Well, not any longer.

Kitty didn't want her daughter to grow up in wartime, but since this was what was happening, she wanted Abbie to see for herself exactly what women were capable of.

'Have you heard from Bill yet?' Naomi asked a day or two later when she came to see how Kitty was getting on. Naomi looked neat and elegant in her Women's Voluntary Service uniform. Oddly, the sober green suited her fair colouring, but then she was the sort who could look good in anything.

Kitty had shown her around the hotel and now they were in the family's private sitting room. Naomi had looked at the new furniture, then at Kitty, with her eyebrows raised; to which Kitty had responded, 'Don't ask.'

Answering her sister's question about Bill, Kitty said, 'He's doing basic training.' Lowering her voice, she added, 'It's making him remember last time.'

Naomi nodded. 'That's understandable. You'd think Congreve's would just have sent the younger men.'

'The army doesn't just need soldiers,' said Kitty in what she

A New Home at the Wartime Hotel 143

hoped was a normal voice. 'There are many different jobs. Bill has years of experience in a shipping warehouse. He knows all about transporting goods from A to B. He has valuable experience to offer.'

'How are you managing without him?' Naomi asked.

'I've got heaps to learn, but the truth is I can't wait,' said Kitty. 'I feel as if my world is opening up. There are so many women now who are doing jobs that used to be seen as men's work. Now I've got a man's job too.'

Naomi gave a little laugh. 'I don't know about that. You can't really compare yourself to the women who are operating cranes or heavy machinery or mending motorcars.'

Kitty lifted her chin. 'All right, so I won't be getting my hands dirty, but Dunbar's has always been run by a man and now it's going to be run by a woman. I'll be setting a good example to Abbie and that means everything to me.'

There was a sharp knock on the door and Mrs Swanson burst in, making the sisters look round in surprise.

'Mrs Dunbar – oh, Mrs Dunbar, come quickly. You won't believe it. The bailiffs are here. The bailiffs – at Dunbar's! Never in all my born days— Oh, Mrs Dunbar, they've come to take everything away.'

* * *

With his black jacket, pin-striped trousers and bowler hat, Mr Clegg, the chief bailiff, looked more like a solicitor.

'Is Mr William Dunbar on the premises?' he asked.

'No. He's been called up,' said Kitty. 'I'm his wife.'

Mr Clegg thrust a typewritten letter at her, followed immediately by another typewritten sheet. Before Kitty could absorb what they said, Mr Clegg brushed past her, rattling off instructions to his men.

Dazed and startled, Kitty hurried after him. 'Stop! What's going on?'

'We're the bailiffs, love,' said one of the workmen. He went by without stopping and walked into the dining room.

'I know that,' said Kitty, trying to sound sharp, though what she felt was desperate.

The guests were angry and upset, the staff shocked and deeply shaken. Mrs Swanson began by being staunch and supportive, but when the piano was wheeled out, followed by the handsome oak sideboard, her eyes hardened.

'Mr Jeremiah Dunbar must be turning in his grave,' she announced before she marched away.

Kitty was beside herself. Naomi put her arms around her and held her tightly for a minute while Kitty fought not to sob.

Naomi eased away slightly, still holding Kitty by the arms. 'There's one good thing. At least Abbie's at school and not here to witness this.'

Kitty nodded, too fraught at that moment to speak.

Mr Clegg went around the building accompanied by a Mr Hawthorn, whom he introduced as his valuer.

'Surely you needn't take *all* the beds from the guest rooms.' Kitty could barely get the words out. 'And you've reduced the dining room to a shell.'

'It's tables, chairs, beds and cupboards that people are most in need of, these days,' said Mr Hawthorn. 'With folk losing all their worldly goods in the air raids, they're desperate for the basics.'

Anger flared inside Kitty. 'There's nothing basic about the furniture here. Everything is of the highest quality.'

'That's true,' Mr Clegg conceded, 'but war regulations

require me to sell to organisations that help people start again after losing everything. They can't afford to pay top whack, which means I have to remove twice as much from you as I would have done before the war in order to recoup the same amount of money. That's so, isn't it, Mr Hawthorn?'

'It is indeed,' his colleague agreed.

By the end of the morning, Dunbar's had been stripped of most of its furniture, or its 'assets', as Mr Clegg referred to them.

Kitty was stunned. Disbelieving. All the breath seemed to have been sucked out of her lungs.

Before Mr Clegg and Mr Hawthorn left, she managed to ask, 'How can we possibly owe so much money?'

Mr Clegg shrugged. 'I believe that before Mr Dunbar inherited this place he was able to take out loans on the strength of being the heir.'

'He *what*?' cried Kitty. What on earth could Bill possibly have bought that could warrant this visit from the bailiffs? It beggared belief. Bill had surprised and infuriated her so many times, but this time she could feel pressure building up inside her chest and realised she had forgotten to breathe.

The two men exchanged glances, then bade her good day and left.

Kitty wanted to sit on the stairs and weep, but then new strength came to her, fuelled by anger. Bill's debts. Bill's *bloody* debts. But there was no time to indulge in these feelings. She had to get to grips with the reality of her situation.

With next to no furniture remaining in the bedrooms, the guests couldn't stay. This was especially hard on the resident guests who had lived here since before Kitty married Bill. They were all jittery with distress. Kitty might be almost dizzy with shock and humiliation, but she lifted her chin and promised to help everyone find alternative accommodation. She had to go over the road to the Grove to see if they had rooms available, leaving Naomi telephoning other hotels.

When Kitty returned, Mr Seton, a guest who was in Manchester visiting family, pounced on her.

'The least you can do is put me up at the Claremont or the Midland,' he declared.

'I'm sorry, sir,' Kitty replied. 'That's out of the question. They are considerably more expensive than Dunbar's.'

'Exactly!' said Mr Seton. 'And you can make up the difference.'

'No, I can't,' said Kitty. 'I will reimburse you for the nights you cannot spend here, and I'll help you find a hotel room of similar value, but that's as much as I can do.'

With Naomi's help, the guests were gradually dispatched to other hotels. Kitty had to raid the petty cash tin to pay for taxis.

'It's your turn, Major.' It was a relief to deal with a friendly face. 'Let me see where I can send you where you'll be comfortable.'

'No, thank you,' was the stiff reply. The major's tone was polite but his eyes clearly stated that he wouldn't be mad enough to trust the assistance of the person who had presided over today's debacle. He apparently assumed it was her fault.

Kitty had to clamp her lips together to prevent herself from landing Bill in the soup. She had never been disloyal to him, except with Naomi, and she wasn't about to start now. Mam had brought her up not to wash her dirty linen in public. Something inside her curled up in dread at the thought of being whispered about behind her back, for being married to a man who couldn't stop spending. She didn't want to be pitied and she didn't want that kind of talk inflicted on Abbie.

Mrs Swanson asked about the staff.

Kitty released a long breath. 'There's no hotel any more. We have virtually no furniture left in the guest rooms – literally no beds. I'm more sorry than I can say, but I have to give everyone notice, effective immediately.' Tears welled and her heartbeat raced.

Naomi stepped in. 'Mrs Swanson, please could you let the staff know.'

Kitty pulled herself together. 'Please tell the staff they'll be paid to the end of next week.'

'Kitty!' Naomi sounded alarmed.

Kitty looked at her. 'I have to.' She turned to Mrs Swanson again. 'You and Cook will receive a month's wages.'

'Thank you, Mrs Dunbar. I appreciate that – though it doesn't make up for the years I've spent here. It's the only place I've ever worked. I started out as the scullery-maid when I was a lass of thirteen. I thought I'd be here until I dropped. Excuse me,' she finished brokenly and hurried from the room.

Kitty expelled an audible breath. If Mrs Swanson had started here at thirteen, that meant she'd been here forty years or more. Kitty longed to race after her and envelop her in a huge hug, but that wouldn't solve the problems the housekeeper faced.

Naomi took Kitty's hand. 'What will you say to Abbie?'

'I'll make up something about death duties,' Kitty answered. 'At her age, she'll believe what she's told.'

'What about Bill's mother?' Naomi asked. 'If it helps, I could drop in on her on the way home and tell her what's happened.'

Kitty shut her eyes for a moment, then opened them again. 'She has to be told – and she's going to come storming round here asking questions. Please don't let anything slip about Bill's debts,' she begged her sister. 'Just say that all you know is that the bailiffs have been.'

Kitty spent ages during the night trying to work out the

kindest way of telling Bill's mother the truth about his financial irresponsibility, but how could you sugar-coat something like that?

When Mrs Dunbar marched in the next morning, her face was set in grim, angry lines. At first Kitty thought this was her way of holding in her distress – but oh, how wrong she was.

'Well, I hope you're pleased with yourself,' was Ivy Dunbar's opening salvo, causing Kitty's mouth to drop open in shock. 'This was the opportunity of a lifetime for my Bill and look what you've done with it.'

'What d'you mean?' Kitty asked, baffled. 'I haven't done anything wrong.'

'Don't give me that.' Mrs Dunbar's voice was loaded with anger and scorn. 'Bill told me years ago what you're like. Spend, spend, spend, that's you, Kitty Dunbar. Money slips through your fingers like water.'

'Bill said *what?*' Kitty spluttered. 'He blamed the spending on *me*?'

'Aye, and with good reason,' Mrs Dunbar retorted. 'New lino and fresh wallpaper in your old house – and don't get me started on that walnut-cased clock on the mantelpiece.'

'But I never—'

'It's been as much as I could do to keep a civil tongue in my head all these years while I've had to stand by and watch you take my Bill for a ride.'

'I've done no such thing,' Kitty insisted. 'He's the one who spends like a maniac. He's the one who thinks that if a shop will give him credit, it's the equivalent of having money in his pocket. He's the one who bought the things you blame me for – including that damn clock. Wait a minute.' She was getting into her stride now. Ivy Dunbar wasn't the only one who'd stayed silent for years. 'Did I say he *bought* them? My mistake. To buy something, you have to pay for it. You have to hand over actual money – and when did Bill ever do that if he had the chance to sign a credit note and spend for evermore paying interest? Don't you dare blame me for this wretched mess I'm now in, Mrs Dunbar. None of it is my fault. It's Bill's.'

Mrs Dunbar jerked her chin. 'So you say.'

'Aye, I do,' Kitty shot back at once. 'If you don't believe me, write and ask Bill. And tell him that if he lies to you, I'll go down to those barracks and shoot him myself.'

14

Before Baby Toby was buried, Lily had imagined herself immediately packing and leaving Rookery House after the little funeral, but now that the time had come she couldn't bear to leave. It would feel like abandoning him. She wanted, needed, to be as near as possible to his grave. Oh, if only she had thought harder about his funeral – but she hadn't been capable of thinking things through. She had been too stunned; and when she hadn't been numb with shock, she'd been distraught. Her precious baby was gone. She'd had him for such a short time, less than a day.

All she had wanted was to hold him, but she'd been gently but firmly discouraged. She had sat beside his cot, pressing herself as close to its side as she could get, as if trying to merge herself with it. With one fingertip she had stroked her little boy's soft cheek, willing him to live, willing the doctor Matron had sent for to have made a mistake, willing her own life to pass into Toby's body. But to no avail. He had simply… slipped away.

She had overheard one of the greenies saying to another, 'At least she didn't have him long enough to get fond of him,' and her skin had tingled painfully all over. She had wanted to grab hold of the greenie, had wanted to slap her and shake her. She'd wanted to let all her grief come storming out in the form of fury against this stupid girl who didn't know any better, who thought that you grew fond of your baby over time, who had no notion of the massive wave of love that changed you for the rest of your life.

Mrs Walters had made the arrangements for the funeral. Making them herself would have been too much for Lily, but afterwards she hated herself. This was the one thing she could have done for her baby – and she hadn't done it.

'Is there anyone you would like me to inform?' Mrs Walters had asked her.

And she had whispered, 'No, thank you.'

Imagine Auntie Nettie and Uncle Irwin receiving a letter from a stranger telling them Lily's baby had died. She couldn't do that to them. She had to tell them in person.

She didn't want Daniel's mother to be informed either. It seemed profoundly wrong that Mrs Chadwick should hear before Daniel did. A powerful bleakness swept over Lily. Daniel would be away for weeks yet and there was no way to get in touch with him.

She imagined him counting the days, checking the calendar, working out whether he was now a father. In his world, his child was still alive. In his world, he was a proud father longing to meet his child for the first time. He was wondering if he was the father of Tobias Irwin or Angela Jeanette.

Lily didn't know what to do. Her thoughts were all jumbled up, though her feelings were jagged edged. The stay at Rookery House that Daniel had paid for wasn't over so she remained there. It wasn't that she chose to stay so much as that she couldn't stir herself to leave.

The only matter that impelled her to act was that of paying the funeral expenses.

'Your husband has listed his mother as your next of kin in his absence,' Mrs Walters had explained. 'Should I approach her to meet the costs?'

Lily was appalled. How could Daniel make his mother her next of kin without telling her – without asking her? She would never have agreed.

After that nasty jolt, Lily had written to Mr Jeremiah Dunbar to beg for a loan that would be repaid upon Daniel's return. He was the only person she could think of. Uncle Irwin and Auntie Nettie didn't have any money.

A kind letter had come from Mrs Swanson, together with the necessary funds. Lily was hurt that Mr Dunbar hadn't written personally, but then she dismissed the thought. What did it matter? Compared to losing Toby, what did anything matter?

There was an air raid, not in the skies over Sale but a couple of miles away. Disturbed by the sound of the ack-ack guns and the distant *crump* of explosions, some of the babies woke up and cried. Matron gave instructions for all the babies to be brought to their mothers to calm them.

Lily was the only one without a baby in her arms. That was the moment when she knew she must leave Rookery House.

* * *

Carrying her suitcase, Lily went to see Auntie Nettie before she went to Daniel's mother's house. It was essential to see Auntie Nettie first. She owed her aunt far more than she owed Mrs Chadwick.

She wore her best pre-pregnancy dress. Its short sleeves puffed at the shoulder and it fastened with buttons from collar to hem, with a belt to define the waist. It used to show off her slim figure but now it hung off her. The other new mothers at Rookery House had carried some extra pounds, but Lily had become as thin as a pencil after Toby died.

Over the top she wore her mackintosh and her felt hat, together with the pretty shoes Daniel had bought her. They were navy-and-white leather with peep-toes and a pattern of perforated dots. He had bought them after she'd told him she only had a pair of sensible shoes because that was what she needed for working at Dunbar's. How swish and grown-up she'd felt when she tried on the new pair in the smart shop Daniel had taken her to.

Arriving at the top of her uncle and aunt's road, she had to stop and take some breaths to fight against the dread of having to explain about Toby. She walked along the street, steadfastly not meeting anyone's eyes.

She knocked at Auntie Nettie's door and waited. She didn't know how to behave. How were you meant to conduct yourself when you turned up on someone's doorstep with news like this? Chin up for courage or shoulders hunched in grief?

'Lily! I didn't know you were back.' Auntie Nettie's kind face brightened at the sight of her. Then her aunt looked past her. 'No baby carriage? Haven't you brought the baby to meet me?'

Lily felt light-headed but she somehow managed not to collapse on the step.

'Can I come indoors? I've got something to tell you.'

'Oh, my lamb.' All Auntie Nettie's children were 'lamb' or 'chick'. 'Something's happened. Come in. Give me that case and sit yourself down.' Sinking onto the place beside her, Auntie Nettie took Lily's hand and gazed into her face. 'Is it your Daniel?'

'Daniel?' Lily exclaimed, startled. In all the versions of this conversation she had rehearsed in her head, this hadn't happened. 'No. No, he's fine – well, as far as I know. He's at sea—'

She couldn't continue. Daniel wasn't here. He didn't know. She needed him with all her heart and soul, but he wasn't here.

And why was she talking about him, anyway?

Shutting her eyes, Lily drew in a sharp breath through her nose and huffed it out through a little O in her lips, as if she was about to blow a smoke-ring. Her lashes were damp on her cheeks. For a moment her eyes seemed to be glued shut, then they sprang open upon the sight of Auntie Nettie's eyebrows squished together in confusion.

'Lily, what is it, chick? You're scaring me.'

Lily looked away. Being scared was nothing compared to a heartbreak that would never end. She returned her gaze to this darling auntie who had taken her in and brought her up.

'I had... a little boy.' Her voice wobbled but she forced herself to continue. If she didn't thrust the words out now, she might never manage it. 'His name... Tobias, known as Toby. Tobias Irwin.'

'Irwin!' Auntie Nettie smiled so widely that her cheeks plumped up. 'Your uncle's going to be so proud. Tobias Irwin Chadwick. That's a grand name. Oh, if your dear mam could be here now...'

Lily's throat was packed solid with emotion. She had to stop Auntie Nettie's happy prattling but she couldn't speak. She flapped her hands.

'What is it, chick?' Auntie Nettie was all concern. Then an uneasy frown appeared. 'Oh my goodness. It can't be...'

'He, um... He...'

Auntie Nettie squeezed Lily's hand almost tightly enough to break her fingers. 'Are you telling me that – that – I can't say it, because if I'm wrong, you'll be so shocked and hurt that I could ever have thought such a thing.'

'He lived for one day.'

'Oh, Lily.'

Auntie Nettie leaned forwards but Lily jumped to her feet to escape the embrace. If she started crying, she might never stop. She had to be strong.

'So here I am. No baby.'

Auntie Nettie looked at her for a long moment. 'I'm so very sorry, Lily, sorrier than I can say.'

Lily held up her hand, like a policeman stopping the traffic. 'I know. You don't have to say it. It's actually better if you don't.'

And then Auntie Nettie said the words that Lily had come to hate more than any other in the English language.

'You're young, chick. There'll be more babies.'

Inside her head Lily screamed. Everyone had told her this. Mrs Walters, the midwife, the proud mothers cuddling their newborns. Even the undertaker had said it.

Lily's jaw was so tight she had to unclamp her teeth before she could say, 'Don't. Don't say that.'

Auntie Nettie looked nonplussed, then she nodded. 'I'm sorry. It's too soon. Let's put the kettle on and make a brew. Keeping your hands busy takes the edge off things. That's what I've always found. Then we can sit and talk about... whatever you want to talk about.' Her gaze went to Lily's suitcase. 'Were you wanting to move back in? We can all budge up and make room if that's what's needed.'

'That's quite possibly the kindest thing anybody has ever said to me,' Lily told her sincerely, 'but I know you don't have the space. It was enough of a squeeze when I was here before, and the children are several years bigger now. But thank you for offering. It means a lot. It means everything.'

'Where will you go?'

'To Daniel's mother's. She doesn't know yet, about Toby. I've got to tell her and... and the plan always was that when I left Rookery House, I would go back to her house with the baby and we'd live there while we waited for Daniel to come home.'

Auntie Nettie said gently, 'I thought you didn't get on with her.'

'I don't,' said Lily, 'but that has faded into insignificance now. And...' She dredged up a colossal sigh. 'Honestly, does it matter where I am, without my baby?'

15

Since her confrontation with Ivy, Kitty's mind seemed to have been split in half with a wall down the centre. On one side was a blazing anger. How *could* Bill have fed all those lies to his mother? No wonder Ivy had never liked her. Bill deserved to be clapped in irons for that.

On the other side of the wall was a deep stillness. Kitty was stunned. She wasn't in love with Bill any longer, but she had carried on loving him in a steady way, feeling safe in the knowledge that, whatever their differences in their attitudes to money, spending and debt, and whatever strain those attitudes caused, nevertheless other aspects of their lives together were solid and true, especially their shared devotion to Abbie. But not now. Not any more.

Kitty had been loyal to Bill all along. There had been so many times when she could have announced his extravagance to the world, but she never had. She could have told the bailiffs; she could have told the residents and guests. But she'd never told a soul. Oh, she'd confided in Naomi, but that was like having a safety valve. She could share her concerns with her sister, knowing Naomi would never breathe a word.

And what good had her loyalty to Bill done her? Where was his loyalty to her? If she had talked about him, she'd have been divulging the truth. Instead, he had talked about her and it had been a pack of lies. How *could* he?

She felt numb, dazed. Across her abiding, residual love for Bill, a crack had appeared that could never be repaired.

How *could* he?

Kitty forced herself to carry on. There was Abbie's birthday to think about. Her little girl was about to turn thirteen. Thirteen! One more year and she'd be leaving school. It was hard to believe, and it was horrible to think that her final years at school had been swallowed up by the war.

And what of Abbie's birthday celebration? Ivy had always been present on her granddaughter's special day. Was that possible this year, after all the things that had been said? But Kitty wasn't about to change the routines of Abbie's life because she'd had a major falling-out with Ivy. She wouldn't inflict that on her daughter.

After a little thought, she made arrangements to take Abbie over to Withington for her birthday, so she could share the day with her friend Martha. Kitty took the girls to a teashop and invited Martha's mum and Ivy to come too. Whatever thoughts Ivy was brewing about her, Kitty knew she would bury them in order to ensure the girls had a good time.

Just now, that was Kitty's focus: her beloved daughter's happiness.

* * *

Kitty had written a fierce letter to Bill, the nib of her fountain pen blazing across the paper. He kept her waiting for a reply. By the time she received it, she was hopping mad at the delay, though she had to hide her tumultuous feelings from the world, especially from Abbie.

Far from offering abject apologies, Bill laid the blame squarely at Kitty's door.

You shouldn't have let the bailiffs over the threshold. You should have told them that the debt was being taken care of. They aren't allowed to enter a property if they are told that – and it would have given me time to sort things out.

Kitty could practically feel the steam pouring out of her ears. How dare Bill make out that it was her fault? A bitter laugh erupted from her lips. *Given me time to sort things out, indeed!* What a load of tripe.

At the end of the letter Bill wrote, *I'm pleased you told Abbie it was because of death duties.* Not *Thank you for saying it was death duties.* Not *Thank you for letting me off the hook.* Just *I'm pleased* – as if he was entitled to have his financial misdemeanours hidden. Kitty could have bashed him over the head with the frying pan. She almost wished she hadn't offered him that reassurance. He didn't deserve it.

But Abbie did. Abbie deserved to believe that she had the best father in the world. Kitty sincerely hoped she would never find out any different.

Unwanted tears welled up behind Kitty's eyes. She had been so happy and excited at the prospect of learning to run Dunbar's – and now there was no hotel left, just an almost empty building. The kitchen was still intact, which was a blessing, and there were still beds, hanging-cupboards and wash-stands in the rooms on the third floor where the live-in staff had slept. A few things remained in the guest rooms but the family flat had been stripped. Bill's precious new furniture had been carried out.

Kitty had begged Mr Clegg to leave Abbie's bedroom alone.

'I am obligated to gather items to a certain value,' he had replied in a tone that made it clear he had uttered these words a thousand times before.

'Then leave her room until last,' Kitty had pleaded. 'Please – she's just a child.'

'It's a pity you and your husband didn't think of that before you plunged up to your ears in debt,' Mr Hawthorn had murmured as if speaking to himself, though his voice was loud enough for Kitty to hear and she could tell he had intended his words to carry.

How she had ached to declare that this was nothing to do with her, that it was all her husband's doing, but as always she held her tongue. In any case, the two men had already moved on.

The staff were all gone now. Mrs Swanson had departed and frankly it had been a relief to see the back of her. She must have been deeply shocked by the events, not to mention more than a little afraid of facing the future at her age, and Kitty would have been glad to offer moral support, but Mrs Swanson had coped by donning a mantle of cold anger at the way Mr and Mrs William Dunbar had let down the memory of dear Mr Jeremiah Dunbar and Mr Ronald in such an appalling way.

Now there were just Kitty and Abbie left in the big old building. The big old *empty* building.

'Are we going to sell it and move?' Abbie asked.

'We can't,' said Kitty. 'Dunbar's belongs to Daddy. He's the only person who can sell it and he's not here.'

The hair lifted on the back of Kitty's neck and her palms felt clammy. Just imagine if Dunbar's was sold and Bill got his hands on all that money! She had to prevent that – but how?

'Do you think it's spooky, the hotel being empty?' Abbie asked.

'No,' Kitty said firmly. 'Do you?'

Abbie shook her head. 'It's not spooky, just echoey. It needs to be full of furniture to make the echoes go away, and not just the real echoes but the echoes of the past.' She looked at Kitty. 'Is that daft?'

'Not in the slightest,' Kitty assured her. 'You're right. Buildings need to be occupied.'

Encouraged, Abbie added, 'They need people and furniture. They need to feel full.'

An idea darted into Kitty's mind. She caught hold of her daughter and hugged her, much to Abbie's surprise.

'You've hit the nail on the head, Abbie. That's exactly what Dunbar's needs.' Kitty laughed as the weight she had been carrying eased a little. 'You clever girl!'

* * *

The first thing Kitty did was turn to Naomi with her idea.

'Oh my goodness!' Naomi burst out. 'You can't possibly!'

Kitty was taken aback and was too surprised to say anything.

'You must admit it's an outlandish idea,' said Naomi, sounding kind now. 'You're proposing to turn Dunbar's into a place for storage.'

'Why not? I've got to do something to earn money and I can't run it as a hotel. And you can't deny there are many people who need somewhere to keep their possessions safe after they've been bombed out.'

'Oh, sweetheart.' Naomi put her arms around Kitty. 'I don't

mean to put you off. It's just that I can't bear the thought of you doing something so... so...'

'Outlandish?'

'You've already been through that dreadful experience with the bailiffs,' said Naomi, 'and now you want to throw yourself into this. Do the words "frying pan" and "fire" mean anything to you? The last thing I want is to see you get hurt.'

'I appreciate your concern,' Kitty told her, 'but at the very least I have to look into this. What else can I do with a building this size?'

'Don't go all defensive on me,' Naomi said coaxingly. 'If I didn't instantly provide the wholehearted support you were hoping for, it's because you took me by surprise. I'm on your side. You know that. I always have been.'

Kitty felt reassured. Naomi's support meant everything to her.

Her next step was to discuss the matter with her WVS colleagues. They were far more than the ordinary housewives they had been before the war. Through their WVS experience, they had gleaned all kinds of knowledge, most of it related, directly or indirectly, to how to get things organised.

'You'll need to talk to the Corporation,' was one piece of advice. 'They run all the local public services and hand out the licences for private services. Various permissions are bound to be involved.'

'You should visit a proper storage place,' said someone else. 'Ask questions. Find out how they work.'

Kitty put through a call to the Town Hall and after playing telephone ping-pong with the Corporation switchboard, finally spoke to a clerk who agreed to send out an official to look at Dunbar's.

After that Kitty contacted a couple of storage warehouses and asked if she might look round.

'I'm sorry, madam,' said the woman who answered her first telephone call. 'We're full to the rafters. You need to get in touch with another storage business.'

'You misunderstand,' Kitty put in. 'I don't need to place my belongings in storage. I hope to make an appointment to visit your warehouse to see how it's run. I'm speaking on behalf of a new storage company that is hoping for advice.'

'I see.' The woman sounded warmer. 'Well, there's plenty of work to go round. I have the diary in front of me. When would your boss like to visit? And what's his name, please?'

Kitty felt as if cold water had been dashed over her, but the woman's assumption was only natural. In the steadiest voice she could muster, she replied, 'I'm not ringing on behalf of anyone else. I will be the boss of the new company.'

There was a tiny silence at the other end. Kitty held her breath.

'Good for you! There's nothing men can do that women can't. The war is busy proving that. What's your name?'

Soon, Kitty had appointments lined up at two storage warehouses. In her WVS work she had helped plenty of the newly homeless who now needed to move in with family for the remainder of the war and who also had to cope with the additional upheaval of finding suitable storage accommodation for whatever possessions they had left. Even so, the sight of all the piled-up goods in the first warehouse took Kitty's breath away.

Everything was here. Large items like beds, wardrobes, pianos, sideboards and dining tables. Bulky things like armchairs, bookcases and linen chests. Small but substantial things like side tables, footstools, coal-scuttles and bedside cabinets. On shelves and in boxes were masses of everyday possessions, everything from candlesticks and vases to bookends and clocks; from fruit bowls and jugs to tea trays and ornaments; from butter dishes and kitchen scales to watering cans and pipe racks.

Tearing her gaze from a grandfather clock and a telescope on a collapsed tripod, Kitty concentrated on what Mr Rickford, the owner of the warehouse, was telling her.

'You must decide whether to accept household linen. If you do, add mothballs to the customers' bills. And there's no such thing as having too many mousetraps in your building.'

Kitty was starting to feel overwhelmed, but that was nothing compared to how all the people whose houses had been destroyed must feel. She pushed back her shoulders. She was going to provide an important service and at the same time give Dunbar's a new lease of life.

* * *

To start with, being in Mrs Chadwick's house had been... Lily struggled to think of the right word. All right? Acceptable? The right word hardly mattered. Being here without Toby shredded her heart.

Mrs Chadwick had been shocked and distressed to learn of the death of her brand-new grandson, and that had drawn her and Lily close together. Lily had even thought that perhaps living here wouldn't be so bad after all.

But after Mrs Chadwick got to grips with her initial grief, her feeling turned to anger.

'Why wasn't I informed at once when the baby was born?' she demanded. 'You were only a few miles away. I could have come. If I'd known that... that time was short, I could have seen him, held him. I could have told Daniel that I held his son in my arms.'

Maybe it was wrong of her, but resentment poured into Lily at the implication that his mother holding Toby would be of greater consolation to Daniel than the thought of Lily holding him.

'You had no right to deprive me of that,' Mrs Chadwick declared.

'I... I wasn't thinking straight.' Lily hated having to defend herself. She hadn't done anything wrong... had she? 'I just wanted every single moment that I could have with my son.'

'And never mind his grandmother,' Mrs Chadwick retorted. 'Never mind what I might have wanted. You didn't even ask me to pay for the funeral,' she exclaimed, her voice cracking with emotion. 'You asked your old employer, of all people. How do you think that makes me feel? How do you think it makes me look to other people?'

'I'm sorry,' Lily whispered. 'I couldn't tell you. I...' She shook her head, trying to remember the thinking behind a decision that had seemed reasonable at the time. 'I thought Daniel should be told first before anyone else.'

Mrs Chadwick cast her gaze up to the ceiling. 'That was foolish. You knew Daniel would be at sea for weeks.'

'I know, but...'

Mrs Chadwick hadn't finished. 'If your aunt and uncle had had room for you in their house, would you even have come here to tell me about Toby?'

'Of course I would!' cried Lily.

Mrs Chadwick's pencilled eyebrows climbed up her forehead. 'There's no "of course" about it, given how you've admitted you wanted Daniel to know before I did.'

Lily couldn't think what to say. Not only had she failed to

produce a thriving baby like all the other mothers, but apparently she had made a mess of her bereavement as well.

* * *

The sun was shining brightly when Kitty visited the second storage warehouse, armed with a list of questions. She had learned a lot from Mr Rickford and now she wanted to glean as much information as she could from Mr Tulip.

Mr Tulip! What a name. It made her smile. He turned out to be a tubby, well-dressed individual with a Burnley accent, which meant he stressed the letter R in his speech. He was happy to show her around and answer her questions.

'Doesn't it worry you that I'm setting up in competition?' Kitty asked.

That made him chuckle. 'My dear Mrs Dunbar, I'm aware of the size of your building compared to my three warehouses. Trust me: you are not competition.'

Far from feeling slapped down, Kitty was pleased. It meant Mr Tulip had no reason not to give her all the information she needed.

'You need to make decisions about insurance,' he explained. 'If you insure your customers' contents, you must pass on that cost to them. Or you can get the customers to arrange their own. You could,' and he coughed discreetly, 'have an arrangement with an insurance company whereby you recommend them and they pay you commission.'

Kitty wrote it all down. Sometimes what she was proposing to do felt scary but mainly she was excited and determined.

'Are you going to provide boxes and packing cases for your customers? If so, make sure you charge for them. Don't do anything for nothing. Everything that passes through your front door needs to be labelled and added to an inventory. Make sure the customer signs every page of the inventory. This matters for insurance as well as to prevent errors or disagreements as to what belongs to whom.'

Kitty made more notes.

'Shall you charge weekly or monthly?' Mr Tulip asked her.

'People get paid weekly so that makes more sense... doesn't it?'

'I could help you get started,' said Mr Tulip.

'Could you really?' It was all Kitty could do to prevent herself from tipping her head back and shutting her eyes in relief and gratitude.

'I could send some consignments of belongings your way,' said Mr Tulip. 'The owners would pay your fees and you would pay me a small commission for the recommendation.' He smiled. 'Never do anything for nothing, Mrs Dunbar.'

'I'll have to think about it,' said Kitty.

Mr Tulip gave her an hour of his time, by the end of which Kitty's head was crammed as full as her notebook.

She walked back to Dunbar's, considering Mr Tulip's offer to put business her way. If she agreed, he would cream off some of her income; but if she decided to go it alone, what if no one felt confident about using an ex-hotel run by a woman with no experience of running a business?

As she walked up the front steps, she heard a voice behind her.

'Mrs Dunbar! May I have a word?'

Turning, she smiled at Mr Barnes from the Grove, the hotel over the road.

'How are you, Mr Barnes?' she asked politely.

'Very well, thank you. Feeling remarkably chipper, as a matter of fact.'

'I'm pleased to hear it,' said Kitty.

'You will be when I tell you the news,' he replied. 'After that unfortunate business with the bailiffs, I had a letter from your husband and we've been corresponding since.'

'Really?' Kitty said again, but in a different tone of voice. She'd heard from Bill only once, when he'd told her off for letting the bailiffs over the threshold.

'Yes, really.' Mr Barnes beamed at her. 'Good news, Mrs Dunbar – the very best. Mr Dunbar has agreed to sell Dunbar's Hotel to me.'

16

Beatrice's workload had doubled since Miss Todd had gone off to work in the canteen in a munitions factory. The time that she previously used to spend helping her ladies to change the sheets was now well and truly eaten up by the rush to get to her next address. She explained that she now had more appointments and most of her ladies understood, but an expression flashed across the faces of one or two that suggested she had let them down.

'It makes me feel bad,' Beatrice confided to Mrs Gates as they enjoyed their weekly meal together, with Beatrice at the old lady's bedside.

'I'm not surprised,' said Mrs Gates. 'These women who benefited from your acts of kindness probably ended up thinking that helping put the sheets through the mangle was part of your job.'

'Do you think so?' Beatrice asked.

'It doesn't matter what I think, an old biddy like me.' Mrs Gates put down her piece of bread and butter on her plate and Beatrice made a mental note to encourage her friend to take another bite in a minute. 'I want to hear about *you*, Miss Inkerman, dear. I'm sure those women aren't the only ones who are disappointed with how things have turned out.'

'Yes, well.' Beatrice almost shrugged her shoulders but straightened them instead. 'Things happen the way they happen. You just have to get on with it.' She'd learned that at a young age, after Dad had buggered off.

'I know how much you loved your job before you were given all these extra people,' said Mrs Gates.

'You're right. I did,' Beatrice agreed. 'I loved all the personal contact. It might sound big-headed but it made me feel I was making a difference. Now all I seem to do is rush from house to house.'

'You're still providing a necessary service,' her friend reminded her.

It was true. Of course she was. But Beatrice was only too aware of what she'd lost. The odd ten minutes here and there to have a natter with one of her ladies had, she was sure, given them a much-needed lift in the middle of a day of drudgery. She had liked feeling she was helping them – because nobody had ever helped her.

She had lost something else too – the time to pop in on Mrs Chapman and young Dora. She always made a point of asking Mrs Williams if the rent was up to date, but she honestly couldn't afford the time to go upstairs and check. All she did these days was hand over the latest consignment of nappies and say, 'Sign here, please.' As soon as she'd done that, she had to get back on her bicycle and start pedalling.

She also had to call in more frequently at the district nurses' station for supplies, and that too ate into her day.

The next time she went there, just as she was fastening the

straps on her trolley to keep her latest bundles safe, a cheerful voice greeted her.

'Miss Inkerman, how nice to see you.'

Beatrice recognised the voice but couldn't think where from. She looked around and saw Miss Brewer, the young woman from the Town Hall who had interviewed her. Her dark red hair spilled onto the shoulders of her linen jacket, where it sat in a plump roll. She looked both professional and attractive in a suit, with suede shoes and the hat Beatrice remembered from last time, with the perky feather. Dangling from one shoulder were her gas-mask box and a bag. In the opposite hand she carried a leather satchel, which looked rather worn and shouldn't have seemed professional but somehow did, presumably because of Miss Brewer's air of genial competence.

Responding to Miss Brewer's friendly smile, Beatrice found herself saying, 'I like your hat.'

Miss Brewer laughed and her hazel eyes sparkled. 'Everyone says that but I'm inclined to think that when they say it, what they really mean is, "I like that feather." It's quite eye-catching. The hat was a gift from my brother.'

'That was kind of him,' said Beatrice.

Miss Brewer grinned. 'I think he wanted me to have the feather.'

Beatrice couldn't help smiling in return. 'He wanted you to receive lots of compliments on your headwear.'

'Possibly,' said Miss Brewer. 'He's a good egg, really. We're twins.'

'Does that mean you're a good egg too?' Miss Brewer tilted her head as she chuckled. Then she looked serious. 'Well, I hope so. I work in welfare and I do the best I can.'

Beatrice hesitated. Should she say what was on the tip of her tongue? Miss Brewer was smart, not just in her appearance but in the brain department as well. Though not posh, she was well-spoken and must be educated. She was exactly the sort of person Beatrice had been brought up to respect. On the other hand, Beatrice had a good ten, if not fifteen, years on her, and that, together with Miss Brewer's smile, gave her the confidence to speak up.

'I think you did your best for me when I was interviewed, Miss Brewer. Thank you for that. Is that your job in welfare? To help women move into war work?'

'No. I was sent to do the interviews because I happened to be available. No offence intended.'

'None taken,' said Beatrice.

'My job has developed somewhat since the war started – since the air raids started, I should say,' Miss Brewer explained. 'I now visit a lot of properties to see what other uses they can be put to – as rest centres or soup kitchens or temporary accommodation, all sorts of things. But everything I do also has a welfare slant. I'm particularly interested in the lives of women and children. Everybody has to adapt in all kinds of ways in wartime, but the basic welfare needs are still the same.'

Beatrice suddenly felt fired up with resolve. She didn't know what she was going to do, but she was jolly well going to do *something*. With luck, Miss Brewer would point her in the right direction.

'I can't stop now,' said Beatrice, 'because I have a rota, and I'm sure you have appointments, but could I please arrange to see you another time – in your professional capacity.' She couldn't have this intelligent, efficient young woman thinking she hoped for a social meeting. 'I'm sorry to put you on the spot, but there's something I've been wanting to do for a while – to help others, you understand – children, actually – and if I'm not being presumptuous, I'd be grateful for your advice.' Heat rose in Beatrice's cheeks. Was she babbling?

'You want to pick my brains,' said Miss Brewer. 'That's fine, but you're right about me being busy.'

Something inside Beatrice slumped in disappointment. 'I understand.'

'Wait. What time do you finish your rounds? We could meet after that over a cup of tea and a bun. How does that sound?'

'Well, if I'm not imposing—'

'Of course you aren't,' said Miss Brewer. 'Are you familiar with the Worker Bee on Deansgate? We could meet there. I'm intrigued by what you've said and I won't let you back out. I told you after your interview that you're the capable sort, so let's see what it is I can help you with.'

* * *

As she went on her way, Beatrice was consumed by panic. What had she let herself in for? Had she just set herself up to look like a prize chump? But the panic soon turned to resolve. She had for some time now wanted to help Dora and other children in the same position. Now, the time had come to stop simply wanting and do something about it.

That gave her the shove she needed to think things through. Why did she want to help Dora and others like her? It wasn't just because it was undesirable to heap responsibilities onto a child to the point where they missed school more often than not. It was because Beatrice remembered from her own childhood what it was like to live like that, to have a never-ending list of jobs, to be desperate to attend school only to wear the dunce's cap when she did attend, never to go out to play in the road with the other children... to miss out on childhood pleasures.

There. Was that something she could organise? She couldn't do anything to improve the school attendance of Dora Chapman and the other children, but might she provide opportunities for them to have a little regular time off from their responsibilities?

By the time she went to meet Miss Brewer, her determination was bubbling over.

The owner of the Worker Bee had been fined early on in the war for showing a light when the door opened and thereby breaking the blackout. As a result of this, there was now a wooden frame inside the door, from which hung more blackout curtains. In dark evenings, the blackouts draped to the floor, creating a darkened lobby for customers to pass through; but in the daytime, the curtains were looped back out of the way.

Walking in, Beatrice looked around. Miss Brewer was already seated at a table.

'I was a child looker-after, you see,' Beatrice explained to Miss Brewer as they sat waiting for their tea and buns to be brought to them.

'I remember from your interview,' said Miss Brewer. 'You missed a lot of school.'

'I've met a girl who's in the same position I used to be in,' said Beatrice, 'and I know she can't be the only one.'

Miss Brewer nodded. 'I'm sure you're correct.'

'I want to help these children, these young looker-afters.'

'They're known as "children with responsibilities" these days,' said Miss Brewer. 'If you imagine you can get them into school, I'm afraid you're barking up the wrong tree.'

'I understand that,' said Beatrice, 'and I've thought of something else. I remember what it was like for me. All those jobs – shopping, cooking, washing, ironing... helping my mum get dressed or get ready for bed. She'd had a stroke and she couldn't tackle the housework, but there was nowt the matter with her eyesight and she could spot dust from the other side of the room. I used to pretend I was Cinderella doing all the work. Don't get me wrong. I wanted to do it. I wanted to look after her.'

'It must have been hard,' Miss Brewer said softly.

'It was heavier work than a child should be required to do day after day and, of course, I missed ever such a lot of school.'

'Did you have friends?'

Beatrice perked up. This would lead them down exactly the right path. 'Yes, but their lives were different to mine. They could play out when they wanted and not go home until their mums put their tea on the table. I never had that freedom. I always had jobs to do.'

'Grown-up responsibilities,' said Miss Brewer.

Beatrice leaned forwards. 'Nobody can magic away these children's responsibilities, but I'd like to give them something to look forward to, a bit of free time.'

'It would have to be outside school hours,' said Miss Brewer. 'What do you have in mind?'

'To be honest, I don't have definite ideas yet. But for instance, I've got what I call my leftovers – you know, a box of fabrics and wool and buttons and braids.'

Miss Brewer shook her head. 'Your personal craft box isn't bottomless. Besides, it isn't good practice to pay for everything yourself. That would cause complications. I don't mean to put you off. I'm just being practical.'

Beatrice thought hard. 'Well... a games evening, cards, word games. I could find some games in a second-hand shop and they could be used over and over again.' She looked earnestly at Miss Brewer. 'What do you think?'

'I think you have the beginnings of a good idea. A lot more thought needs to go into this, but if you don't mind giving up your sitting room for a couple of hours one evening a week, this could develop into what you want.'

'Oh.' Beatrice felt flat. 'I don't have a sitting room. I don't have my own house. I just have a bedroom.' Not even that, she thought. Just half a bedroom.

'That puts a different slant on it,' said Miss Brewer. 'You can't do this without a room.'

'I suppose not,' said Beatrice.

She could have wept. How could she help Dora and the other children now?

* * *

Typical shower: ten minutes of light rain, then the May sunshine emerged again, its rays bringing a sparkle to the raindrops covering the privet hedge. The effect was beautiful but it filled Lily with despair. The world was continuing as normal and she felt distanced from everything. She wanted it all to stop, so that the world could get used to the loss of Toby Chadwick.

But there were the same queues outside every butcher's and every grocer's; there were air raids at night. Lily felt as if the world was running away and dragging her with it when what she wanted, what she needed… She didn't know what she wanted or needed. She wanted Toby not to be dead, but she could never have that.

How she wished she wasn't living under Mrs Chadwick's roof, but Daniel had insisted that this was where she must come after she left Rookery House. Back then, they'd expected her to have their new baby with her. Daniel had been so sure that the new baby would make a strong bond form between the two women in his life.

As it was, after Mrs Chadwick's initial grief, things had

grown strained. Lily felt increasingly aware that she didn't belong here. Every time she looked at the grand piano, or the dinner service with the maroon-and-gold pattern around the rims, or the bone-handled cutlery, she knew that a simple girl from her station in life should be here as a maid, not as the daughter of the house.

It would have been only too easy to spend her days and nights nursing her broken heart. Instead, in the interests of not going mad, Lily threw herself into WVS duties. She measured, cut and hemmed bandages; worked in the canteen where they cooked meals for people who had been evacuated from their homes because of unexploded bombs; filled sandbags, swept up glass from broken windows; and helped look after people who had been discharged from hospital to convalesce at home.

She did all that was asked of her and was constantly surrounded by people, yet she had never felt more alone in her life. She thought a lot about how things had changed for her in such a short time. This time last year, none of it had happened. No Daniel. No baby on the way.

Coming in earlier than usual from her WVS shift one afternoon, she heard voices in the sitting room – plummy voices, her mother-in-law and someone else posh. Tempting as it was to scamper straight up the stairs, Lily knew she must be polite. If she stuck her head round the door to say good afternoon, would that suffice?

The door was ajar. As she went towards it, she heard Mrs Chadwick's voice.

'Daniel still has no idea about the baby.'

'Poor chap,' said the visitor and Lily recognised Lady Ingrid Campbell's voice. 'What dreadful news for him to come home to. How is his wife coping?'

'Credit where it's due,' said Mrs Chadwick. 'Lily is being brave.'

Lily was pleased to be praised. It gave her a boost to know that her mother-in-law thought well of her.

Then Mrs Chadwick lowered her voice, though not so low that Lily couldn't hear.

'Of course, she does hail from the lower echelons of society and they don't have the same fine feelings as we do.'

'All the same,' said Lady Ingrid, 'it's a terrible thing to lose one's own child. Poor—' and Lily expected her to say, 'Poor Lily,' but what she said was, 'Poor Daniel.'

'The most desperate part of it,' said Mrs Chadwick, 'is that he only married her because she was in the family way. As things have turned out, he needn't have put a ring on her finger at all.'

A dark chill hit Lily right in the core of her being. That settled it. She absolutely could not remain here.

There was one place left where she could go.

17

Beatrice's expanded inco area took her close to the centre of Manchester. Would Sister District let her make some alterations to her schedule so she could deliver her signed sheets to the Town Hall as part of her routine instead of having to make a special journey? That would be a big help. But she feared that Sister District's attitude would be that the convenience of the people using the inco service was of greater importance than making life simpler for Beatrice.

Still, there was no harm in asking, was there? Or was there? Would asking make her look as if she wasn't dedicated to her job?

Oxford Road was one of the main routes into the city centre. Beatrice had always assumed this area was all shops and offices, but, as she was finding, once you left Oxford Road itself, there were some residential parts – aye, and some of them had taken a hammering from old Adolf. In the Christmas Blitz, perhaps? Other damage was obviously newer. You could tell how old the damage was because of how much of it had been cleared up or, in older patches, how many weeds had grown.

Beatrice cycled along one road that was freshly strewn with roof tiles, timber and chunks of rubble. On her right, the houses were still standing, although there wasn't a windowpane to speak of. On her left was a shop with no roof and no windows, in between two demolished buildings, each a mass of wood, bricks and lumps of plaster, with a chimneystack sitting at a wonky angle on top of one of the heaps. Pasted to the front wall of the shop was a notice saying MORE OPEN THAN USUAL.

Concentrating on cycling around the paving stones that lay scattered in the road, Beatrice came to the end of the street and found, on a large corner plot, a bomb site where children were playing, girls as well as boys. Some were bent over, sifting through the rubble, no doubt in search of shrapnel. Collecting cigarette cards had been all the rage before the war, but now shrapnel was the thing to have. Other children were engaged in a lively game of chase, leaping from one pile of debris to the next. One girl in particular caught Beatrice's eye because her fair hair shone in the spring sunshine. She was a slip of a thing, clearly with bags of energy.

Beatrice experienced a tug of envy on Dora Chapman's behalf. Poor little Dora. What chance did she ever get to muck about like this? Beatrice pushed steadily on the pedals as she steered around a pile of broken bricks that had spilled out into the road. Her thoughts remained with Dora and all the other children whose young lives were crammed full of grown-up responsibilities.

She had wanted so badly to help them – but she'd failed.

* * *

Kitty stood at one of the windows in what used to be the residents' sitting room, peering between the criss-crossed lengths of anti-blast tape. She clutched her elbows, her tummy turning over and over. Would this visit make a difference – could it? It was her only hope. If the man from the Corporation declared that Dunbar's was to be used for vital war work, would that prevent Bill from selling?

She had sent Abbie out to play, not wanting her to know what was going on. Abbie was excited about Kitty's plans for Dunbar's, all the more so because, as Kitty had made a point of telling her, the inspiration for the idea had come from Abbie herself. The child knew nothing of her father's plan to sell up. If this appointment went the way Kitty hoped, she never would.

Across the road, old Miss Winspear, leaning on her walking stick, went up the steps into the Grove. After living for years in Dunbar's, she was now one of Mr Barnes's resident guests. Kitty had gone to call on her and found her civil but not warm.

'Moving isn't easy at my time of life,' she'd said 'I don't know what dear Mr Jeremiah Dunbar would have made of it. Such shenanigans.'

Kitty had felt guilty and embarrassed. She would have liked to drop Bill in it, but pride forbade it.

Now she waited anxiously for the arrival of the Corporation official. A good-looking young woman came walking along Lily Street. Kitty's eyes were drawn to her dark red hair. She carried a leather satchel and wore a hat with a feather. There was an air of confidence in her step. She was obviously looking for somewhere, but scrutinising each building didn't slow her down.

She came up the steps to Dunbar's. Someone in need of a room who didn't know this was no longer a hotel? Or could this be the expected 'man' from the Corporation?

The front doors were no longer left unlocked all day. Kitty hastened to unfasten them and greet her visitor.

'Good afternoon,' said the redhead. 'Mrs Dunbar? I'm Fay Brewer from Manchester Corporation.'

Kitty smiled and shook hands. 'Thank you for coming. I feel I ought to apologise for expecting a man. We should all be used to women being in all kinds of jobs by now. I keep telling my daughter that women are capable of anything.'

Fay Brewer laughed. 'And then you go and spoil it by expecting a man. Never mind. I won't tell tales if you won't.'

Kitty warmed to Fay Brewer, feeling sure they were going to get along. 'There are some hooks over here if you'd like to hang up your gas-mask box. I know that being empty makes the place looks strange, but the kitchen is still in one piece so I can offer you tea. I even have a few bits of furniture left, so we can sit down and discuss matters, Mrs – Miss? Brewer.'

'Miss.' Fay Brewer hung up her gas-mask box, then undid the buckle on her satchel and produced a sheet of paper. 'Shall we start by looking round? I need to assess the building. I gather you wish to make a change-of-use application to turn Dunbar's from a hotel to a building for storage.'

'That's right,' said Kitty. 'With so many people having to up sticks and move in with family after losing their homes, there is a great need for the storage of possessions. I've met with two gentlemen who run storage warehouses—'

'Their names, please?'

'Mr Tulip and Mr Rickford.'

'Mr Tulip? What a wonderful name.'

'I thought so too,' Kitty agreed. 'He and Mr Rickford were both generous about sharing information with me.'

'Shall we start our tour?' Miss Brewer requested. 'I need to see how much space you have and make sure the rooms are secure.'

'All the former guest rooms have locks, obviously,' said Kitty.

They went from room to room, ending up back in the foyer.

'Forgive me for being nosy,' said Miss Brewer, 'but how did you come to lose all the furniture?'

Kitty had hidden the truth from everyone but Bill's mother and Naomi, but she had to reveal it now. She couldn't lie on her application to the Corporation.

'Dunbar's is – was – a family business. My husband unexpectedly became the heir shortly after war broke out. He's never been responsible where money is concerned. I've been told he was able to borrow on the strength of being the heir. Then his uncle, the owner, died and – well, the debts came home to roost. The first I knew of it was when the bailiffs came knocking.'

'I'm sorry to hear it,' said Miss Brewer. 'It's rotten luck on you.'

'My husband was called up,' said Kitty, 'and I want to make a fresh start.'

'Good for you.' Miss Brewer gave her a warm smile. 'I'm pleased to tell you that the Corporation will approve your change-of-use application. There will be a few hoops to jump through, but I'll ensure the matter is dealt with speedily.'

'Thank you.' The tension in Kitty's body faded away. 'You've no idea how much this means. It isn't just a matter of setting up in business. To be honest, I also need to prevent my husband from selling to the hotelier over the road.'

Miss Brewer frowned. 'Getting Corporation permission won't prevent that.'

'Oh, but I thought—' Kitty stopped.

'If the Corporation had some sort of stake in the building, then the sale could be prevented for the duration of the war,' Miss Brewer explained, 'but I'm only here to authorise change of use. When you set up your storage business, you won't be working for the Corporation. It'll be a private business.'

Kitty could have kicked herself. 'I should have thought of that.'

Miss Brewer glanced around the foyer as if seeking inspiration. 'I'm sorry not to be able to help. Dunbar's isn't big enough to be of interest to the Corporation as a storage facility. You'd need a warehouse for that.'

'I see that now,' said Kitty.

There was nothing she could do to prevent Bill from selling Dunbar's.

* * *

After delivering a couple of consignments of nappies, Beatrice cycled back the way she had come. The children were still playing on the bomb site. For a brief moment, Beatrice was appalled at the sight of what looked like a dog wearing a gas mask. She was all set to leap off her bicycle and rescue it from the children's thoughtlessness, then realised it was actually a large toy dog on wheels. Her pulse settled. Mind you, what a grand toy. Did the mother know it had been taken to the bomb site?

Beatrice toiled on alongside the site. Because it occupied a large corner, she had to cycle past one side, then turn the corner and do roughly the same distance again. In this part of the site were the children she had noticed earlier, including the fair-haired girl who had caught her attention. She had a real *brightness* about her. That was the only word Beatrice could think of to describe it. It was more than energy and nimbleness. It was something in her general bearing that denoted a sunny nature.

If Beatrice had ever had an imaginary friend when she was a child, she'd have wanted one like this girl. And what a stupid thought that was. Positively bizarre.

She cast one final look in the girl's direction – and witnessed her suddenly drop out of sight. Beatrice braked hard to the sound of cries from the other children, who came swarming from all directions. Beatrice laboured across the site, her feet sinking and sliding, waving her arms inelegantly to maintain her balance.

As one, the children turned to her.

'Abbie's fell down a hole, miss.'

'So I saw,' said Beatrice.

'The ground just vanished beneath her feet,' said another child.

'Well, if you will play on bomb sites,' Beatrice responded. She winced inwardly. What a spoilsport.

She made her way to the edge of the hole and just had time to glimpse a little face peering up at her when she had to retreat suddenly because the ground slithered into a miniature landslide.

'Are you all right?' Beatrice called. Turning to the crowd of children, she asked, 'Did you say her name's Abbie?'

'She's Abigail Dunbar from Lily Street, two roads along.'

'Is she going to get buried alive, miss?'

'Of course not!' said Beatrice. She raised her voice. 'Abigail! Abbie! Can you hear me? Can you climb out?'

'She's already climbing out,' said a girl who was balanced precariously on the edge of the hole.

'Then if a couple of you could lie down and stretch out your hands for her to grab onto,' Beatrice suggested.

All the children instantly threw themselves on their tummies and leaned over the edge, causing an ominous creaking sound. Panic raced through Beatrice accompanied by a vision of the hole swallowing everyone, but before she could issue fresh instructions, Abbie appeared, batting away numerous helping hands.

'Come away from the edge – all of you,' Beatrice ordered, trying to sound authoritative and not at all panicked.

As the children moved away, making a great show of leaping for their lives, Beatrice noticed Abbie wince as she put the weight on her foot.

'Are you hurt?' Beatrice asked.

'I'm fine, thank you,' said the child.

'Maybe I should ask your foot if it's hurt,' Beatrice replied drily.

'My foot's fine too, thank you.'

'You and your foot have beautiful manners, but I recognise an injury when I see one. Is it your ankle?'

A small hesitation, then, 'Yes, miss.'

'One of the others said you live nearby,' said Beatrice. 'If you can hop onto my bicycle and sit on the seat, I'll push you home.'

'I can manage, honestly.'

'I'm sure you can,' said Beatrice, 'but why risk making your ankle worse by hobbling home when you can ride in style?'

In reply she received a shy smile, which, once Abbie was perched on the bicycle, was transformed into a real dazzler.

'Lily Street,' said Beatrice. 'Do we go right or left at the end of this road?'

Not two minutes later, they were in Lily Street, a very different road to the one with the bomb site. Here there were smart hotels, rather grand-looking even though they weren't massive in size.

Following Abbie's directions, Beatrice halted outside one with DUNBAR'S HOTEL over the door. She helped Abbie down from the bike.

'Can you manage the front steps? You can hold my arm if you like.'

Together they reached the doors. Abbie knocked and one of the doors opened.

A good-looking, dark-haired woman exclaimed, 'Abbie!' and drew them both inside.

Before Beatrice had a chance to get her bearings, she found herself looking straight at Fay Brewer.

'Miss Inkerman.' Miss Brewer gave her a broad smile. 'We meet again.'

* * *

Kitty had a split second to realise that Miss Brewer knew this stranger who had brought Abbie home, before all her attention zoomed in on her daughter, who was limping.

Soon Abbie was lying on her bed, her bandaged ankle and foot raised from the mattress by a heap of cushions.

'Here we are. Let's try this.'

A couple of minutes ago, Miss Brewer had asked for a man's handkerchief and Kitty had provided one of Bill's. Miss Brewer had disappeared and now she was back, the handkerchief transformed into a bulky little parcel dangling from her fingers.

'Ice,' she said. 'It'll help reduce the swelling.'

Kitty positioned it across Abbie's ankle, then smiled at the other two women. 'Thank you both.'

Miss Brewer laughed. 'It seems all three of us have had first-aid training. We all swooped on her in one go, poor child.'

'You should say thank you for the attention,' Kitty prompted Abbie. 'This lady is Miss Brewer from the Corporation and this – I'm sorry,' she added, turning to the stranger. 'You brought home my injured daughter and I don't even know you.' She recalled that Fay Brewer had used her name, something unusual, but couldn't bring it to mind.

'I'm Miss Inkerman,' said the stranger. 'Beatrice Inkerman.'

She was a good ten or more years older than Kitty, plainly dressed and rather dowdy. Her dark hair was starting to fade and her brown eyes were serious. Above all, as far as Kitty was concerned, she had come to Abbie's aid, and that was all Kitty needed to know.

She beamed at Miss Inkerman, shaking her hand warmly. 'Kitty Dunbar, mother of this one.' She gave her daughter an affectionate glance. 'I can't begin to thank you, Miss Inkerman.'

'It was nothing,' said Abbie's rescuer. 'I'm sure she and her playmates would have managed perfectly well if I hadn't come along.'

Abbie looked at Kitty, silently seeking permission to speak. Kitty gave her a tiny nod.

'Miss Inkerman brought me home on her bicycle.' Receiving another glance from her mother, Abbie added, 'Thank you, Miss Inkerman.'

'It was no trouble at all,' Miss Inkerman replied.

Kitty looked from one adult to the other. 'And you two know one another?'

'We both work for the Corporation,' said Miss Brewer.

'I ought to return to my rounds,' said Miss Inkerman.

'Could you spare another minute?' Miss Brewer asked her. 'You too, Mrs Dunbar? I've had an idea that could be of benefit to you both.'

Leaving Abbie, they went downstairs to the foyer.

'I'll come straight to the point,' said Miss Brewer. 'Mrs Dunbar, you need the Corporation to have some sort of stake in this building in order to prevent its sale. Miss Inkerman, you need a room in which to hold activities for children with responsibilities.' She waved her hand between the two of them, as if performing an introduction. 'Mrs Dunbar, will you make one of your rooms available to the Corporation so that I might, for example, send Miss Inkerman your way for the accommodation her friendship group needs?'

Kitty caught her breath. She and Miss Inkerman looked at one another.

Before anything could be said, someone tried to open the front doors. After a moment, there was a knock and Kitty opened the door. A skinny girl immediately entered. She stumbled and had to put down her suitcase quickly in order to steady herself. Blue eyes looked around in surprise at the empty foyer.

'Oh,' she said. 'Pardon me for bursting in. Is Mrs Swanson available?'

'She no longer works here,' said Kitty.

'Oh,' the girl said again. Her face fell. 'Mr Dunbar, then. Please may I speak to Mr Dunbar?'

'He was called up,' said Kitty, baffled.

The girl stared incredulously and Kitty saw the misunderstanding.

'My husband, Mr William Dunbar, was called up,' she explained. 'I think you mean his uncle, Mr Jeremiah Dunbar.'

The girl nodded.

'I'm sorry to tell you he passed away.'

'He—? But I've only been gone a few weeks.' The girl's face, already pale, drained of colour. 'I thought – I hoped—' With a visible effort, she pulled herself together. 'I'm Lily Chadwick. I came here as a chambermaid in 1936 and I lived in until... Anyhow, I'm back and I need a job and a roof over my head.'

'I'm sorry,' said Kitty, 'but Dunbar's isn't a hotel now. I'm about to set up a new kind of business.'

'Then let me work for you.' Lily's eyes were suddenly over-bright. 'I won't even need paying until you're established, as long as I can have my old room back.'

18

What a day! So much had happened, and so quickly. This morning Kitty had been in fear of losing Dunbar's. Now she had an agreement with the Corporation to accommodate a weekly children's club, and she'd acquired a lodger. Kitty had discreetly let Lily know that she already knew her tragic story. She'd wanted to hug the girl. Offering her old room back seemed the very least she could do.

Kitty sat on Abbie's bed, telling her about their unexpected new housemate.

'Her name is Lily Chadwick – Mrs Chadwick – and she worked here from when she left school. She had a little bedroom on the top floor. Last year she met a handsome young man called Daniel and they fell in love, but he has to be away at sea most of the time because he's with the merchant navy.'

'Bringing us food from Canada and America,' said Abbie.

'Exactly. They're very brave men, because Hitler's U-boats are out to get them,' said Kitty. 'Mrs Chadwick had a baby—'

'A boy or a girl?' Abbie asked immediately.

'A little boy called Toby.'

'Not George after the King?'

'I told you: Toby. Unfortunately, Toby died.'

'In an air raid?' Abbie asked.

'No. He had something wrong with his heart, apparently. His father is still away at sea and has no idea, which makes it even harder for Mrs Chadwick.'

Abbie nodded wisely. 'She must feel very sad.'

'She does, so we need to be kind to her. She's come back here because she needs somewhere to live.'

Abbie smiled. 'So even though we aren't a hotel any more, we've got someone staying with us.'

'Yes, I suppose so.'

The bailiffs hadn't needed to take anything from the old staff quarters and Lily's room was intact. Kitty had offered her a larger room, but the girl had politely refused. Maybe she would find it a comfort to be in her old, familiar surroundings. Kitty hoped so.

Abbie clearly liked Lily, and Kitty was horrified to hear her daughter calling the newcomer by her first name.

'It's quite all right,' said Lily. 'I'm not that much older than Abbie. I grew up in my aunt and uncle's house and I have five younger cousins, so I'm used to being the big sister.' Smiling sadly, she added, 'I feel more like Lily than I do Mrs Chadwick.'

So Abbie acquired a big sister and Lily was Lily to both the Dunbars.

Determined to earn her keep, Lily offered to spring-clean, and she set to with a will.

'There'll never be another chance like this to get all the skirting boards washed and polished,' she said.

'Now that all that pesky furniture has gone, you mean,' Kitty answered with a smile.

Fay Brewer came to see her to finalise arrangements.

'I need you to sign an agreement to accommodate the club for children with responsibilities,' said Miss Brewer. 'I may ask you to make that room available for other purposes too, but let's not worry about that just now.'

'You said something about the Corporation having a stake in Dunbar's,' Kitty prompted.

'Not in the sense of part-ownership or having a say in your decision-making,' Fay Brewer answered. 'It simply means the Corporation will expect you to cooperate if a room is needed for a meeting – things like that. The change of use from hotel to storage building has gone through, but there are certain conditions.'

'What are they?' Kitty felt a stab of worry.

'They're cosmetic,' said Miss Brewer. 'The building's frontage mustn't change. It has to remain in keeping with the rest of Lily Street. Broadly speaking, no stranger walking down the road should really think Dunbar's isn't a hotel.'

'I can see to that,' said Kitty.

'And if your clients need assistance bringing their furniture and what-have-you here, you must hire a Corporation van.'

Kitty was happy to agree. 'It'll help me, actually, to be on the Corporation's official list for transporting goods.'

Feeling fluttery with happiness and hope, she signed and dated the agreement. Now all she had to do was tell Bill his plan to sell up had been thwarted.

* * *

As Beatrice soon learned, Fay Brewer was nothing if not speedy when it came to getting matters sorted out. Before Beatrice knew it, she'd received a letter on Corporation paper, offering her the use of one of the downstairs rooms in the former Dunbar's Hotel for one evening a week.

'The headed paper makes it look very official,' said Beatrice, impressed.

'It's intended to,' Miss Brewer replied.

'I've been wondering how to find the names of other children who are kept off school to run the home,' said Beatrice. 'The only one I personally know of is Dora Chapman.'

'I'll ask the truancy officer for his list,' said Miss Brewer, 'and I'll go around the schools and find out the reason behind the truancy. Then it's just a matter of asking the mothers if the children may have the evening off.'

'Thank you for taking such an interest.'

'Welfare: it's what I'm here for. These children are sorely in need of some free time.'

Beatrice nodded, remembering. It made her all the more determined to make a success of her club. She used her all-too-brief dinner-breaks to trawl through second-hand shops and jumble sales in search of jigsaws and board games, but things like that weren't to be found because new ones weren't being made, so folk were hanging on to their old ones.

Just when she was getting desperate, her friend Mrs Gates weighed in.

'I have an old compendium of games, you know, a box with Ludo, Snakes and Ladders, that sort of thing – that you could have; and I'm sure there's an old ping-pong set. That might be fun.'

'Won't your daughters mind?' Beatrice asked.

'Why would they? They've never asked to have any of them. There's a perfectly ancient board game called "Aerial Derby" or some such, which dates back to the early days of aeroplanes.'

'Thank you,' said Beatrice. 'It all sounds splendid.'

A New Home at the Wartime Hotel

'My pleasure,' said Mrs Gates. 'On the subject of giving you things, have you thought any further about the brooch I want you to have?'

Beatrice hadn't given it another thought. 'Much as I appreciate your kind offer, you know I can't accept it.'

'If you say so,' Mrs Gates replied. 'Here's an idea for your children's club. Next time you go to a jumble sale, go right at the end when they're wondering what to do with what's left. Buy some old clothes as cheaply as you can to start a dressing-up box.'

'What a good idea.' Beatrice smiled at her friend.

Every time she pictured her new club, she lifted her chin and gave a crisp nod. It was good to have something to look forward to, and she of all people knew what a difference it would make to the children. It felt far more important to her than the news of Rudolph Hess parachuting into Scotland, although the destruction of the chamber of the House of Commons in a bombing raid shook Beatrice as much as anyone. The MPs duly took their work into the House of Lords instead, showing that, just like the rest of the population, they intended to get on with the job. It was a feeling Beatrice understood. That was how she felt about her children's club.

When she took the board games and the ping-pong paraphernalia donated by Mrs Gates over to Dunbar's, Mrs Dunbar let her in and showed her the spacious room at the front of the building that her club was to occupy. Lily was up a stepladder, wet-dusting the picture rail.

'Are you sure I can use this room?' Beatrice asked Mrs Dunbar. 'It's rather grand.'

Mrs Dunbar laughed, a hollow sound. 'It would be if it contained furniture.' Although she spoke lightly, pain shadowed her hazel eyes. Perking up, she added, 'I can provide some chairs and a couple of tables, including one big enough for ping-pong. The built-in cupboards in the alcoves have locks. You can have one of them to store your things.'

'Thank you,' said Beatrice. 'I just wish I had more to offer the children.'

'Children?' Lily turned round.

'Miss Inkerman is going to run a children's club,' said Mrs Dunbar.

'For children who need time off from looking after the home and sick parents,' Beatrice explained.

'Why didn't you say so?' Lily's wan, determined face brightened. 'There are plenty of games in the attic, along with all the Christmas decorations. Christmas used to be a big event here. Did the bailiffs go into the attic?'

'No,' Mrs Dunbar answered. 'They took everything they needed from the public rooms and the guest rooms. And the family flat.'

'Well, you might not have guest-beds left,' said Lily, 'but you've got board games coming out of your ears. There are extra card tables as well, and a bagatelle board, a set of skittles and a billiard table. All we have to do is screw its legs back on.'

Delight rose inside Beatrice. She clamped down on it in case Mrs Dunbar refused, but a smile and a nod told her it was safe to be happy.

'It's going to be splendid,' she said, 'so much better than I'd dared to imagine. So far Miss Brewer has found a dozen children with responsibilities – ten of them girls, which comes as no surprise.'

'More might come out of the woodwork when words gets around,' said Mrs Dunbar. 'She's given me a small allowance for drinks and biscuits.'

Beatrice huffed out a breath of pure satisfaction. 'All the club needs now is a name.'

'You said it yourself,' said Lily. 'These are kids who need time off. You should call it the Time Off Club.'

* * *

Ivy Dunbar marched inside the moment Kitty opened the front door. Kitty might be taller but Mrs Dunbar had a way of thrusting her shoulders back and walking in a swift, decisive way that gave her presence, especially when she was vexed.

She was vexed now. Her eyes positively snapped with it – and was that scorn in her expression too? Kitty felt riled. It was obvious that her mother-in-law had come here to lay down the law about something, though Kitty couldn't imagine what.

Yes, she could.

Kitty got the first word in. 'I take it you've heard from Bill. He's had my letter about Dunbar's Storage and instead of writing back to me, he's roped you in on his side. I expect he's told you that I've blocked the sale of Dunbar's.'

Mrs Dunbar – no, not Mrs Dunbar, not any more. Kitty would call her that to her face because she was entitled to the courtesy, but from this moment on, inside Kitty's head, she would be plain old Ivy. It would be Kitty's private way of cutting her down to size.

Ivy looked taken aback by Kitty's attack, but she quickly recovered. 'Stopping my Bill from selling. What game d'you think you're playing?'

'I'm not playing games. I'm starting a business.'

'As if you have the know-how for that sort of thing,' snorted Ivy.

'Then I'll have to learn, won't I?' said Kitty.

'Aye – using my son's inheritance to do it.'

'And what do you imagine would happen if Bill had sold Dunbar's?' Kitty demanded.

'He'd provide an income for you and Abbie and he'd patriotically invest in war bonds.'

'Is that what he told you?' Kitty laughed, but it wasn't funny. 'You said Bill always told you I was the one doing the spending and that was why you blamed me for the bailiffs. I told you then to write to Bill and demand the truth. Are you saying he wrote back and still claimed it was all my fault?'

The corners of Ivy's mouth pulled downwards. 'I never wrote. Well, why would I? I trust my son.'

'Give me strength,' Kitty muttered.

'If I'd written that letter, it would have been tantamount to saying I doubted him.'

'And now he's told you that I've committed the terrible crime of preventing him from selling his own property, and he's sent you round here to sort me out.'

'You can't deny that's what you've done,' snapped Ivy.

'I wouldn't dream of denying it.' Kitty strove for a calm voice. 'I'm doing it to keep the family finances intact.' She gave a huff of exasperation. 'You want proof, Mrs Dunbar? Come upstairs to the flat and I'll show you.'

'There is no proof. There can't be, because Bill never did all that spending.'

'Then there's no harm in coming upstairs, is there?'

Kitty led the way without looking back. If Ivy followed, she'd see the evidence with her own eyes. If she didn't, good riddance.

Kitty entered the flat, leaving the door open. She went straight to the bedroom, where she opened a built-in cupboard. Standing on a chair, she reached to the back of the top shelf, pulling a box forward. This she took into the sparsely furnished parlour, where Ivy stood waiting, looking stroppy and self-righteous.

Kitty placed the box on the table and waved a hand at it.

'Help yourself.'

Ivy didn't move. Her face was set like stone.

Kitty waited. When Ivy still made no move, Kitty opened the box. It contained a number of statements of account from various shops. Kitty tossed them onto the table.

'I've only got a few of these that I managed to get hold of and squirrel away. Goodness knows how many more there have been over the years. Take a look. Statements of account made out in Bill's name – *Bill's* name, not mine.'

At first it seemed Ivy would be too stubborn to look. Kitty felt like shaking her. Then Ivy edged closer, tilting her head, obviously determined not to pick anything up for a close look.

'What of it?' she said. 'You could have opened the accounts in his name.'

Kitty stared in disbelief. 'No, I couldn't. They wouldn't have let me – and you know it.' She thought anger was going to surge to the surface, but instead something inside her slumped as a cloud of resignation settled over her. 'You're never going to believe me.' Putting on a bright voice edged with insolence, she said, 'So you and Bill can have a lovely correspondence for the duration of the war, all about what a nasty piece of work I am. But d'you know what? None of it will alter the fact that I'm telling the truth.'

* * *

'Don't put all the games out,' Kitty Dunbar advised Beatrice as she prepared for the first Time Off Club session. 'Have a different selection each week.'

'And make it clear that billiards is a girl's game as much as a boy's,' Fay Brewer added. 'I'll teach them how to play it. But it's your club, Miss Inkerman, and you must be in charge.'

The children arrived in dribs and drabs. A couple of pairs already knew each other, but all the rest were strangers. Beatrice was pleased to see that Dora Chapman had come. She hoped the child would benefit from the evening – she hoped they all would.

She introduced herself, trying to strike the right balance between authority and welcome.

'I'm Miss Inkerman and I run the Time Off Club. I hope you'll enjoy coming here. You're all in charge of various things at home and I know what that's like because I was in charge when I was a girl. But when you're here, I want you to relax and have fun. There are various games, or you might prefer to sit and have a natter. If there's anything you'd specially like to do,' she added, her tongue running away with her, 'tell me and I'll see what I can do.' Before she could say anything else inadvisable, she said firmly, 'Let's begin with an air raid drill, and I'm sorry to sound like school but I also have to take the register.'

The evening went well. The children enjoyed a mixture of activities and the session ended with everyone dividing into teams for skittles. The children were full of beans as they departed.

Fay Brewer got ready to leave shortly afterwards. 'Congratulations.' She shook Beatrice's hand. 'I think we can claim that as a success. I won't come every week, but I'll drop in from time to time. Please can you make notes every week in the back of the registration book? You don't need to write an essay, just say what the children enjoyed, things like that. Because the Corporation is involved, we have to keep records.'

After Miss Brewer left, Mrs Dunbar sent Abbie to prepare

for bed. Lily disappeared too, leaving Beatrice and Mrs Dunbar sitting together over a cup of tea, the ashtray between them.

'Those poor children,' said Mrs Dunbar. 'It makes me realise how lucky Abbie is. Fancy losing your childhood to all those responsibilities.'

'And your education,' Beatrice added. 'That's what happened to me. My mother had a stroke when she was young, not quite thirty. My father coped for a while, then he said, "It's up to you now, Beatrice," and off he went.'

'That's awful,' Mrs Dunbar said sympathetically.

'It was all right to start with,' Beatrice told her. 'I loved my mum and I wanted to look after her. Looking after the home made me feel grown-up, but somewhere along the line I realised it was never going to end. I was very resentful – but I still loved my mum.'

'I'm sure you did.'

'I didn't mind missing school at first, but then I fell way behind. When I did manage to attend, I had to stand in the corner wearing the dunce's cap, so that was something else to resent.'

'But you still loved your mum,' Mrs Dunbar said quietly.

'I did, but – oh, it was complicated. She wanted to boss me about because she was the adult, but I didn't see why she should when I was the one with all the responsibility. Then I'd feel rotten for being a bad daughter.'

'It sounds to me as if you were a very good daughter,' said Mrs Dunbar. 'It can't be easy when the roles are reversed.'

Beatrice snapped her mouth shut to prevent herself from saying how she'd hated it when her mother was proud of not being pursued by the truancy officer even though Beatrice missed school most of the time.

'It shows we're respectable,' her mother used to say. 'If you were off school because I was blind drunk, the truancy would haul you along to school every day and have me up before the magistrate.'

'I wonder what the future holds for the Time Off children,' said Mrs Dunbar.

'That's what worries me,' said Beatrice. 'I ended up without an elementary leaving certificate. It wasn't because I couldn't read and write. It was because I didn't have the attendance record – yet the headmaster had agreed to me having the time off.'

'That was unfair,' Mrs Dunbar commented. 'It must have made it hard for you to get a job.'

'I hate to think of that happening to these children,' said Beatrice. Aside from Dora, she hadn't met them until this evening, but already a feeling of protectiveness was growing inside her.

'You're doing what you can for them,' said Mrs Dunbar. She leaned forward. 'Tell me if I'm being nosy, but is it because of devoting yourself to your mother that you're a spinster?'

Beatrice fiddled with her cup and saucer as a flush crept across her cheeks. 'No. As a matter of fact, I used to be engaged and my mother was perfectly happy about it.' She laughed. 'I can see in your face that you're trying to work out how old I am, so that you can ask without offence if he died in the last war.'

Mrs Dunbar pressed her hand to her chest. 'No, really—'

'Yes, really,' said Beatrice. 'It wasn't that at all.' Sometimes she thought it would it have been easier if it had been. 'Goodness, I haven't thought about Frank in ages.'

'And there's no need to now. I apologise if I intruded.'

'It's all right.' The words were a polite response but, to her surprise, Beatrice found they were true. 'Frank didn't want children. He wanted a wife but not a family, whereas I wanted a family very much. After a lot of heart-searching, I broke it off.'

'That was brave of you.'

'Was it?' Beatrice asked. 'But I never met anybody else, you see. So not only did I never have children, I don't have a husband either.'

'There must be many folk who don't get the life they thought they were going to have,' Mrs Dunbar said softly.

'Most people, I imagine,' said Beatrice. 'Heavens, how glum.' Seeing her companion glance at her wristwatch, she rose to her feet. 'I ought to go home.'

'I'm sorry. I didn't mean to be rude, but I must go and kiss Abbie goodnight and switch her light off,' said Mrs Dunbar. 'I've enjoyed our chat, Miss Inkerman.'

'So have I,' said Beatrice. 'Sorry for monopolising.'

'Maybe I'll monopolise next time,' Mrs Dunbar answered with a smile.

Beatrice cycled home feeling she was well on the way to making a friend.

19

Lily might have the sensation of being in her own world, distanced from much of what went on around her, but she was as taken aback as anyone when clothes rationing started at the beginning of June.

'My teacher says it's been the best kept secret of the war,' said Abbie. 'Nobody knew about it beforehand or they'd have rushed out to the shops to buy up the clothing. That's why it started the day after a bank holiday, too – to give the shops an extra day to get ready.'

'You're quite the expert, aren't you?' Lily remarked. It was impossible not to be drawn to Abbie. She was a real sweetheart, helpful and good-natured and interested in everything.

'It's important to be informed,' Abbie said seriously.

'Did your teacher tell you that, too?'

'It makes sense when you think about it. That's why I want to know all about the storage work at Dunbar's.'

Several of the old guest bedrooms were now occupied by what remained of various families' belongings after their homes had been severely damaged or destroyed. Lily felt torn. It saddened her to see Dunbar's in its new guise, but at the same time it was good to think of the dear old place doing its bit for the war effort. Given how her own life had been turned upside down so brutally, there was something appropriate about Dunbar's also having unwillingly had a new direction forced upon it. It added to Lily's sense of her world being broken and out of kilter.

She was immensely grateful to Mrs Dunbar for taking her in and she was fond of Abbie, liking her chirpy good nature. Being cast in the role of big sister felt familiar, though it also, when she thought about it, which she tried not to, left a leaden feeling in her chest. When she had left Dunbar's a matter of weeks ago, she'd been looking forward to becoming a mother. Now here she was back again, motherhood torn from her, once more the big sister.

She worked hard for Mrs Dunbar, not simply to earn her place in the household but also in the vain hope of tiring herself to the point of getting some proper sleep. As well as her work at Dunbar's, she also had the Women's Voluntary Service. She had thought of offering herself to a different service – fire-watching, perhaps, or first aid – but, aside from her absence since getting married, she'd been with the local WVS since the outset and it felt right to return. Mrs Dunbar kindly ensured that the other women knew about Toby, so Lily was spared the agony of explaining.

She took on as much WVS work as was compatible with her duties at Dunbar's. She joined one of the working parties that darned soldiers' socks, and the other women soon twigged she wasn't keen on conversation. She went netting twice a week – forming camouflage nets on a huge frame on the floor. Although plenty of women did it regularly, it was a much-disliked job. The dust and fluff that flew up when the knots were tied got down your throat, up your nose and in your eyes, while crawling about on the floor inevitably led to sore knees and aching backs. But who cared about any of that when it was all being done to help the British Army?

At Dunbar's, Lily cleaned as if her life depended on it. Certainly it felt as if her sanity did.

'Just because we aren't a hotel any longer is no reason to let standards slip,' she declared. 'We must still do things the Dunbar way.'

She came up with an idea for Mrs Dunbar to earn a little extra.

'Everything that comes from the bombed-out houses is filthy,' she pointed out. 'Coated in dust. I could clean everything when it arrives and your customers can pay you for the service.'

'That's a good idea,' said Mrs Dunbar, looking impressed, 'if you're prepared to do it.'

'I'm a chambermaid. I know the correct way to clean everything.'

'The Dunbar way,' Abbie chimed in.

'Exactly,' said Lily. 'You could offer a spring-cleaning service too. People will probably be glad to have their precious belongings refreshed once a year. In fact, I expect plenty of people would pay for it once a month.'

'I'll help, Lily,' said Abbie. 'You can make sure I clean the Dunbar way.'

'I like the idea,' said Mrs Dunbar, 'but let's wait and see, shall we?'

It was only later that Lily realised that Mrs Dunbar, looking to the future, wasn't taking it for granted that Lily was going to stay here indefinitely. That brought her up short. She had suggested spring-cleaning and monthly cleaning without thinking it through. Where would she be in a few months? She

A New Home at the Wartime Hotel

had no idea. Compared to the overwhelming importance of losing her little boy, nothing else mattered. She didn't have a future, not one she could face. Living in the present was hard enough.

She ached to see Daniel again, yet at the same time she dreaded it. Sometimes she hated him for not being with her when she'd needed him most. She envied him too, because in his world his family life was perfect. Sometimes her feelings were so intense that her flesh seemed to tighten all over her body to hold the emotions in.

One morning a new consignment of household goods was delivered by a Corporation van. The driver and his assistant carried everything indoors, where Mrs Dunbar wrote out a detailed inventory as each item came through the front doors. A member of the unfortunate Miller family was present as well.

The Millers were paying to have their belongings cleaned, so Lily was there too, running a practised eye over everything. There would be plenty of wet-dusting to do. She had made furniture cream, which would be a nice finishing touch.

Everything would stay here in the big entrance foyer for cleaning, after which men from Mr Tulip's warehouse would ferry it all upstairs. They were experts at storing in the smallest possible amounts of space and Mrs Dunbar reckoned it was worth her while to pay for this service.

Later, when the Millers' possessions had been safely locked away, Lily got the carpet sweeper out and swept the carpets in the foyer and on the stairs and the landing. According to Mrs Swanson, some jobs were meant to leave you hot and bothered, and the foyer, stairs and landing was one of them. It was a sign you'd done your work properly and given the carpets a thorough sweeping. It was the Dunbar way.

At the end of it, Lily had flushed cheeks and sticky armpits.

She returned the sweeper to the cupboard in the lobby beside the kitchen in the basement. When she came back upstairs to the foyer, she found Mrs Dunbar answering the door to somebody.

Mrs Dunbar looked at Lily over her shoulder, tilting her head with a frown that made her appear unsure of herself, which wasn't like her at all. Lily stepped forward to see if she could help – and there on the front steps was Daniel.

* * *

Just when Lily ought to have crumpled, shock held her bolt upright. She led Daniel upstairs. Mrs Dunbar had told her to use the family flat. Lily used to come in here to clean when it was occupied by Mr Dunbar – the real Mr Dunbar, as Lily privately thought of him, and poor Mr Ronald, both of them dead and gone now, both of them unexpectedly too. Like Toby.

In Mr Jeremiah Dunbar's day, this parlour had been occupied by heavy old Victorian furniture. Handsome, no doubt, but it had made the room dark. According to Abbie, her parents had bought a lovely new sofa and matching armchairs.

'Brand new?' Lily had asked.

'Yes. One of the very last brand-new suites until after the war,' Abbie had told her proudly. 'Possibly even the actual very last one.'

But that hadn't been what Lily had meant. She'd been expressing astonishment at the idea of people shelling out for brand new. She'd never met anybody before who could afford to do that – well, aside from Daniel's mother, but she took pride in having old family pieces – and it wasn't as though this new Dunbar family could be rolling in money.

Now, the flat was furnished in a basic sort of way with bits and bobs left over from the bailiffs' visit.

And what was she doing, thinking about Mrs Dunbar's accommodation, anyway? Oh, the answer to that was simple. All the things she should be thinking about were too difficult, too painful, too *huge* to contemplate.

Daniel shut the door behind them and took her in his arms. A feeling of recognition flooded her. Had she forgotten how it felt to be held by him – by her husband?

Clasping her firmly to him with one arm, he stroked her hair with his free hand, bending his head. 'Lily… Lily… I can't believe it. Our baby… our son.'

Lily clung to him as hot tears poured down her cheeks. Then, without knowing what she was about to do, she pushed against him to open a space between them before she delivered an almighty shove that made him step back. Anger, despair and grief surged up inside her. Fists clenched, she pounded his chest.

'Lily! Lily…'

Daniel captured her fists, but she dragged them free. Turning on her heel, she put a few paces between them before turning around to face him.

'I'm sorry,' she whispered. 'I'm sorry. I shouldn't have done that. I didn't know I was going to.'

'I'm your husband.' There was uncertainty in his voice. 'You're supposed to be able to lean on me. It's my job to take care of you. Why would you want to attack me like that?'

Lily shook her head. 'I don't know. It just happened. Does it matter?'

'Does it matter that my wife wanted to hit out at me? What were you thinking?'

'I wasn't thinking,' Lily answered brokenly. No – just feeling. Just being overwhelmed.

Daniel moved his hands in a gesture of frustration. 'I can tell you what I've been thinking. I've spent weeks picturing a blooming young mother with a baby in her arms, waiting at the docks to meet the proud father. That's what I've been thinking – and all this time...'

'Don't say it,' Lily begged.

'You didn't even come to meet me.'

'I didn't know your convoy was due back.' She honestly hadn't thought about it.

'It was left to my mother to meet me – and tell me—'

A frown tugged at Lily's brows. 'I should have... You're right. I should have paid attention, but...'

How to explain? How to describe that it was all she could do to put one foot in front of the other? That returning to Dunbar's had given her a place of safety that she needed to cling to? The thought of the outside world, beyond Dunbar's and Lily Street and the WVS, was too much.

'What happened?' Daniel asked. Taking her hands, he guided her to a chair and sat beside her. 'The baby – our poor little boy.'

'They thought it was his heart. You'd never have known it to look at him. He was perfect. He was everything we wanted. I'm so sorry I couldn't...'

'Couldn't what?' Daniel asked softly.

'He grew inside me so if there was something wrong with him...'

'Did they say it was your fault?'

'No,' Lily answered, but it was still something she battled with every day.

'And... did they tell you...?'

'Tell me what?' Lifting her face, Lily saw the pain etched in Daniel's features.

'Did they tell you if you'd be able to have another baby?'

Lily's mouth dropped open. She jumped up. Oh, she hadn't known she was going to hit him when she'd done it before but, by crikey, she could have clobbered him good and proper right now.

'Have another?' It was all she could do to force the words around the massive lump in her throat. 'We've just lost our son and you want to know if we can have another? A quick replacement and forget Toby ever existed?'

Daniel scrubbed his face with his palms. 'I didn't mean it that way. I just meant to ask whether there's any reason why another baby might have the same problem.'

Lily's jaw hardened. 'I don't know. They never said and it didn't occur to me to ask. I was too busy grieving for the baby I'd just lost.'

'Please don't say it like that.'

'Like what?'

'As if the loss is yours alone.'

Lily caught her breath in a great gasp. 'But it has been mine to bear on my own, hasn't it? You weren't here. I needed you so much and you weren't here.'

'I was at sea. I had no idea what had happened. Even if I had known, I couldn't have done anything about it. I couldn't have sprouted wings and flown home.'

Pulling out a packet of Woodbines, Daniel offered one to Lily. She shook her head. Daniel lit his cigarette and put it to his lips, dragging in a lungful before blowing out a fierce stream of smoke.

'This is getting us nowhere,' he said. 'I'm still shocked at learning of the baby's death. I only found out this morning.'

From his mother. Something slumped inside Lily. She should have been the one to break the news. She should have found out when his convoy was due. She should have been a better mother and kept her baby alive.

Daniel swiped a hand across his eyes, dashing away tears. Lily went to him, hands outstretched as she reached out to him with all her heart and soul, but now it was his turn to get to his feet and move away. He kept his back to her. She heard his ragged breathing, then he produced a handkerchief. Sniffing a few times, he mopped his face before turning to her, stuffing the handkerchief into his pocket.

'He was beautiful,' Lily said softly. 'He had blue eyes and wisps of fair hair, and he had the tiniest fingers and toes you can imagine. The first time I saw him, it was like falling in love.' She heard the wonderment in her voice as she re-lived that moment, that revelation.

'I wish I'd seen him,' said Daniel. 'I wish I'd had the chance to fall in love as well.'

This time when Lily came to him, he opened his arms. They stood together for a long time, locked in an embrace.

At last Daniel eased away slightly, so he could look down into her face.

'I just can't believe this has happened,' he said. 'It's so much to take in all at once.'

Lily's brittle soul, which had started to yield, hardened again. It was her only form of protection. She dropped her face so he couldn't see her expression. How was she to bear his grief? His bereavement had only started this morning. He was in the first stages of shock, but she had left the shock behind some time ago. She had lived through – floundered through, more like – the first part of her own loss. Was she now meant to live through the first part of Daniel's? All that raw pain...

She stepped away from him. 'I know how hard it is to believe.'

'All this time, I thought I had a baby to come home to.'

The anger came from nowhere. 'Then you're lucky! You had that luxury – you had that gift. All the time that Toby was gone and I was alone and desperate, you were playing happy families in your head.'

'You can't blame me for not knowing.'

'You weren't here.'

'It's my work – my war work, in case you hadn't noticed. And for your information, imagining returning to my new family was what kept me going. You've no idea what it's like crossing the Atlantic—'

'I don't *care* what it's like,' Lily flared. Looking away, she pressed a palm to her face. 'I'm sorry. I shouldn't have said that.'

'No, you shouldn't.' Daniel's voice was so rigidly controlled that it almost vibrated. 'It's probably for the best that I have to go away again.'

With a jerk of her head, Lily looked at him. Her heart bumped. 'Already? You have another crossing already? But you've only just got back.'

'Not another crossing – not yet, though the next one will be soon. I can't go into detail but when I was in America, I had a job to do.'

'What?'

'I can't give you any details. Suffice it to say that I was under orders from my father.'

'So it was for the War Office?'

Daniel didn't give a direct answer. 'I have to go to London to see him.'

'When?' Lily asked quietly.

'Tomorrow.'

'*Tomorrow*?'

'I'm sorry—'

'What about me?' Lily asked. 'What about Toby?'

'Lily, I'd have had to go even if—'

'—even if Toby had still been alive,' Lily finished. The part of her that had begun to open up froze over again. 'Well, you'd best go, then, hadn't you?'

She couldn't look at him. There was a long silence and then she heard the door open softly and shut again.

20

The initial success of the Time Off Club led to Miss Brewer granting permission for the club to meet twice a week instead of once, which was a source of deep satisfaction to Beatrice. She couldn't wait to tell Miss Oates about it.

'It does me good to hear you sounding so pleased and cheery,' the old lady declared. 'Your eyes are shining too. It suits you, Miss Inkerman.'

It was so long since Beatrice had received a compliment that she didn't know what to say. She took refuge in providing more information.

'The best thing is that one of the children, a girl called Agnes, knows another girl who is kept off school to look after her bedridden mother and two bedridden grandparents, if you can believe it. Anyway, originally this other girl – Rosemarie – was refused permission by her mother to go to the Time Off Club, but Agnes's mother is so pleased with what Agnes has had to say about it that she sent a neighbour round to persuade Rosemarie's mother. She couldn't go herself, of course, as she's not a well woman.'

'So you've got an extra child,' said Mrs Gates. 'Lucky thirteen.'

'Lucky fourteen, actually,' said Beatrice. 'A girl who wasn't on Miss Brewer's list, because of living further away, has asked to join.'

'Word is getting round. How gratifying for you.'

'I'm not interested in being gratified,' said Beatrice. 'I just want to help as many children as I can. Lord, how pompous that sounds. But it's true.'

'It's not pompous at all,' her friend replied. 'It's something to be proud of. Have you time for a cup of tea? Would you mind putting the kettle on?'

This was a little fiction that Mrs Gates went through each time, saying, 'Would you mind?' when the fact was that she needed whoever was with her to do it.

Over tea, Mrs Gates asked about Dunbar's.

'How intriguing to think of a respectable old hotel taking on a new identity,' she said, 'but we all have to adapt, I suppose. If you'd told me ten years ago that I'd see out my final years from my bed, I'd have laughed at you. I've never met this Mrs Dunbar but I do admire her. Women are always far more capable than men think they are. I was pretty capable myself in my day.'

Beatrice smiled. 'I can imagine.'

When it was time to go, Beatrice quickly washed up, then took her jacket from the back of the bedside chair and slipped it on as she said goodbye to her friend.

'I'll see you again soon,' she promised.

As she cycled away, she warned herself to be discreet in what she passed on about Dunbar's. She'd been careful to say only what was becoming common knowledge and she must stick to that, especially if she hoped for a friendship with Mrs Dunbar and they started exchanging information on a personal level.

Speaking of which – fancy her opening up about Frank! Ought she to feel shocked at herself? But she wasn't, because she felt certain she could trust Kitty Dunbar.

She intended to pop into Dunbar's on her rounds this afternoon, because Mr Trent, who lived downstairs from Dora Chapman and her mother, had given her half a dozen old packs of playing cards and she wanted to drop them off. When she got there, Abbie had just got in from school and took them from her, promising to ask her mother for the key to the Time Off Club cupboard so they could be put away.

Feeling a sneeze coming on, Beatrice delved in her pocket for her hanky and honked into it.

'This fell out of your pocket,' said Abbie when Beatrice put her hanky away. She held out a tiny packet in pretty paper.

Beatrice frowned. 'That's not mine.'

'It came out of your pocket,' the child insisted. 'I saw it.'

Reluctant but intrigued, Beatrice took it. 'I don't remember the last time I saw proper wrapping paper.'

'Open it,' Abbie urged her. Then, 'Is it for your birthday? Are you supposed to save it?'

'I've no idea what it is.' Beatrice opened it carefully so as not to tear the patterned paper. 'Oh.'

Abbie came closer. 'What is it?'

'A brooch.'

A wing-shaped brooch set with red stones. Beatrice didn't know whether to feel pleased or vexed or what she was supposed to feel. It was very naughty of Mrs Gates – but also generous and kind. She must have slipped it into Beatrice's pocket when her jacket was over the back of the chair while Beatrice went to make the tea.

She'd have to return it, of course. Or would she? Mrs Gates obviously wanted her to have it and it was so pretty. Beatrice yearned for it – not for the brooch itself so much as what it represented. A gift. When had she last received a present? Not for years.

She handed the small piece of wrapping paper to Abbie. 'Please will you put this in your salvage box, though it hardly looks enough to be of any use.'

'Lots of little bits add up to one big bit,' Abbie said virtuously, which made Beatrice smile.

'I must be on my way,' she said, 'or I'll be late and that would never do.'

She set off, trying not to think too much about the brooch. It was a tricky subject. The last thing she wanted was to cause upset by returning it, but it didn't feel right to keep it. Then again, why shouldn't she keep it? It wasn't as though Mrs Gates used the inco service. Nevertheless, they had met because of the Blackers, Mrs Gates's downstairs neighbours, and they did use the service.

Beatrice fixed her thoughts on the Time Off Club instead. Mrs Gates was right. It was indeed something to be proud of.

By the time the next meeting came around, the group had grown yet again. This time there was an additional boy called Cyril. Beatrice was delighted because they were very top-heavy with girls, though that was inevitable. Cyril was a quiet, serious boy, rather bookish, with a sweet smile.

Halfway through the time, Mrs Dunbar came into the room and signalled to Beatrice with her eyes.

Beatrice left the uproarious game of ping-pong she'd been scoring and made her way across the room, the sound of young voices ringing in her ears.

'You've got some visitors,' Mrs Dunbar told her.

'Visitors?' Beatrice repeated.

'Well, not so much visitors as a deputation.'

A New Home at the Wartime Hotel 219

What on earth was going on? Beatrice followed Mrs Dunbar to the front doors and stepped outside. At the foot of the steps were— her heart sank. Tommy Abbott, Joseph Simpson and others. The young louts from her road. The 'Inky Stinky Inkerman' song started running round and round in her head.

Joseph nudged Tommy and he stepped forwards, snatching his grubby school-cap off his head and clutching it in both hands.

'Please, Miss Inkerman, it's us. We've heard about your club and – and – if we promise not to sing that song about you ever again, can we join?'

* * *

It was a WVS day for Kitty, who was on duty at the British Restaurant. The menu at dinnertime was either fish pie or beef with dumplings, with sultana sponge or milk pudding afterwards, and a cup of tea, all for under a shilling. Kitty spent the morning peeling potatoes and carrots, then helped serve the meals, keeping an eye out for any ladies in the family way, because they were always given extra.

Later in her shift she cleared and wiped tables, and scraped leftovers into the pig-bin. Most of the washing-up was done by the next shift of women before they made a start on the teatime meals.

When she got back to Dunbar's, Lily met her in the foyer.

'You've got a visitor. She says she's Mr Dunbar's mother. I put her in the family flat.' Lily looked unsure. 'I hope that's all right. The only other place is the kitchen and I wasn't sure that would be polite, given as it's down in the basement.'

'It's fine, Lily,' said Kitty, taking off her WVS hat and shaking her head to loosen her hair.

Oh glory, what did Ivy want? Another row, presumably. Heading upstairs, Kitty braced herself.

But when she entered the flat, Ivy didn't look geared up for mortal combat. Instead she looked awkward. She stood up at once.

'I haven't been noseying around, if that's what you're thinking,' was her stiff greeting.

'It never occurred to me,' said Kitty. 'Sit down and I'll put the kettle on.'

'No – wait. I've got something to say.'

Kitty considered making her mother-in-law wait while she changed out of her uniform. Dismissing the idea, she sat down. So did Ivy, who then made a fuss out of smoothing her skirt and pretending to remove a stray thread.

'I take it this is about Bill,' said Kitty.

Ivy nodded.

'What has he told you this time?'

'I haven't been in touch with him,' said Ivy. 'It's been so nasty with him saying one thing and you saying the opposite. It's had me all hot and bothered, so I decided it was time for me to find out something for myself.'

Kitty waited.

Ivy said, 'I went to see about the motorcar.'

'The *what*? What motorcar?'

'The one Bill told me you'd insisted on having.'

Kitty gasped. 'I never—'

'It was an Austin 7 Ruby and it cost over a hundred pounds. A hundred and twenty-five, to be precise.'

Kitty gasped. '*A hundred and*—' Disbelief tingled inside her chest. 'He only earned three pounds ten a week.' She pressed her splayed hand to her breastbone.

'He told me you'd set your heart on it,' Ivy went on, 'and his life wouldn't be worth living if he didn't buy it.'

Kitty's heart thumped. 'This is the first I've ever heard of it, I swear.'

'I know that now,' said Ivy, 'but I didn't then. Then, I just thought what a shabby piece of work you were. Spoilt, demanding, spending money your husband didn't have. The trouble I've had over the years keeping my opinion to myself, but Bill was adamant I must never say a word to anyone, and I never did. The first time I breathed a word was—'

'—when the bailiffs came round,' Kitty finished. Things were starting to slot into place. 'Tell me about this motorcar I'm supposed to have wanted so badly.'

'Bill bought it.'

'But he didn't have that kind of money,' Kitty exclaimed. But when had the lack of money ever stopped him? 'Anyway, he couldn't possibly have bought it. I think I'd have noticed an Austin parked outside our house.'

'He told me that he'd insisted to you that he couldn't afford it, and that he was going to buy it as a surprise.'

'It would have been that, all right,' Kitty said darkly.

'So he bought it,' Ivy said, and stopped.

'On the never,' supplied Kitty.

'But he was in a traffic accident on the way home. Both motors were damaged. It was Bill's fault, so he had to pay for the other motor to be repaired. The damage was extensive, apparently. Bill didn't have insurance. He'd told me he'd been going to sort that out later.'

Kitty's jaw tightened. Just like Bill. Concentrate on the expensive stuff and leave the sensible things for afterwards.

'Don't tell me,' she said crisply. 'He had to sell back the Austin – at a loss – to pay for the other chap's repairs.'

'It was worse than that,' said Ivy. 'The Austin was so badly damaged that it wasn't worth mending. Bill was left with the bill for a brand-new vehicle and nothing to show for it.'

Kitty spread out her fingers in a fan against her breastbone. When the bailiffs had barged in, she'd been unable to comprehend how Bill's debts could have been so bad. She'd been completely stumped. Now she knew how his financial situation had become so dire. Not that knowing brought any comfort.

'He swore me to secrecy,' said Ivy. 'He said you'd be heartbroken if you knew how close you'd come to having the Austin.'

Kitty's muscles quivered with anger. She was appalled at the tale of the Austin, but oddly she was more vexed at the way Bill had misrepresented her to Ivy all these years.

'There's more,' said Ivy.

'Honestly, I think I've heard enough for one day.'

'Don't you want to know what the motorcar people told me? I was hopping mad the last time I left here. You and your pathetic little scraps of paper with Bill's name on: what sort of proof were they? I decided to find my own evidence. Before he bought the Austin, Bill said he'd told the men at the garage about you insisting on having a motor, so I thought that if I asked them, they'd confirm it, and you would have to stop pretending to be the innocent little miss. That was my plan.'

'What did they say?' Kitty asked quietly.

'They said he never mentioned his wife. They said he was full of how much he wanted a motor. They said... they said he knew all about buying on the never and didn't bat an eyelid when he heard what the repayments were.' Ivy looked straight at Kitty. 'All these years I've loathed you for leading my boy up the garden path, and it was him all along. It's taken a few days to build up to coming here and saying this, and now I won't be surprised if you never want to see me again.'

Kitty thought for a few moments. 'It seems to me I've got two choices. I can tell you to sling your hook or I can put the kettle on. I know which one I'd prefer. How about you?'

* * *

Daniel had been gone for a week. When he returned, he asked Lily to come to his mother's house. She didn't relish the thought but knew it was something she had to do.

Mrs Dunbar encouraged her. 'It's such a desperately unhappy situation. It would mean a lot to your husband if he could go back to sea knowing that his wife and mother are on better terms.'

Lily felt a little flare of annoyance. That was Daniel's trump card, wasn't it? He had to return to his work, which involved being out of communication for weeks on end, and it put everyone else under an obligation to send him on his way without a worry.

Then she felt ashamed. How could she be so mean? She loved Daniel and didn't want him to suffer. Making peace with his mother was a small thing to ask of her – or was it? Mrs Chadwick regarded their marriage as a mistake. She had told her friend Lady Ingrid that Daniel had only married her because of her being in the family way.

Lily had meant to keep that to herself but it had proved impossible. The words seemed to fizz on her tongue like sherbet and when she saw Daniel after he returned from London, she found herself asking, 'When we got married... did you only do it because of the baby?'

The look of shock on his face had made her want to bite off her tongue.

'Of course not,' he'd said. 'How can you ask? I thought you

knew how much I love you.' Frowning, he shook his head. Then his frown darkened. 'Did you marry me because of the baby? Is that what you're saying?'

'*What*? No!' It seemed all she could do to protect herself was attack his mother. 'It was something I heard your mother say to somebody. She said you only married me because you had to.'

And instead of being shocked, instead of raging against his mother, Daniel said, 'You must have misheard.'

Lily had been so vexed she had clammed up. She was furious that he'd taken his mother's side. She thought about it more when she was alone. Had he sided with Mrs Chadwick – or had he neatly taken no side at all? And if so, was that better or worse?

Now Daniel wanted her to go to his mother's house. Lily understood the need for it, but she also thought that smoothing things over with Mrs Chadwick was a lot less important than her and Daniel navigating the unhappy and difficult situation they were in.

But if it had been her own mother, wouldn't she have wanted Daniel to have a loving relationship with her? Of course she would. That meant she owed it to Daniel to swallow her anger and visit Mrs Chadwick.

* * *

Beatrice felt torn in two. The brooch was so very lovely and this was the first time in years that she'd received a present. On top of that, Mrs Gates was dear to her, and that alone gave the brooch deep sentimental value.

She sighed. She knew she had to return it. The thought produced a grimace, not for the loss of the jewellery, but at hurting her friend. Mrs Gates just couldn't understand that it was inappropriate for Beatrice to accept the brooch. Couldn't understand? Refused point blank to understand, more like.

Beatrice smiled to herself. More than once she had humorously accused her friend of being obstinate – to which Mrs Gates's immediate reply had always been, 'I'm not obstinate – I'm cantankerous!'

Well, now it was Beatrice's turn to be obstinate. She would call on her friend on her way home from work and explain why it was impossible for her to keep the piece of jewellery; and she would bring the brooch back in a day or two.

Pulling her trolley along behind her bicycle, she made her way along Fig Street, slowing as she saw a priest going into the house shared by the Blackers and Mrs Gates. She drew up alongside a couple of housewives, who were talking quietly on the pavement.

'Pardon me for interrupting but did I just see a priest enter the Blackers' home? I'm not being nosy. I know the family.'

'You're the inco lady, aren't you?' said one of the women. 'I'm afraid there's been a death.'

'I'm sorry to hear it,' Beatrice said sincerely. 'Poor Mrs Blacker.'

'It isn't Mrs Blacker, love,' said the other woman.

'I mean old Mrs Blacker, the mother-in-law,' Beatrice said quickly.

'No, it's not her.'

Beatrice's skin prickled. 'Not young Mrs Blacker, surely?' A picture filled her mind of Mrs Blacker unable to cope with the strain a moment longer and dropping dead.

'It's not one of the Blackers at all,' said the first woman. 'It's old Mrs Gates upstairs.'

21

Lily spent the morning doing an extra stint at netting. By the end of it, her back was practically screaming with pain and she had to keep twitching her nose like a rabbit to try to clear the dust and fluff. The discomfort didn't really bother her, though. Who cared about sore muscles when their heart felt as if it had been put through the mincer?

As she walked back to Dunbar's, the summer skies were duck-egg blue with wisps of cloud, but the air smelled of smoke and cordite left over from last night's raid. Lily had been out with the mobile canteen last night, dispensing tea, sandwiches and ciggies to firemen and rescue parties, though she knew not to offer cigarettes if there had been a gas leak in the vicinity.

Now she must have a bite to eat and get changed, ready to call on Daniel's mother. Daniel had asked her if she wanted him to collect her and she'd said no. Not because she didn't want him to, but because he shouldn't have asked. He should just have announced he was going to collect her. By asking, he'd made it sound as if he would be doing her a favour if she accepted. She knew she was being daft; she knew she was nit-picking; but she couldn't help it.

At Dunbar's Lily made herself a sandwich, then prepared some parsnip fritters for her and the Dunbars to have, heated up, for tea with fried bread and bacon. She was good at cooking; she'd had plenty of practice at Auntie Nettie's.

Soon it was time to go to the Chadwicks' house. Lily's heart picked up speed. Would Daniel meet her halfway? But he didn't. Nor did he come running to answer the door when she knocked. That job was left to the maid.

When Lily walked into the drawing room, Daniel stood up, smiling, and crossed the room to meet her. Although her heart leapt at the sight of him, being here made Lily feel awkward and out of place.

'Lily,' said Daniel, her name on his lips sending a little shiver through her. He drew her towards the sofa. 'You came.'

'You asked me to.'

'Now then, Lily,' said Mrs Chadwick, her voice sounding warm and humorous. 'We all know you're here under sufferance, which is quite understandable if you think I've been talking about you behind your back. Daniel told me what you thought you overheard. I'm so sorry if you misunderstood.'

Lily wanted to say she knew precisely what she'd heard, thank you very much, and there hadn't been any misunderstanding, but no words would come. She knew that, whatever she said, Mrs Chadwick would outfox her.

'But you're right in thinking I spoke out of turn to an acquaintance,' said Mrs Chadwick in the same honey-filled tone, 'and I shouldn't have done that. I've promised Daniel it won't happen again. Can we please put it behind us?'

Daniel gave Lily a beseeching look and she suddenly saw the situation through his eyes. He had such limited time here at home before he had to go back to sea. Of course he wanted – needed – all to be well.

She made an effort. 'Of course.'

Daniel took her hand, his relief obvious in his smile. 'Thank you, darling. I know how hard the past few weeks have been for you.'

How could you know? You weren't here.

Lily caught her breath. She felt light-headed.

Time for another effort.

'I'm sure all three of us miss Toby every day.'

Emotion lent depth to Daniel's voice. 'I only wish I'd had the chance to meet my son.'

'I wish you could have met him too, Daniel, dear,' said his mother. 'Dear little Tobias.'

'Toby,' said Lily. 'He was going to be known as Toby.'

'How sweet,' said Mrs Chadwick, 'but he would always have been Tobias to me. It's a family name.'

Lily went hot and cold. She remembered her and Daniel laughing as they considered various names. They'd been so happy. Then Daniel had suggested Tobias and she'd instantly loved it.

She closed her eyes for a moment. She had loved the name. That was all that mattered. So what if Daniel hadn't mentioned it was in his family? She'd wanted Irwin, hadn't she? Family names mattered.

Make an effort.

'It's nice to think of my little Toby coming from a long line of Tobias Chadwicks,' she said.

'Oh – didn't Daniel tell you?' asked Mrs Chadwick. 'Tobias isn't a Chadwick name. It's from my side of the family. That's how I know it shouldn't really be shortened.'

A New Home at the Wartime Hotel

* * *

Daniel took Lily back to Dunbar's. At least, that's where she thought they were going but instead he got off the bus at a different stop.

'Where are we going?' Lily asked.

'The Claremont. Do you know it?'

Surprise showed itself in a burst of laughter. 'Everyone knows the Claremont. It's one of the best hotels in Manchester.'

'That's where we're going,' said Daniel.

'I can't go there.'

'Why not?'

'You asked if I know it,' said Lily. 'I know *of* it. There's a difference. Girls like me only go to the Claremont if they work there as maids or waitresses.'

'Lily, you're my wife and you get your status from me.'

Try telling your mother that.

'We need to talk privately,' said Daniel. 'You wouldn't be comfortable talking at my parents' house and Dunbar's is hardly the appropriate venue.'

'It's where I live,' said Lily.

'We can go there if you prefer.' A touch of crispness edged Daniel's tone. 'Where should we have our talk? In your bedroom? There'd be nothing wrong in that. We are married.'

Lily flushed, feeling caught out.

Daniel ushered her into the Claremont. The pillared foyer was handsomely furnished. On the far wall, alcoves with tables for two offered privacy. Daniel took Lily towards one of these. A waiter appeared and Daniel ordered tea.

He gave Lily an earnest look. 'I'd like you to come back to the family home.'

'It's not that simple,' said Lily.

'My mother has apologised. There's no reason for you to stay away.'

'We didn't really get on even before I heard her talking about me,' said Lily.

'Then you'll both have to make an effort, won't you? What am I supposed to do, Lily? I can't stay here to be the referee.'

'Don't speak to me like that,' said Lily, stung.

'I apologise,' said Daniel. 'There: you've had two apologies in one afternoon.'

'What's that supposed to mean?'

'It means maybe you should be more... amenable. You were happy enough to fall in with my mother's wishes before we were married.'

'Don't you like me as much now I'm thinking for myself?'

'Don't you see, Lily?' Daniel asked. 'This is about where you live. I'm your husband. It's my duty to provide you with a home. We haven't got a place of our own and no billeting officer will give us one. You know that. I would dearly love to have our own house or flat, but right now the only home I can offer you is the one where my brothers and I grew up.'

Lily's eyes swam. 'I'm sorry. I can't, I just can't.'

'Because of my mother? She's apologised.'

'When I lived there before, it never felt right,' said Lily. 'It's a grand place, filled with beautiful things. I admired the china one day – except that I made the mistake of calling it "crockery", which your mother didn't appreciate. I said how nice it was and she said it was her second-best china because she'd had the best set packed away and put in storage until the end of the war.'

'What's your point?' Daniel asked.

'Auntie Nettie doesn't have best and second-best. She just has what she has – and it isn't china. It's crockery, plain and simple, that was bought off the market.'

'You've gone up in the world, Lily. I've told you. Your rank in life comes from me.'

'When I was in your mother's house, I didn't feel like Mrs Daniel Chadwick. I felt like Lily from Auntie Nettie's.'

The tea arrived and they both sat back until the waiter withdrew. Lily poured and offered Daniel his cup.

In a gentler voice, he said, 'I imagine there will be a lot of unequal marriages throughout the war. You must learn to live up to my position.'

'It would be different if you were here,' Lily whispered.

Daniel returned his cup to its saucer with a clatter. 'Not that again. I'm in the merchant navy.'

'And the work you do is essential. It's the merchant navy that helps keep the country fed. Folk say, "God bless the merchant navy" when they say grace before meals. I'm not asking you to change what you do.'

'Good, because I wouldn't change.'

Daniel lifted his cup again. They both drank, Lily because it saved having to speak. Was it the same for Daniel?

Presently he said, 'I'll ask you one more time. Will you move back into my family home? Please?'

'I'm sorry,' Lily said softly.

'Then where do you suggest we live? In a hotel? In the Claremont?'

'Don't be silly.'

'What's silly about it? You're my wife. We're supposed to live together.'

Lily stiffened. 'I've barely seen you since our baby died and all you want is for us to sleep together.'

'Don't twist my words.' Colour appeared along Daniel's cheekbones. 'I want us to live under the same roof. We're married and that's how it's meant to be. Instead, you've got your room in Dunbar's and you refuse to live in my home, so what are we to do? If you don't live in my family home, that's like saying – it's like saying we're separated.'

Lily set down her cup. She was trembling. 'Is that what you care about? Appearances? What the neighbours think? None of that matters to me. How can any of it matter? Compared to Toby, how can any of it matter? That's what I care about, and it's all I care about: Toby, my beautiful baby boy.'

22

Beatrice was able to take the time off to attend dear Mrs Gates's funeral, but she couldn't stay for the do afterwards. She was needed back on her rounds. Besides, it wasn't as though she knew Mrs Gates's daughters. They'd met a few times in passing, but that was all. When one of the girls arrived when Beatrice was in the middle of a visit – Mrs Gates had always referred to them as 'girls' even though they were older than Beatrice – she had always got up to leave, not wanting to intrude on the family. And neither Renee nor Olive had ever pressed her to stay.

The funeral was a simple but heartfelt service and Beatrice shed tears for the friend whose company she had always enjoyed. She'd brought the brooch with her, but when everyone left the church, the idea of handing it over seemed crass. It was entirely the wrong moment. It would have been different if she'd been able to join everybody afterwards, but she couldn't.

Well, she would return the brooch another time. Just now she needed to concentrate on her new club even though, having lost her friend, she didn't altogether feel like it. But Beatrice was used to doing things she didn't feel like doing. As the young daughter and only child of an invalid mother, it had been part and parcel of her childhood.

'I don't think I was ever more taken aback in my life than when those boys asked to join the Time Off Club,' she had confided to Mrs Dunbar before explaining about the Stinky Inkerman song.

Mrs Dunbar was shocked. 'That's appalling, cheeking an adult like that. They shouldn't be allowed to get away with it. I'm surprised you didn't send them away from here with a flea in their ears.'

Beatrice had been surprised too. It was undoubtedly what those boys had deserved, but something had stopped her. Even more surprising, she'd told them she would think about it.

And she had – at considerable length. Hence the Gentlemen's Club was about to open.

'Do you think they'll come?' Abbie asked that evening when she was helping to set up the club room.

'Oh, they'll come all right,' her mother said drily. 'Whether they end up staying is another matter.'

Beatrice swallowed. She was taking a risk, she knew, but if these lads wanted to belong to a club, they would have to abide by her rules.

When they arrived, she made them all wipe their feet before they came in.

'And put these ties on, please,' she added, holding out her arm, over which were draped some ties she had bought cheap from a bombed-out gentlemen's outfitters.

'You what, miss?'

They all gawped at her.

'If you want to come to Dunbar's and take part in one of the clubs, then you have to obey the rules, which are as follows. When you arrive, you wipe your feet and put on a tie. Then you raise your caps to Mrs Dunbar and me and wish us good evening, after which you may hang up your caps on those pegs over there and enter the club room, with no jostling. I will tell you which games and activities are available on any particular evening. At the end of the evening, you must help to put everything away, then line up to shake hands with Mrs Dunbar and me and say thank you. Then you take off your ties, put on your caps and leave the building quietly. No yelling or cavorting until you reach the pavement.'

The boys continued to stare at her.

Beatrice found their consternation rather enjoyable. 'One more thing. This club is the Gentlemen's Club. Hence the ties and the good manners.'

'The *Gentlemen's* Club?' whined the boys.

'Yes, because gentlemen behave nicely and don't poke fun at people in the street.' Beatrice gave the group a steely look. 'If you wish to join the Gentlemen's Club, there will be skittles, ping-pong, billiards and bagatelle as well as a variety of board games, and I'm on the lookout for old comics and annuals. I know plenty of card games and will be happy to teach you. So that's the Gentlemen's Club, but you can only join if you agree to obey my rules. Is anyone interested?'

The lads shifted from foot to foot, exchanging glances.

'Yes, miss,' said Tommy Abbott.

'Me an' all,' Joseph Simpson added.

'No, that won't do.' Beatrice shook her head with an elaborate sigh. 'Gentlemen don't say, "Me, miss." They say, "Please may I join, Miss Inkerman?" I can't have just anybody playing billiards and skittles in Dunbar's. This is an old establishment with an excellent reputation dating back many years.'

The boys gazed at her, open-mouthed. Did they think she'd lost her marbles? Then Tommy Abbott cleared his throat and a couple of the others stood up straight. Joseph Simpson took his hands out of his pockets.

'I'd like to join the club, please, miss – I mean, Miss Inkerman.'

'Please can I join too, Miss Inkerman?'

'I'd like to be a gentleman an' all, Miss Inkerman, please.'

Beatrice smiled.

* * *

What remained of Mr John Kenwood's household goods occupied Dunbar's large entrance foyer and former dining room. Everything had arrived yesterday and a detailed inventory had been made. Yesterday afternoon and this morning had seen Kitty and Lily giving everything a thorough clean. All wooden pieces had been wet-dusted, then dry-dusted and polished. The crockery, cutlery and ornaments had been washed and dried, though the glassware, after being washed, was rinsed in hot water and left to drain.

'Only when the glasses had dried was I allowed to wipe them,' Kitty murmured now to Naomi, 'and then only with a dry cloth, not a damp one. That way they end up looking really bright.'

Naomi's lips twitched. 'When you say "that way", I take it you mean the Dunbar way.'

'I thought I had a good grounding in housework from Mam,' said Kitty, 'but I've learned plenty since Lily arrived.'

'She seems a sweet girl,' said Naomi. 'It's such a shame that – well, I don't need to say it, do I? Poor thing. But I hope she's earning her keep.'

'Naomi!' Kitty exclaimed.

'I'm sorry if that sounds harsh,' Naomi replied, 'but you've only just set up in business and you've hardly got off the ground yet. I'm sure you can't afford staff.'

'She works for me for bed and board,' said Kitty.

Now it was Naomi's turn to exclaim, 'Kitty! That's disgraceful. You're taking advantage.'

'You said you wanted her to earn her keep. Well, that's exactly what she's doing. I can't afford to give her any wages – yet. But I will, starting next month. In any case, she doesn't really need wages off me. Part of her husband's salary is paid to her.'

'But you said she arrived here desperate for work.'

'She did – but the need was to keep herself busy, not because she was destitute,' said Kitty. 'I'm glad she's here. She's worth her weight in gold.'

'If you say so,' Naomi remarked.

'That sounds rather grudging,' said Kitty.

'It wasn't meant to,' her sister answered. 'It's just that I worry about you.'

Kitty gave her a hug. 'I'm glad you're here today so you can see a part of what we do. The furniture came yesterday and I wrote the inventory, which was sent over to Mr Tulip's—'

'—the storage warehouse man—'

'—to be typed up. That's a service I pay for, but not for long, I hope, if I can get hold of a typewriter. Mr Kenwood is due here soon to check and sign the inventory, then Mr Tulip's men will carry everything upstairs.' Kitty consulted her wristwatch, feeling a tug of anxiety. 'They should be here by now. They're supposed to arrive before Mr Kenwood.'

'Does it matter if he gets here first?' Naomi asked.

'Mr Tulip's men will have the invoice with them. It'll look bad if Mr Kenwood is kept waiting. It'll look…' Kitty hesitated. 'It'll look as if I can't manage my business properly.'

The front doors were standing open in readiness, but it was Abbie who walked in, her eyes lighting up at the sight of her auntie.

'Have you come to see the system for storing furniture?' Abbie asked.

Naomi smiled. 'The system? That sounds very grand.'

'It's the Dunbar way,' Abbie said seriously.

'I thought the Dunbar way was to do with cleaning,' said Naomi.

'It is,' Abbie replied, 'but now it's also to do with storage. We have to show customers that we know what we're doing,' she added, quoting Kitty.

'Then you'd better hope the warehousemen get here before Mr Kenwood,' said Naomi, sounding amused.

A movement made all three of them look towards the open doors. This time it was Miss Inkerman, a cloth shopping bag dangling from one hand.

'Goodness me,' she said. 'All this furniture. It's quite the Aladdin's cave.'

Kitty introduced her to Naomi.

'You must be the lady who runs the children's club,' said Naomi. 'My sister was telling me about it.'

'Yes. Actually, I have two clubs now.' Miss Inkerman glanced around at the furniture. 'I hope I haven't called at an inconvenient time, but I've brought these.' She handed the bag to Abbie. 'Would you pop these into the cupboard for me, please? It's a selection of comics I've been given.'

Abbie caught her breath in delight. Holding up the bag in one hand, she delved inside it with the other.

'Oh, Mummy, look. *The Dandy, The Beano, The Magnet* – that's got Billy Bunter stories in it. What else? *The Rainbow*...'

'There's also a couple of copies of *The Modern Boy*,' Miss

Inkerman said wryly to Kitty and Naomi, 'though the boys who read them first time around must be grown-up now.'

'And probably fighting for their country,' Naomi added.

'Is this Mr Kenwood's reception committee?' asked Lily, walking in with a couple of library books under her arm.

Kitty introduced her to Naomi, then saw that Miss Inkerman was hovering, evidently looking for a polite moment to leave. Just then Mr Tulip himself walked in, looking dapper, followed by a couple of his men.

'I wasn't expecting you, Mr Tulip,' said Kitty, surprised.

'I thought I'd take the liberty of seeing how you're getting on,' he answered. 'Here is the inventory.' He produced it with a flourish.

As Kitty took it, Mr Kenwood walked in. He was a sharp-featured middle-aged man with grey eyes behind round spectacles.

Feeling self-conscious in front of her audience, Kitty showed him the inventory and got him to sign each page.

'Now your belongings will be taken upstairs and put into storage,' she said.

'Thank you,' said Mr Kenwood.

Another figure marched in.

'There you are!' A middle-aged man in tweeds confronted Mr Kenwood. 'I might have known!'

'You can't barge in here,' said Kitty but the newcomer ignored her.

'Thought you'd take everything for yourself, did you, John? That's typical of you, that is.'

Kitty tried again. 'Mr Kenwood, do you know this man?'

The fellow in tweeds turned to face her. 'I'm the other Mr Kenwood. John here didn't tell you he had a brother, did he?'

'Why should he?' asked Kitty.

'Because that furniture isn't his to do with as he pleases,' replied the new Mr Kenwood in a loud voice. 'Everything here belonged to our late father, who died last week in an air raid.'

'I'm sorry to hear that,' said Kitty.

'He left everything to me,' Mr John Kenwood declared, 'so I'm within my rights to remove the lot and make appropriate arrangements.'

'Not when I'm going to contest the will,' his brother flung back at him before addressing Mr Tulip. 'I take it, sir, that you are the owner of this storage service. I'm Stanley Kenwood and if you take these items into storage, you could find yourself on the wrong side of the law.'

Kitty's mouth dropped open and she snapped it shut. She knew that however she conducted herself next would set the tone for Dunbar's for the rest of the war. Forestalling Mr Tulip, who was about to reply to Mr Stanley Kenwood, she stepped forward.

'Mr Kenwood, I run Dunbar's, so please address yourself to me; but before you address anyone, kindly listen to what I have to say.' Kitty straightened her spine. To John Kenwood, she said, 'You allowed me to believe that these possessions are yours.'

'They are mine, according to my father's will.'

'A will I have every intention of getting overturned,' his brother snapped.

Kitty faltered. What exactly was the legal position? But she couldn't afford to show indecision. She had to demonstrate to these warring brothers – and to Mr Tulip and his men, to Naomi, to Miss Inkerman, Lily and Abbie – that she was in charge and that, no matter what happened, she could rise to the occasion.

'You won't be the only one going to a solicitor,' she informed

Stanley Kenwood. 'I shall too, because I also now have a claim on your father's estate.'

'You *what*?' demanded Stanley Kenwood.

'Now see here,' blustered John Kenwood.

Kitty had spent years trying to be reasonable with Bill and it had got her precisely nowhere. A sudden fire burned inside her. It was time to lay down the law.

'No, *you* see here, both of you,' she said. 'I don't care about your family squabbles, but I do care about my business. If the will is disputed, then your father's estate will be frozen and I doubt that Mr John Kenwood will feel it worth his while to pay my storage bills out of his own money if there's a chance of Mr Stanley Kenwood receiving half of everything. That means I'll need to see a solicitor to lodge my own claim on the will, so that when it's settled one way or the other, I, as a creditor, will have first crack at the proceeds.' She airily waved a hand, indicating the late Mr Kenwood senior's household goods. 'Who can say how much of this will have to be sold to meet my storage expenses?'

Kitty looked from one Kenwood to the other. She had no idea at all whether what she'd said was true, but she could tell from the two men's expressions that she had spoken with sufficient confidence to make them believe her, or at least to question their own positions.

'Gentleman, I have no wish to be dragged into this matter,' said Kitty. 'It would bring trouble on me if I stored these things at Dunbar's and so I request that you remove them from my premises.'

'You can't do that!' John Kenwood exclaimed. 'We have an agreement—'

Kitty pressed the tip of her forefinger to the side of her mouth and pretended to think. 'Are you referring to the agreement in which you allowed me to think that all these articles are yours? The agreement in which you failed to mention your brother's intention to get what he can?'

Both brothers uttered explosive sounds of indignation.

'As I said,' Kitty ploughed on, 'I want all your father's things taken away from Dunbar's. You have twenty-four hours to do this. After that I shall charge you by the hour. But, of course, nothing can be removed until Mr John Kenwood pays what he owes.'

'I *beg* your pardon,' said that gentleman.

'You've already paid the deposit,' said Kitty. 'You also need to pay for the Corporation van, the cleaning service and the first storage fee. But I'll let you off the storage fee if everything is gone by this time tomorrow.'

'This is outrageous,' said Stanley Kenwood.

'No,' said Kitty. 'It's good business practice.'

'I suggest, gentlemen,' said Mr Tulip, 'that you go and make arrangements. The clock is ticking.'

The brothers glared at him, then at Kitty and finally at one another before they barged through the doorway, each of them trying to be the first one out of the building.

'Bravo, Mrs Dunbar,' murmured Mr Tulip.

Kitty felt a surge of self-confidence, but then she saw Abbie's eyes, wide and shining with interest, and euphoria was replaced by a stab of guilt. Children weren't supposed to witness adult disputes. She ought to have sent Abbie away as soon as the unpleasantness started. Belatedly she caught Naomi's eye and gave a tiny nod in her daughter's direction.

Naomi understood at once. 'Shall I go and put the kettle on? Come and show me where everything is, Abbie. Have you time to stay for tea, Miss Inkerman?'

'No thank you. I must get going.'

Miss Inkerman moved aside to let Naomi and Abbie disappear, but before she could herself depart, more people walked in. Kitty could hardly believe her eyes. A woman in a nurse's cap and cape. A flinty-eyed middle-aged woman in a headscarf and clumpy shoes. And – a policeman.

'Miss Inkerman,' said the nurse. 'We've found you at last.'

'There she is.' The headscarfed woman jabbed a finger towards Miss Inkerman. 'That's her.'

'Miss Beatrice Inkerman?' asked the bobby. 'I'm Sergeant Wakefield and I'd like to ask you some questions.'

Kitty had no idea what was happening, but of one thing she was absolutely certain. She liked Miss Inkerman and thought well of her. Moving forward to stand beside her, Kitty asked, 'What about?'

The woman in the headscarf glared at Miss Inkerman.

'About her being a lousy thief – that's what!'

23

When Beatrice saw Sister District walk into Dunbar's accompanied by a policeman, her first thought – as stupid as it seemed afterwards – was that Sister had come to accuse her of skiving off work and the bobby was here to make it official. The policeman was some years older than Beatrice herself and carried himself with an air of quiet authority. Then she saw Renee Shotton, one of Mrs Gates's daughters. She didn't exactly know Renee personally, but she knew a lot about her and her sister Olive from their mother. Beatrice automatically reminded herself, as she'd done on previous occasions when she saw one of the daughters, to call this one Mrs Shotton even though she would always think of her as Renee.

And then – and then Renee had pointed at her and uttered the extraordinary words, 'About her being a lousy thief – that's what!' and consternation had gone streaming through Beatrice's veins, followed a moment later by fear.

'Now then, Mrs Shotton.' Sergeant Wakefield's voice held both patience and authority. It was undoubtedly a tone he employed all the time in his line of work. 'I'll deal with this. Miss Inkerman, I believe you knew the late Mrs Gates. Correct?'

'Yes.' Beatrice's heart beat hard.

'According to Mrs Shotton and her sister, Mrs Judd, a brooch belonging to Mrs Gates has gone missing.'

Beatrice's shoulders tightened and she blinked rapidly. She missed the policeman's next words. It took her a moment to realise the room was quiet and everybody was looking at her.

Mr Tulip cleared his throat. 'Officer, my men are here to do a job that has been – um – put off. I suggest we leave.'

'Very well, sir. And you are?'

Mr Tulip introduced himself and his men and handed over a business card, which Sergeant Wakefield put in his pocket.

When the men had left, Renee Shotton gave Beatrice a dark look before saying, 'This is an official matter and I would like it to be conducted at the police station.'

'I'm sure there's no need for that,' said Sister District. 'We can use my office in the district nurses' station.'

'That's further away,' Renee snapped. 'I want this dealt with *now*.'

Mrs Dunbar intervened. 'Why don't you use the club room?'

'I knew Dunbar's had shut down as a hotel,' said Sergeant Wakefield, 'but I didn't know it had been turned into a club. One of those places where foreign servicemen can get a bite to eat and a spot of company, is it?'

'No, it's—' Mrs Dunbar shook her head. 'It doesn't matter what it is. I have a room you can use.' She indicated the closed door. 'It isn't particularly comfortable but you can sit around a table.' To Beatrice she said, 'Would you like me to come with you?'

'There's no need,' Sister District said before Beatrice could answer.

In any case, Mrs Dunbar's sister, whose name Beatrice was too flustered to remember, and Abbie appeared with a tray of tea just then. Their eyes widened with curiosity.

'Let's take the tea up to the family flat,' said Mrs Dunbar. This time when she addressed Beatrice, her words were soft enough to be for her ears alone. 'Don't worry. I shan't tell them anything. This is a private matter.' Her glance flicked towards Renee. 'Disagreeable woman.'

That buoyed Beatrice up more than anything else could have done. The policeman opened the door for the three women. Renee was about to march in first but then she made a point of waiting for Beatrice as if Beatrice might make a run for it.

The table still had the ping-pong net fastened across it. Beatrice wondered if she ought to remove it, but Renee got going right away.

'You took my mother's brooch. It looks like a wing and it's set with red stones. You can't deny it. You are the only person who could have taken it.'

'Hold your horses, Mrs Shotton,' said Sergeant Wakefield. 'Miss Inkerman, do you know this brooch?'

'Yes,' said Beatrice. 'Mrs Gates showed it to me. We were friends. I used to go and see her.'

'And now we all know why.' Renee tightened her lips into a circle. 'Sneaking around, looking for things to pinch.'

Sister District sat up straight. 'Miss Inkerman has been a member of the inco service for many years and her honesty has never before been called into question.'

Renee snorted. 'She's too clever for that. I know all about her job because my mother told me. When she goes to the houses of the afflicted, there's always a member of the family present, so she wouldn't have the chance to take anything. But when she saw my mother, they were alone – the perfect opportunity.'

Beatrice forced herself to speak calmly. 'Instead of talking about me as if I'm not here, why not simply ask me about the brooch?'

Sergeant Wakefield raised an eyebrow at her. 'Well, Miss Inkerman?'

'Mrs Gates gave it to me.'

'No, she didn't,' Renee stated.

'She most certainly did,' said Beatrice. 'She popped it into my jacket pocket when I was out of the room.'

There was a brief silence. Beatrice intercepted the glance that passed between Sister District and the policeman.

'She did *what*?' Renee demanded. 'Well, I suppose it makes a better story than saying it fell into your pocket by accident.'

'It's the truth,' Beatrice said stoutly.

'It's a load of old codswallop,' Renee replied scornfully.

'Miss Inkerman,' said Sergeant Wakefield, 'are you claiming to have received the brooch as a gift from Mrs Gates?'

'I'm not claiming it,' said Beatrice. 'I'm stating it as a fact.'

'And where is the brooch now?' he asked.

'At home,' said Beatrice.

'I will accompany you there,' said the sergeant, 'and collect it. It is now a piece of evidence. Mrs Shotton and Mrs Judd will have to come to the police station to identify it, and we'll take matters from there.'

'But Mrs Gates *gave* it to me.' Beatrice's voice was dangerously close to a wail.

'That remains to be seen,' said Sergeant Wakefield.

'You'll have to collect it from me later,' said Beatrice. 'I haven't finished my rounds yet. My bicycle and trolley are parked outside.'

'I'm sorry, Miss Inkerman,' said Sister District. 'I cannot have you working for the inco service while you're under suspicion of theft.'

Beatrice's head jerked back. 'But Mrs Gates wasn't an inco patient. She was a personal friend.'

'It makes no odds,' Sister said gravely.

'Are you...?' Beatrice could scarcely breathe. 'Are you sacking me?'

'I'm removing you from your duties, effective immediately, while this matter is under investigation,' said Sister District. 'If your reputation is restored, I will reinstate you, but in the meantime, you cannot work – and that means you shan't get paid.'

* * *

Beatrice sat on the bed in her cramped slice of bedroom, rubbing her upper arms for comfort, her mouth dry with despair. It was all very well for Sister District to say she hadn't been sacked, but she had, because how could she ever prove her innocence – or 'restore her reputation', as Sister had put it?

Why hadn't Mrs Gates accepted it when Beatrice said she mustn't take the brooch? More to the point, why hadn't Beatrice immediately returned it after she found it in her pocket?

There was a knock on her door and Beatrice stood up to answer it. Stretching out her arm was all she had to do. Her room was so small that she didn't even need to take a single step.

Her landlady, Mrs Thornton, stood on the landing. She had a stout, straight-up-and-down figure over which she wore a wraparound apron every morning until midday.

'Is it true?' she asked without preamble.

'Is what true?' Beatrice asked, though her sinking heart already guessed the answer.

'Word is, you've been caught stealing from the elderly and the infirm.'

Beatrice breathed in so sharply that she burned the back of her throat. 'Absolutely not.'

Mrs Thornton shrugged. 'That's what the gossips are saying.'

Beatrice stood tall. 'I hope you told them you know me better than that.'

'Aye, I did. I keep a respectable house.'

'Thank you.' Beatrice wanted to speak clearly but it came out as a whisper.

'So you haven't lost your job, then?' asked Mrs Thornton. 'Only that's what's being said; that you've been sacked for thieving.'

Oh, glory be. There was nothing for it but to explain.

'There's been the most horrible misunderstanding.' Beatrice explained about the brooch and how it had ended up in her pocket. 'Mrs Gates obviously didn't tell her daughters she'd given it to me. Now she's passed away and they've been sorting through her things—'

'—and the brooch is missing and they've accused you.'

'And spread rumours, by the sound of it,' Beatrice added. She needed to be strong but she felt raw and vulnerable. 'Now there has to be a police investigation.'

'It all sounds most unpleasant,' said Mrs Thornton, 'but I'm sure you'll be acquitted.'

'Acquitted!' Beatrice exclaimed. 'It's people who go on trial who get acquitted, not people who are victims of misunderstandings.'

'It won't come to a trial,' said Mrs Thornton. 'You're an honest woman, Miss Inkerman. What I want to know is, are you still in your job? I've heard they chucked you out on your ear.'

Heat flared in Beatrice's cheeks. 'I'm not allowed back to work until this matter is sorted out.'

'And how long will that take?'

'I can't say,' Beatrice answered, trying not to sound as wretched as she felt.

Mrs Thornton nodded slowly, then shook her head. 'It grieves me to say it, it really does, but I can't afford to be sentimental. No job means no wages, and that means you can't pay your rent. I'm sorry, Miss Inkerman, but you'll have to leave.'

* * *

The Time Off Club was in full swing. Kitty glanced in through the open door, smiling to see Abbie chatting animatedly with a couple of the girls. Abbie had begged to be allowed to join in. At first Kitty had been reluctant, not wanting to push her way into Miss Inkerman's territory. But it had seemed such a shame to deny Abbie this chance of making more friends, so she had asked Miss Inkerman on Abbie's behalf, and Abbie had been warmly welcomed.

'Abbie lives here,' Miss Inkerman had said simply. 'It's only natural to include her.'

Kitty was more than happy to accommodate the Time Off Club, and not just because doing so had given the Corporation a formal interest in Dunbar's, which had placed Bill in the position of looking unpatriotic if he attempted to sell up. That was important, of course, but Kitty was also glad to help these children who carried so much weight on their young shoulders. She was grateful that Abbie could lead a normal life.

As for the Gentlemen's Club, merely thinking the name brought a smile to Kitty's lips. Gentlemen's Club! After their initial astonishment, the boys, faced by Miss Inkerman's determination, had fitted in with her wishes. They put their ties on when they arrived and politely said good evening; and at the end, they lined up to shake hands and say their thank yous.

It was amusing but also touching and Kitty gave Miss Inkerman credit for having the vision to make the rules she had. After the name-calling she had endured in the past from some of these boys, setting up this club for them had been both generous and brave.

Now, Kitty removed her gaze from her daughter and looked at Miss Inkerman instead. She was in the club room watching a billiards game and uttering a congratulatory word now and then in response to a clever shot. Kitty noted how pale she looked – well, that was understandable after what had happened earlier on.

Kitty made up her mind. She went to Miss Inkerman's side. After watching the billiards for a minute or two, Kitty spoke softly.

'I'm about to make a cup of tea. Would you like one? The children are all occupied. We could sit in the foyer and keep an eye on them from there.' She added wryly, 'We still have the use of Mr Kenwood's furniture.'

Soon the two of them were seated on upholstered dining chairs at a circular table a short distance from the door to the club room.

Miss Inkerman spoke quietly, her voice tired but steady. 'You want to know what happened when I was in there with Sister District and the others.'

'I don't want to know anything that you don't want to tell me,' Kitty replied kindly. 'I just wanted you to know how sorry I am that you're in a fix. You strike me as being a good person, Miss Inkerman. Just look at what you've done for these children

– not to mention your Gentlemen's Club. That was a stroke of genius.'

'It's good of you to say so.'

To Kitty's alarm, Miss Inkerman's brown eyes filled with tears, but before Kitty could so much as extend a hand in sympathy, there was a knock at the front door.

'Drat.' Kitty stood up.

Who could this be? She'd already checked that they weren't showing any slivers of light around the blackout curtains, so it couldn't be an ARP warden wanting to tell her off.

Kitty flicked off the foyer light and opened the door a crack. Spying Fay Brewer, she opened up a little more for her to squeeze inside, then shut the door and flicked the light back on. Seeing Miss Inkerman, Miss Brewer went straight to her.

'I heard what happened to you. I'm very sorry. For what it's worth, I have faith in you.'

Miss Inkerman dashed a hand across her eyes and cleared her throat. 'Thank you.'

'I hope everything is cleared up soon,' said Miss Brewer, but instead of the warm, encouraging tone Kitty expected to hear, her voice held uncertainty – discomfort, even.

'What is it?' Kitty asked.

Miss Brewer's hazel eyes were troubled. 'I'm sorry to be the bearer of bad news, Miss Inkerman, but the accusation against you is serious, as I'm sure you realise. The thing is, the Time Off Club is linked to the Corporation through the arrangement whereby Mrs Dunbar permits the Corporation to make use of the club room.'

'What are you getting at?' asked Miss Inkerman.

'You can't run the Time Off Club while you have this accusation hanging over you,' said Miss Brewer. 'It could bring the Corporation into disrepute.'

Miss Inkerman tilted back her head and looked up at the high ceiling. Then she heaved a deep breath and looked from Kitty to Fay Brewer.

'I quite understand.' Her voice was calm and controlled and Kitty could only guess at the effort behind it. 'I should have expected it, really, after what happened earlier. Sister District has sacked me. She says it's temporary, but how I can prove I didn't steal that brooch? If I can't, then it's permanent and I'll never get another job, not with this hanging over me.'

'I'd no idea it was so bad,' said Kitty.

With a choked exclamation, Miss Inkerman bent right over, then reared up again, the fingers of one hand splayed across her mouth and chin.

'Is Miss Inkerman all right?' came a scared young voice from the club room doorway, where some girls, including Abbie, now clustered.

Miss Brewer took charge. 'She's fine. Go back to what you were doing and you can show me.'

She shepherded the girls back inside, tactfully pulling the door shut behind her.

Kitty sat down and placed her hands on top of one of Miss Inkerman's. 'I know what my mam would have said. "What a palaver." That's what she said when things got complicated.'

Miss Inkerman managed a watery smile. 'Mine would have said, "You brought it on yourself, Beatrice," and she'd have been right.'

'You don't deserve this,' said Kitty.

'I should have returned the brooch the instant I found it in my possession,' said Miss Inkerman. 'Because I didn't, I've lost my job, my digs and now the Time Off Club.'

'Wait a minute,' said Kitty. 'You've lost your digs?'

'No job, no pay. No pay, no rent.'

'And yet you still came here to run the Time Off Club,' said Kitty.

'Please don't admire me for it,' said Miss Inkerman. 'I wouldn't let the children down. Anyway, I needed the distraction. My rent is paid until the end of the week. After that—'

'After that,' said Kitty, 'you'll come and live here in Dunbar's. In fact, I suggest you don't wait. Move in immediately.'

Miss Inkerman stared at her.

'I mean it,' said Kitty. 'I can't do anything about the brooch, but I can do something about a billet. Why not? I took Lily in when she needed it and now I want to do the same for you.'

'Oh, Mrs Dunbar,' was the whispered reply.

'Lily has become Abbie's big sister and you can be her Auntie Beatrice, if you don't mind,' said Kitty matter-of-factly. 'And you can be my friend Beatrice and I'll be your friend Kitty.'

* * *

Beatrice was more grateful than she could express to Kitty for taking her in. Abbie welcomed her without question into the Dunbar's household.

'She doesn't know about the theft business,' Kitty assured Beatrice, 'and she won't hear it from me.'

'Thank you,' said Beatrice. The fewer who knew, the better.

She handed over her ration books for Kitty to register her with the butcher and grocer Dunbar's used and the two of them took turns to do the daily shopping.

On a warm morning towards the end of June, Beatrice headed for the butcher's with her shopping basket, hoping to get some lamb to make a lamb and vegetable stew, or, failing that, maybe a rabbit for a hotpot. The sunshine gave her spirits a boost. Her nerves were in turmoil much of the time, but she tried to focus on the good things. She had hoped that she and Kitty might become friends and that had happened, and never mind the circumstances. If anything, the fact that Kitty had not just stood by her but had actually offered her a home showed what a staunch friend she was going to be. Beatrice vowed to be an equally worthwhile friend.

There was a long queue outside the butcher's, going all the way around the corner. Beatrice tacked herself onto the end of it. The two women in front of her looked round and she gave them a nod.

'Morning,' she said. 'Lovely day.'

'Morning,' said one of the women.

The other was about to speak but then her eyes narrowed. 'I know who you are. You're that inco lady that stole from her old and infirm patients.'

'This is *her*?' asked her friend, scandal in every syllable. Pursing her lips, she inhaled sharply, making a hissing sound that sent chills through Beatrice.

Fighting to maintain a steady voice, Beatrice said, 'I've never taken anything that doesn't belong to me.'

'Oh aye? Tell me you haven't lost your job, then.'

Several women in front of the first two now also turned round. Beatrice's face grew hot.

'It's true that I left my job—'

'Left it? Got given the boot, you mean. Stealing from poor helpless invalids.'

'Is that what she did?' broke in one of the new women.

'And she stands in this queue, looking like butter wouldn't melt. Sinful, I call it.'

'A false accusation has been made against me,' said Beatrice, 'but it has nothing to do with anyone using the inco service. It was made by...'

'Go on. Finish what you were going to say. It was made by...?'

'The daughter of a friend,' Beatrice whispered.

'You *stole* from a *friend*?'

'I didn't steal from anyone,' Beatrice said desperately. 'She gave me a present.'

To her surprise, her principal tormentor laughed.

'Aye, that's right, she gave you a present. Did you hear that, everyone? That's her story and she's sticking to it.'

It was more than Beatrice could bear. As the tears started to flow, she turned and hurried away.

* * *

The last thing Beatrice wanted was to go running home to Kitty with her tale of woe, but she had no option. She would have given anything to go to a different butcher, but you could only use the one where you were registered. Besides, she might get the same welcome in another queue.

'I'm sorry I couldn't get the lamb,' she told Kitty, 'but I couldn't stay in that queue a moment longer.'

'You poor love, what a thing to happen,' said Kitty. 'I'll do the shopping in a while – after we've had a cup of tea.'

'The cure-all,' Beatrice said wryly.

They went down to the hotel kitchen. Beatrice had been surprised to learn that the family flat didn't boast a kitchen of its own, but apparently, with men at the helm in the old days, they hadn't seen the need for it. Beatrice wondered what the Dunbar wives had made of that.

'Even if I had a little kitchen of my own,' Kitty had told Beatrice when she moved in, 'I'd still be using the big kitchen now that you and Lily live here. Much friendlier.'

No sooner was the kettle on than the doorbell rang and Kitty went upstairs to answer it. A minute later she returned with Sergeant Wakefield. Beatrice's heart sank when she saw his sober expression.

'Good morning, Miss Inkerman,' he said. 'Might I have a private word?'

'I'll leave you to it,' Kitty said at once.

'Don't go,' said Beatrice. 'I'm happy for Mrs Dunbar to hear whatever you have to say, Sergeant.'

'Very well. It's the matter of the brooch. I've had one of my constables call on the other ladies who used to visit Mrs Gates to ask if she gave any of them presents – and she didn't.'

'That's a shame,' said Kitty, 'but it doesn't prove she didn't give one to Miss Inkerman.'

'Agreed,' said the sergeant. 'According to my constable, one lady became rather indignant when she was questioned, demanding to know what was wrong with her that she didn't get a present. Got quite huffy about it, she did. Then she said that since she hadn't been offered a gift, that showed you haven't either and you must have helped yourself. But as you say, Mrs Dunbar,' he added quickly, 'it doesn't prove anything of the kind.'

'You mean,' said Beatrice, 'that if Mrs Gates had given someone else a present, it would have shown she'd wanted to give me the brooch.'

'It wouldn't have proved it,' said Sergeant Wakefield, 'but it would have been good enough for me. I would have been happy to let the matter drop.'

'As it is,' said Beatrice, 'she didn't offer a gift to anybody else, which makes my story look even worse.'

She rubbed her arms. How was she ever going to dig herself out of this hole?

'The lack of presents to other people doesn't prove anything,' said Sergeant Wakefield.

'On the contrary,' said Kitty, 'it provides definite proof of one thing.' She looked at Beatrice. 'It shows how highly Mrs Gates valued your friendship. It shows how much she cared about you. I know it doesn't seem like it now, but one day, when this is all over, you'll think of that and be grateful.'

24

June had started with the introduction of clothes rationing and it ended with multiple changes to food rationing. Eggs were now rationed to one a week, and the amount of butter per person came down from four ounces to two; but cheese was increased to two ounces, and there were to be double rations of sugar for the next four weeks for jam-making.

The new rules made Beatrice remember her unpleasant encounter in the butcher's queue. In the same way, the July sunshine seemed to warm everyone else but it failed to seep into her skin. For the first time in her life, she was at a loose end. She'd had a busy childhood, rushing around the shops, cleaning out the grate, heaving sopping wet washing out of the copper and struggling to put it through the mangle, not to mention fetching her mother's medicine and measuring it out, emptying the spittoon after Mum coughed her lungs up when her chest was bad... oh yes, and attending school when she could manage to squeeze it in, though she'd spent more time in the corner wearing the dunce's cap than she had in her place in the long row of battered, joined-together desks.

Now, though, after years of working five and a half days a week, she had nothing to do. She hadn't just lost her job. She'd also lost the Time Off Club, which was now run by Kitty, overseen by Fay Brewer. Well, it wasn't strictly true that she had nothing to do. She did what she could to pull her weight at Dunbar's, though that seemed to be precious little. She couldn't do the cleaning because she didn't want to tread on Lily's toes, and while Kitty shared the daily shopping trips, these were agony for Beatrice, who lived in fear of more accusations.

And of course she had her WVS duties. She had resigned from her original branch on the grounds of moving house, though the fact that that group had been based plumb in the middle of a triangle formed by the homes of Mrs Gates, Renee Shotton and Olive Judd had provided a more compelling reason for leaving.

Now Beatrice was part of the same branch as Kitty and Lily, which brought some comfort.

Kitty had taken her to meet Mrs Ford, the branch organiser, and Beatrice, steadied by her friend's presence, had explained her reasons for wanting to join.

Mrs Ford, a headmistressy type with a no-nonsense manner, had given her the once-over.

'Very well. Thank you for your honesty. I'll accept you but you'll have to have a WVS member with you at all times and you can't do any work that involves entering private houses. I stand by the principle of innocent until proven guilty, but I also have a duty to my members and to the many people who rely on us. Welcome aboard, Miss Inkerman.'

Beatrice vowed to throw herself into her war work more deeply than ever, but it was unsettling and humiliating to realise just how many jobs she wasn't permitted to do. She spent a lot of shifts at the British Restaurant, but only preparing meals, never

A New Home at the Wartime Hotel 261

handling money. Even when she went out during air raids, it was only her partner – she always had a partner – who was allowed to step inside a damaged house to comfort an injured person.

After just such an eight-hour shift, which had lengthened to ten hours, Beatrice arrived back at Dunbar's in the familiar post-air raid state of feeling both tired and fired up. As she walked up Oxford Road towards Lily Street, she passed men in pin-stripes and bowlers, shopgirls in black dresses and white collars and cuffs, women in crisp jackets and skirts, men in donkey-jackets and caps – all going to work.

Not long ago that would have been her as well, hauling her trolley onto the road and hitching it to her bicycle, whatever the weather. The bike and trolley had been returned to the district nurses' station and Beatrice no longer had a job to fill her days.

Her shoulders curled round towards her chest. She had moments like this, when her circumstances overwhelmed her. How was it ever to end? When a person did something bad, they might leave evidence of their wrongdoing, but what if you hadn't done anything? How did you prove a negative? Especially when the 'evidence' seemed so damning.

Beatrice let herself into Dunbar's. A cup of tea first, then a wash and maybe a snooze. No – not a snooze. Folk who'd been up all night doing their voluntary war work – the ARP, the Auxiliary Fire Service, the rescuers who spent long hours digging people and bodies out of the rubble, the gas men who saw to the ruptured mains – wouldn't have a snooze before heading off to their daytime jobs, and Beatrice wouldn't snooze either.

But she would have a cup of tea. Going downstairs to the kitchen, she heard voices. Kitty was seated at the table with an older woman whose blue eyes looked like they missed nothing and whose straight mouth looked like she wasn't afraid to say so.

Kitty turned round. 'Beatrice, come and meet my mother-in-law. Mrs Dunbar, this is Miss Beatrice Inkerman, who has come to live here.'

Mrs Dunbar shook hands. 'Pleased to meet you,' she said in a tone that made Beatrice wonder whether it was entirely true. 'You're not a friend I've heard of before – and I've known Kitty since shortly before she married my son.'

'We met when Beatrice helped Abbie after she had a fall,' said Kitty.

Mrs Dunbar nodded. 'That was neighbourly of you. How come you've moved in here? Bombed out, were you?'

'We all know plenty of people who have been bombed out,' Kitty said ambiguously.

'But I'm not one of them.' Beatrice squared her shoulders. Maybe it was the post-air raid mixture of fatigue and being gingered up, or maybe it was the way she'd been pushed around by others recently, but all at once she'd had enough. Mrs Dunbar senior was undoubtedly a formidable woman. Well, maybe it was time for Beatrice to have a go at being formidable too.

'You don't have to explain,' Kitty said softly.

'Yes, I do,' said Beatrice. 'I live here now and I'm sure Mrs Dunbar is a regular visitor, so I'd rather be honest – as long as it's kept from Abbie. I wouldn't want her thinking ill of me.'

'Good heavens,' said Mrs Dunbar. 'What have you done?'

'She hasn't done anything,' said Kitty. 'That's the point.' She patted the chair beside her as an invitation to Beatrice. 'Do you want to explain or shall I?'

'I'll do it,' said Beatrice.

Mrs Dunbar's eyes sharpened as she listened, her gaze flicking between the two younger women.

'That's a pickle to be in,' she said at the end.

They discussed the 'pickle' for a while, but Beatrice had soon had enough. In the beginning, she'd seemed unable to talk about anything else, but she didn't feel that way now.

'How are you keeping yourself busy without a job?' Mrs Dunbar asked.

'Lots of WVS.'

'Very commendable,' said Mrs Dunbar.

Beatrice sighed. 'But it's not enough. Don't get me wrong. It's essential work and I'm dedicated to it, but I miss going out to work.'

The sides of Mrs Dunbar's mouth tugged down thoughtfully. 'Then you know what you need to do. Find something to fill the work-shaped space.'

* * *

As soon as Kitty's mother-in-law offered her advice, Beatrice knew exactly what to do. She might have lost the Time Off Club but she hadn't lost the resolve that had made her set it up. She still cared about those children and her heart ached every time she pictured their lives – cleaning, preparing meals, very likely being in charge of pills or tonics, having to help their mothers keep clean, which might involve looking after bedsores, not to mention being responsible for younger brothers and sisters.

Beatrice made her way to the Chapmans' house, which was where it had started.

Mrs Williams, the daughter of Mr Trent who sublet downstairs, answered the door.

'Oh, it's you. I thought you'd left.'

'Only temporarily,' said Beatrice.

'Gone to a different area, have you?' asked Mrs Williams. 'I hope you come back here soon. The new inco lady isn't anything like as helpful. Hands over the supply, says "Sign here" and off she goes.'

There was nothing Beatrice could say to that. Mrs Williams had just described what she ought to have done as an inco lady. By doing extra, she had unwittingly set up her replacement for criticism and resentment.

'I'm here to visit Mrs Chapman upstairs,' said Beatrice.

Up she went. She knocked, gave it a moment, then opened the door, calling, 'It's Miss Inkerman. Do you remember me? Can I come in?'

There was no sign of Dora. Mrs Chapman lay propped up, wheezing, in her bed. Her skin was grey.

'How are you?' asked Beatrice.

'Fine, thanks.'

'I can see that's stretching the truth,' said Beatrice.

Mrs Chapman lifted her thin shoulders a fraction. 'I've been better.'

Yes, and she would undoubtedly get a lot worse as the months progressed.

Beatrice pinned on a smile. 'Is Dora not with you? Is she at school?' She strove to keep the hope out of her voice, adding gently, 'She really does need to go, you know.'

'And I want her to go, honest I do, but I need her here. My mam died when our Dora was a babe in arms and both my sisters got evacuated because they were in the family way, so I've nobody but Dora left to look after things at home.'

'I understand,' said Beatrice.

'I need her here,' said Mrs Chapman.

'I stayed at home when I was a child and it's affected my

whole life. I know you don't want Dora to be held back when she's grown up.'

'You're blaming me for what's going to happen in years to come?' As well as wheezing, Mrs Chapman now had to combat tears that threatened to choke her. 'I never asked to be like this. For your information, I wish our Dora could go to school, but she's needed here.'

An idea formed in Beatrice's mind.

'What if she went to school part-time?'

'Like half the week here and half there? That wouldn't work.'

'I know it wouldn't,' Beatrice agreed, 'because you need her here every day, but could you manage if she was here part of every day instead? Mornings at school, afternoons here.'

Mrs Chapman eyed her suspiciously, then shook her head. 'The greatest need is for her to be here in the mornings.'

'The greatest need is for Dora's future,' Beatrice replied. 'Mornings are when they write compositions and do spellings and arithmetic. Those are the lessons she needs most, so that's when she needs to go to school. I know it's a lot to ask, Mrs Chapman, but if you agree to this now, Dora will get her elementary school leaving certificate and that'll make all the difference.'

Mrs Chapman turned her face away, but not before Beatrice had seen the tears that spilled over.

'Please at least think about it,' she urged. It was as much as she could do.

25

Lily stood at the window of Dunbar's former dining room. It had been a gracious room in its day. When she had first come here as a fourteen-year-old chambermaid, she had marvelled at the handsome, well-appointed bedrooms and thanked her lucky stars for giving her the chance to look after them. But the first time she had seen the downstairs rooms – the dining room and the residents' sitting room – she had held her breath in awe. She hadn't imagined that anything could ever eclipse the wonder of the bedrooms, and yet these rooms had done exactly that. For a long time, her greatest ambition had been to be asked to clean these two rooms.

The dining room floor had been of polished oak – it still was, of course, but these days you couldn't see it because it was covered by a thick oilcloth to protect it when a new consignment of furniture arrived. Back in the days of the hotel, a wide border of floor had been on display around the edges of a luxurious dark-blue carpet. The white marble chimneypiece was still there, but the mantelpiece was empty of ornaments, thanks to the bailiffs' men. Gone also were the grandfather clock, the mahogany tables, the dining chairs upholstered in bronze-coloured leather, the oak cabinet with glass doors and the vast sideboard where the snowy tablecloths and napkins had been kept along with the best glass dishes, the punch bowls and all the cutlery.

And what cutlery! Lily had never seen the like of it before. Knives and forks with rosewood handles, different knives for fish. Pudding spoons – only they were called dessert spoons – and separate spoons for fruit. Special scissors for cutting grapes, if you please, as if the toffs were too important to pull them from the bunch. Proper nutcrackers: Uncle Irwin had always used pliers. And different small spoons for stirring tea or eating boiled eggs. Cheese knives, cheese scoops, lemon saws, tartlet servers, sardine tongs, tongs for asparagus and larger ones for picking up sandwiches. Crikey! Getting the chance to learn all those things had been like being at school, only harder.

Now this was just a big empty room with an oilcloth. Could you feel sorry for a room? Lily did. She felt sorry for the whole building. It had survived the horror and devastation of the Christmas Blitz, only to be laid low by the bailiffs. Lily felt a deep loyalty to the old hotel where she'd not just worked but also lived.

Truth be told, she seemed to feel more for Dunbar's than she did for herself. She, Lily Chadwick, didn't deserve to be on the receiving end of good feelings, not after the way her baby had died. There were special wartime rules about giving mothers-to-be extra milk and eggs and even orange juice so that they could nourish the babies growing inside them. Lily had eaten everything she was supposed to, but Toby had still died, so she must have done something else wrong. It was the only explanation that made sense.

With a sigh, she looked out of the window once more onto

Lily Street. A faint smile touched her lips as she remembered the schoolgirl who had longed to work in Lily Street because it seemed like fate. Well, coming to Dunbar's had certainly been good for her.

Until she'd met Daniel and fallen rapturously in love. She seemed to have been in turmoil ever since.

Daniel was coming to collect her this morning. They had seen one another a couple of times since he had taken her to the Claremont. They had gone to the Worker Bee café on Deansgate. Had Daniel decided it was a more appropriate place to take her than the Claremont? No, she wasn't being fair. Maybe he had taken her there knowing she would feel more comfortable. If so, he'd been right.

Lily's heart gave a little lurch as he came striding along the pavement. Every time she saw him, her heart beat faster, even though these days her feelings were mostly frozen. Something inside her had turned to ice when Toby died and she was certain it would never thaw.

As Daniel arrived at the foot of the steps, Lily left the window and went to open the door just as he reached it. It took him by surprise and they both ought to have laughed but neither of them did. Lily picked up her home-made jacket and felt hat from the chair near the doors. Daniel took the jacket from her to help her into it. Would his fingers linger on her shoulders? No. Had she hoped they might? She couldn't answer that.

'You look nice,' he said.

Lily glanced down at herself, at the blue-and-cream striped dress with its narrow belt beneath the simple jacket. When she was as big as a house waiting for her baby to be born, she had longed for the days when she could once again wear pretty clothes. Now, she couldn't care less.

'Are we going to the Worker Bee?' she asked.

'I thought we could go back to the Claremont,' said Daniel. 'I've got something to tell you and – well, I'd like a more formal backdrop than the Worker Bee.'

'What is it?' Lily experienced a streak of panic. 'Tell me now and get it over with.'

Daniel looked at her. 'If you lived with me at my parents' house, we wouldn't need to go elsewhere to talk.'

Lily felt slapped down, but she couldn't deny he had a point.

They left Dunbar's. At the foot of the steps, Daniel offered her his arm and she took it. When they had first started seeing one another, and he had wanted her to take his arm in public, she'd felt both thrilled and embarrassed, knowing a simple girl like her had no business cosying up to a well-to-do fellow like him. Now, as with most things in her life, she didn't notice one way or the other.

They walked to the Claremont and sat in one of the alcoves in the grand foyer. Daniel placed his trilby on the table and ordered tea for them. The waitress suggested the chef's homemade honey biscuits and he ordered those too.

Lily looked at him. They had known one another for a year and a month, that was all, but it was more than long enough to get married and have a baby – and lose the baby. Most of their married life had been spent apart from one another, and their baby had died. So much for marriage.

Till death us do part. That was the vow you made in church. Lily and Daniel hadn't made it because they'd got wed in a registry office, but everyone knew the vow. No one had told Lily that it might not be one of their deaths that would part them. It might be the death of their child.

'What did you want to talk about?' she asked, though at this point she didn't mind whether he told her or not. She felt distanced from the situation.

'My leave is being shortened. I'm due to go back to sea.'

Had he asked for his leave to be shortened? Did it matter if he had? It wasn't as though they could continue with things the way they were.

'When?' she asked.

'I'm going to Liverpool tomorrow.'

'Tomorrow,' she repeated, suddenly unsettled.

'I wanted to tell you something that happened at sea last time, on the way back to Britain. Will you let me tell you?'

'Of course,' said Lily.

Daniel was quiet for some moments, then he drew a long soft breath before he began to speak. 'My ship was at the rear of the convoy. Jerry opened fire on us on the port side, from a range of one mile. The alarms rang for action stations. It was a cruiser attacking us and it closed in rapidly. There were other vessels as well, attacking other ships in the convoy. Shells hit our poop deck and destroyed the gun. The men in the cabins below never stood a chance.'

Daniel fell silent, his eyes clouding with memories. Lily's fingers twitched as if about to reach out to him, but then he resumed speaking and the moment was lost.

'There was no chance of saving the ship. The captain headed for the side to dump confidential documents in weighted canvas bags into the sea. The lifeboats were all riddled with machine-gunfire. There was just one small jolly-boat that was safe to use. It had a few essentials in it, just in case. When we lowered it into the sea, it was dragged through the water because the ship still had headway. We swung ourselves down, burning and ripping our hands. I remember that when we slipped the painter, the stern of the ship loomed over us like the face of a gigantic cliff – and then the Jerry shells blew it up.'

'Oh, Daniel,' Lily whispered, though she had no idea if he had heard her.

'We had water, biscuits, some tins of meat and condensed milk, and a small first-aid kit,' said Daniel. 'The men had various injuries, shrapnel wounds, a broken arm, a foot that was no more than a bloody pulp. The only good thing about a jollyboat is that in fair weather, it sails better than a lifeboat. We were at sea for six days and five nights before we were rescued. Our ship had gone down so quickly, you see, and with no lifeboats being launched, it looked as if all hands had been lost. The pulped foot putrefied. Everyone's skin dried out and our mouths burned. Do you know what kept me going, kept me alive? It was the thought of coming home to my wife and child. It was the thought of being a father.'

Lily closed her eyes for a long moment. She didn't want to open them again, but she supposed she had to.

'I'm sorry,' she said softly. 'I'm so sorry that that happened to you, but I can't...'

'Can't what?' Daniel asked when she fell silent.

'I'm sorry that this terrible thing happened to you. I'm sorry about all the deaths caused by the air raids. I know bad things are happening all around me, but I can't think about them.'

Daniel frowned. 'What do you mean?'

'There isn't enough space inside my head for all of it,' Lily whispered. 'What happened with Toby was so important, so *huge*, that I haven't got room for anything else.'

After a pause, Daniel asked quietly, 'Not even for what happened to your husband? I was lucky not to go down with the ship. I was lucky to get picked up afterwards.'

Lily released a long, slow breath. What was she meant to say?

'And now I've come home to a wife who won't live with me because she doesn't get along with my mother.'

'It's not that simple,' said Lily. And yet it was that simple. Toby was dead: it was as simple as that. 'It's all too much,' she said softly. 'I just need to be on my own.'

'Fine,' said Daniel. 'I've tried, Lily. I've tried so hard to get through to you, but I can't. And now you say you want to be on your own. Well – fine. I won't trouble you again. Clearly our marriage wasn't meant to be.'

He rose to his feet. Picking up his trilby, he held it by the brim, his hands moving so that the hat turned round and around.

'One last thing, Lily,' he said, 'and I hope you'll make some room for it inside your head. It was you and my child who kept me alive when I was potentially lost at sea. And when I heard that my son had died, I felt as if he had given his life to save mine. Rationally, I know that can't be true, but I can't stop thinking it. It grieves me that I wanted to live so much that the only way it could happen, the only way it could be paid for, was through the death of my son. On second thoughts, I sincerely hope you don't have the room in your head for that. I don't want it to torture you the way it tortures me.' He gave her a formal little bow and placed his trilby on his head while she stared at him, too stunned to utter a sound. 'Goodbye, Lily.'

26

Beatrice spent the day on British Restaurant duty. It seemed that Mrs Ford, the branch organiser, believed that peeling veg, rolling pastry and stirring the vat of soup of the day was the safest way of filling Beatrice's time on duty. The British Restaurant was always busy, and it was important to offer the public nutritious meals at favourable prices, but even so, Beatrice did get tired of her work behind the scenes, knowing that it was the dark cloud hanging over her that kept her in that role.

This evening there was going to be a Time Off Club session at Dunbar's. She seriously considered putting herself forward for an extra WVS shift so as to be out of the building, since she wasn't allowed to have anything to do with the club now, but that would have felt like running away and she didn't want to be a coward.

After a day spent on her feet in the British Restaurant kitchen, she trudged up the stairs in Dunbar's. She had been given a little bedroom on the third floor, where Lily too had a room. Kitty had also given Beatrice the room next door to her own.

'We can make it into a sitting room for you,' Kitty had said. 'I can't offer much in the way of furniture for it at present, but we'll put it together gradually. If you're going to live under my roof, I want you to be comfortable.'

'Does Lily have a sitting room as well?' Beatrice had asked.

Kitty shook her head. 'She doesn't want one, but don't let that stop you. I don't think she cares, poor love.'

'She does have an air of don't-care about her,' said Beatrice, adding quickly, 'I don't mean to say she's slapdash or she can't be bothered.'

'I know what you mean,' said Kitty. 'Not so much don't-care as can't afford to care.'

'In a very controlled way,' said Beatrice.

Now, she changed out of her WVS uniform into her own clothes, a plain blouse and tweed skirt. Very middle-aged, she thought, but then she was middle-aged, wasn't she? A middle-aged spinster. Very unprepossessing.

Oh, this wouldn't do at all. She gave her shoulders a little shake.

It was nearly time for the evening meal. Kitty organised her days so that she was always here to make Abbie's tea, but Beatrice and Lily couldn't always be there because of their WVS commitments. Today, though, all four of them sat around the table in the basement kitchen for sardine fritters and jacket potatoes followed by apple pie made with potato pastry.

Afterwards, Kitty sent Abbie upstairs to the family flat to finish her homework while the three women relaxed around the table with tea and cigarettes.

'I can say this now Abbie's gone,' said Kitty. 'Lily, you ate barely anything.'

'Abbie didn't mind polishing off the sardine fritter for me,' said Lily.

Kitty looked at her. 'If that's your way of saying, "Mind your own business," I'd rather you came right out with it.'

Lily didn't say anything and the other two waited. The look in Lily's eyes showed she'd withdrawn into herself and was deep in thought.

Finally, she said softly, 'My marriage ended today.'

Beatrice and Kitty both reached out to her.

'Lily, I'm so very sorry,' said Kitty.

Lily shrugged. *Can't afford to care*, thought Beatrice.

'It was bound to happen, I suppose,' Lily said in the same small voice. 'We've hardly seen one another and... Toby...'

'Isn't there any hope of reconciliation?' Beatrice asked. 'You're both young. You've got years ahead of you.'

'Years that aren't going to be spent with one another,' Lily replied. 'Now can we please talk about something else?' After a moment she added, 'I need time to get used to it, although compared to Toby...'

Beatrice and Kitty looked at one another. Beatrice's heart swelled with sorrow for the young couple. Ordinarily she would have been shocked and disapproving at the ending of a marriage, but the baby's death trumped all other considerations. She wished for Lily and Daniel's sakes that the bereavement could have brought them closer together, but it had clearly had the opposite effect.

'Nearly all the old guest rooms are full of stored furniture now,' said Kitty, complying with Lily's wish. 'As soon as we no longer need the old dining room as a space for cleaning newly arrived things, we can see about turning it into a parlour for the three of us and Abbie. I'd like us all to live together properly.'

'I for one would appreciate that very much,' Beatrice chimed in. 'I'd enjoy both the parlour and the company.'

Kitty smiled. 'That's settled, then – though how much of a

parlour it will be, with furniture so hard to come by, I don't know.'

'I'd like it too,' Lily said unexpectedly.

Upstairs the doorbell rang.

Kitty stood up. 'That'll be Miss Brewer wanting to set up the club room.' She threw Beatrice a look of sympathy.

Lily stubbed out her cigarette and pushed back her chair. 'I'll go and fetch Abbie. She loves getting the room ready. Is that all right with you?' she asked Kitty.

'She'll have finished her homework by now,' said Kitty. 'She did most of it before tea.'

Beatrice cleared her throat. 'Has she – has she asked why I'm not running the Time Off Club any more?'

'I just said you're concentrating on your Gentlemen's Club,' said Kitty, 'and Miss Brewer is doing the Time Off Club.'

Beatrice nodded. 'I'll stay down here and wash up.'

If she hoped thereby to avoid Fay Brewer, she'd made a mistake, because Miss Brewer came down the stairs a few minutes later.

'Good evening,' she said brightly. 'I'm bunking off. I've left the others setting up the room. How are you getting on, Miss Inkerman?' Her voice was cheerful and matter of fact but her hazel eyes held compassion.

'Fine, thank you,' said Beatrice, keeping a stiff upper lip. 'I'm very busy with the WVS.'

'Good show,' said Miss Brewer.

Beatrice's stiff upper lip crumpled beneath the need to confide. 'I can't tell you how worried I am. I need this to be over so I can get my job back. Mrs Dunbar is very kind to have me here and she says I don't need to pay rent because we're friends, but I insist on giving her a small sum out of my savings, only I've never earned much so my savings aren't impressive.'

'And it's scary to watch them dwindling,' Miss Brewer finished.

'Exactly,' said Beatrice. Making a grab for her stiff upper lip, she went on, 'Anyway, you don't want to hear all that. I went to see Dora Chapman's mother the other day. I couldn't think of any reason why it wouldn't be allowed.'

'One private citizen calling on another,' said Miss Brewer. 'Nothing wrong with that.'

'I tried to make her see how important Dora's education is. The trouble is, she knows it's important but she still needs Dora at home so much of the time. I even came up with an idea for Dora to attend school half-time.'

'How would that work?' Miss Brewer asked her.

'When I was at school – I'm going back to before the last war now – there was a system in place whereby once a child turned twelve, they could get a job in the afternoon and just come to school in the morning. I wondered about that sort of arrangement for Dora and the other children who do looking-after at home.'

'What did Mrs Chapman say?'

Beatrice smothered a sigh. 'If I'm honest, she wasn't keen. I said Dora would need to be at school in the mornings for the three Rs, and Mrs Chapman insisted it was more important for her to be at home then.' Beatrice pressed her lips tightly together in pure frustration. 'But, you see, even regular half-day attendance wouldn't be enough if the attendance was only ever in the afternoons. If these children are to get their leaving certificates, they need the three Rs.'

Miss Brewer nodded. 'Mrs Chapman sees it from her own point of view and you're looking at it from Dora's, and that of the other children with responsibilities.' She shook her head. 'There are no easy answers, I'm afraid.'

'I'm sorry to bend your ear,' said Beatrice, 'but I feel strongly about it.'

Miss Brewer smiled. 'I can tell.'

'You'd best get up to the club room,' said Beatrice. 'The children will arrive soon.'

Miss Brewer headed for the stairs, then stopped and looked back.

'I hope your situation gets resolved, Miss Inkerman. You're an asset to the community.'

* * *

On Saturday afternoon, Abbie came home earlier than Kitty was expecting. She was busy doing the accounts for Dunbar's, something she worried about getting wrong, and she'd been only too happy for Abbie to go out to play, reckoning that she had ample time to get her work finished and checked before Abbie came home at teatime.

The door to the family flat flew open and Abbie rushed inside.

Kitty looked up from her paperwork, one finger holding her place in the column of figures. 'What's the hurry?'

'Mummy, why isn't Auntie Beatrice in charge of the Time Off Club any more?'

'I told you. She's concentrating on the Gentlemen's Club.'

'Joe Simpson from the Gentlemen's Club says she's a thief.'

Kitty played for time. 'How do you know what he says?'

'We play on the same bomb sites. I can't believe Auntie Beatrice is a thief. She isn't, is she?'

Kitty sat up straight. 'Of course she isn't. Do you think I'd have her living here with us if I thought that for a single moment?'

'That's what I said to Joe, but he said everybody's saying it round his way.'

'That's just nasty gossip.' Kitty tried to sound dismissive.

'But what if people believe it?' cried Abbie. 'Poor Auntie Beatrice. How did it happen?'

Kitty sighed. So much for trying to keep Abbie in the dark. Quietly she explained about Mrs Gates's brooch.

'So you see, Auntie Beatrice has no way of proving that Mrs Gates gave it to her,' she finished.

Abbie went very still. Then she said, 'I can prove it.'

* * *

In the cramped, windowless room at the police station, Beatrice and Kitty sat on wooden chairs at a scuffed table. There was no seat for Abbie, who stood at her mother's shoulder. On the other side of the table sat Sergeant Wakefield and in the centre of the table lay a small piece of creased patterned paper.

'Are you sure about this, Mrs Dunbar?' asked the policeman.

'Positive, Sergeant. Let my daughter tell you in her own words.'

Beatrice's tummy was churning with anxiety but she was beginning to feel excited too and her pulse increased its speed as Abbie, at a nod from Sergeant Wakefield, told her tale.

'Auntie Beatrice came to Dunbar's and she found something in her pocket. It was quite tiny and was wrapped in nice paper. She opened it up to see what it was and it was a brooch.'

'Did you see it?' Sergeant Wakefield asked quietly.

'Yes,' said Abbie. 'It had red stones and was shaped like a wing. I liked it.'

'What happened then?' asked the sergeant.

'Auntie Beatrice gave me the wrapping paper to put in with

the salvage, but I kept it. I knew I shouldn't, but it was so pretty and I thought I could wrap something small in it for Mummy at Christmas.'

'The piece of paper is just the right size for a brooch,' said Kitty. 'I believe if you place the brooch against the creases, it would show exactly how it was wrapped. Also...' She pointed. 'As you can see, on this yellow bit of pattern, in tiny writing, it says *To B.I.* Surely this provides the proof you need,' she ended, her voice warm with hope.

Beatrice held her breath, only letting it go when Sergeant Wakefield permitted himself to smile.

'It certainly looks like it. Let me go and have a word with the superintendent.'

When the door shut behind him, Abbie bounced up and down in excitement. To Beatrice's astonishment, and also to her complete delight, the child left her mother's side and threw her arms around Beatrice's neck. Beatrice could have cried – not because she was relieved, not because her prolonged ordeal looked like it could be over, but because a child had hugged her.

Sergeant Wakefield returned, smiling broadly. Then he looked at Abbie and his expression became stern. 'Normally, young lady, I would tick you off good and proper for keeping to yourself something that ought to have been put into the salvage box – but in this case, I'll let you off.' Back came the smile. 'The superintendent agrees with me that this closes the matter satisfactorily.'

Relief emerged in the form of a shaky laugh. 'Thank you, Sergeant,' said Beatrice. She wanted to say so much more but was afraid of bursting into tears.

'That's wonderful,' said Kitty. 'Who's going to tell Renee Shotton and her sister?'

'I will,' said Sergeant Wakefield, 'and the superintendent

says he'll come too just to make sure that the ladies take it seriously. The superintendent will also inform Sister District and ask her to tell anyone at the Corporation who needs to know. I imagine you've been on the receiving end of some highly unpleasant gossip, Miss Inkerman, but you won't be after this. Excuse me, ladies. I'll go and fetch the brooch and you'll have to sign to say you have got it back.'

'Thank you,' said Beatrice, blinking back tears as the policeman left the room once more.

'It sounds as if Mrs Gates's daughters are going to hear the truth in no uncertain terms,' said Kitty, sounding pleased. 'I'd like to be a fly on the wall for that conversation.'

Beatrice gave a little shudder. 'I wouldn't. If I never see them again, it'll be too soon.'

Abbie gave her another hug, whispering in her ear, 'It's over, Auntie Beatrice.'

'All thanks to you,' Beatrice answered.

* * *

Sister District came to Dunbar's on Monday morning.

'Why don't you take Sister up to the family flat?' Kitty said to Beatrice. 'You can talk in private there. Should I bring up a tray of tea?'

'Not for me, thank you,' said Sister District. 'I can't stay long.'

'This way,' said Beatrice, ushering her old boss towards the staircase.

When they entered the flat, Sister District looked around, interested, but made no comment on the sparseness of the furnishings. They sat down.

'I'm sure you know what brings me here, Miss Inkerman,' said Sister. 'The district nurses' station received a telephone call concerning your unfortunate situation – which is no longer unfortunate, I gather.' For once in her life, Sister District cracked a smile. 'Congratulations, Miss Inkerman. I'm pleased everything has been resolved.'

'Thank you, Sister,' said Beatrice. 'It's a great relief.'

'It's a shame you had to be removed from your post because of it,' said Sister.

'I understand why you had to do that,' Beatrice said diplomatically.

'And now, of course, I can reinstate you. Welcome back to the inco service, Miss Inkerman. You may collect your bicycle and trolley today and fetch a supply of nappies, then resume your rounds this afternoon.'

'Thank you,' said Beatrice.

There was a tap at the door and Kitty walked in.

'Excuse the interruption,' she said to Sister District. To Beatrice she said, 'You have another visitor.'

'Can't they wait?' Sister District enquired crisply.

'I don't think so,' Kitty answered. 'Please come in, Miss Brewer.'

To Beatrice's surprise, in walked Fay Brewer, complete with jaunty feather in her hat. After swift pleasantries, Miss Brewer addressed Sister District.

'May I assume you're here to offer Miss Inkerman her old job back?'

'You assume correctly,' said Sister.

'Then it's your lucky day, Miss Inkerman,' said Miss Brewer, smiling, 'because I'm here to offer you a job as well, with the Corporation, in children's welfare. You'd have to be interviewed, but as long as you don't make a complete pig's whisker of it, the job's yours.'

'Doing what?' Kitty asked. It was just as well she posed the question as Beatrice was too stunned to string a sentence together.

Fay Brewer addressed Beatrice. 'You're obviously interested in children because you set up those clubs, and you have a particular interest in children with responsibilities. Your idea that they might go to school half-time needs work and discussion, but it's high time something was sorted out. This isn't a problem that's going to go away. There will always be children like these. After the war, there will very likely be even more of them, because of handicaps and failing health caused by war injuries.'

'Would that be my job?' Beatrice asked. 'Looker-after children?'

'Not just them, no,' said Miss Brewer. 'You'll require general training and you'll learn on the job. I want you to understand that this is a big opportunity.'

Beatrice caught on at once. 'You mean because I never got my elementary school leaving certificate.' She didn't need to make a question out of it.

'That just goes to show you've achieved this entirely on your own merit.' Kitty beamed at her. 'I'm proud of you.'

'Do you need some time to think it over?' Fay Brewer asked.

'No, thank you.' Beatrice turned to Sister District. 'Thank you for offering me my old job, but I shan't be returning to the inco service.' Warmth spread through her body as happiness bubbled up inside her. 'I'm going to work in children's welfare instead.'

27

AUGUST 1941

Kitty spent two hours in the queue for the grocer's, her wicker basket over her arm and her gas-mask box dangling by its string from her shoulder. It was already hot and it was only the middle of the morning, so goodness knew what it would be like this afternoon. The sunshine brightened everything it touched, adding a twinkle to shop windows. There hadn't been a raid last night, but the lingering smell of smoke added a sharp note to the air, mingled with the aroma of damp soot, from the one the night before last. Kitty could feel the layer of the minutest grit beneath the soles of her shoes each time the queue shuffled forwards. All the pavements were like that now: grit so tiny you couldn't see it – but you could feel it.

The headscarfed woman next to Kitty stretched her spine. 'D'you know, I can spend hours on my feet on the production line, and then spend all night out and about with the mobile canteen, and I can cope just fine with all that, but stand me in a queue and suddenly I'm ready to give Rip Van Winkle a run for his money.'

'I know what you mean,' Kitty agreed with a smile.

'It ought to be restful, standing in a queue,' another woman joined in, 'but it isn't.' She wore a straw hat with a band around the brim.

'Though I do enjoy a good chinwag,' added an elderly woman whose dark skirt came down to her ankles.

'Aye,' agreed Mrs Headscarf beside Kitty. 'What about this Atlantic Conference, then? I thought that Mr Churchill meeting President Roosevelt would mean that America was going to declare war on Germany, but no such luck.'

'We can manage without the Yanks,' chimed in another voice. It belonged to a willowy girl in a swing-jacket that spoke of pre-war fabric quantities. 'Britain can take it.'

Britain can take it. It had become a kind of slogan. Britain can take it. London can take it. Manchester can take it – that was what was said in the aftermath of the Christmas Blitz. Look at poor old Coventry: they'd taken it to the point where there was hardly anything left of the place, and the word 'coventrated' had entered the language.

'But we wouldn't have to take it for so long if the Americans would join in,' said Mrs Straw Hat. 'Join in properly, I mean. Join in the fighting instead of just sending us food. Not that the food isn't welcome,' she added and there were murmurs and nods of agreement.

After that, the conversation moved on. As was always the case in a queue for the grocer, butcher or fishmonger, food rationing was a regular topic.

'I'm looking forward to the cheese ration being increased at the end of the month,' said the old lady in the Queen Mary-length skirt. 'I've always been partial to a bit of cheese.'

'Up to a whole three ounces a week.' Kitty put on a humorous voice, as if the extra ounce represented a massive increase.

'I've got a vegetarian girl billeted on me, if you please,' said Mrs Headscarf, 'and she'll get eight ounces a week. It'll make my life easier, having to cater for her, I can tell you.'

'Manual labourers and workers on the land are getting extra an' all,' said Mrs Swing-Jacket.

They all moved forward a little. The shop door was now in sight. A buxom woman with roses in her cheeks came out and stopped to talk to the women near the front of the line. Then she moved along and stopped again, obviously passing on information.

Kitty stopped her when she drew level. 'Excuse me. Are you passing on what Mr Pargeter has on his shelves today?' She smiled. 'I hope you're going to say there are plenty of tins of tuna to go round.'

'If only,' the woman replied. 'The delivery is late this week so if you're hoping to stock up your cupboards, you're out of luck.'

As she moved on to spread the word further along, Kitty was about to comment but young Mrs Swing-Jacket fanned her face with her hand and Kitty noticed she looked a bit green about the gills.

'Are you all right, love?' she asked.

'I'm fine,' said the girl. 'I'm just...' She held her jacket against herself by way of finishing the sentence.

'Eh, lass, you shouldn't be queuing up,' said Mrs Headscarf as the women looked at the girl's bump.

'I don't like to take advantage,' she said.

'Nonsense,' Kitty said briskly. 'It isn't taking advantage and nobody will mind. Have you got your green book? Give it here.'

The moment Mrs Swing-Jacket produced her green ration book, Kitty twitched it out of her fingers and took her by the arm.

'Come on, love.'

Waving the green book at anyone who looked like objecting, Kitty escorted the girl to the front of the queue and into Pargeter's.

'May this lady sit down for a minute, Mr Pargeter?' Kitty asked, taking the girl to one of the pair of wooden chairs over to one side of the shop. 'I think the heat is a bit much for her.'

Mrs Pargeter came out from behind the counter, taking charge. 'Dear me, yes. You sit there and gather yourself, Mrs Norton, while I fetch you a cold drink. We'll have you right as rain in no time, and then I'll serve you.'

The young mother-to-be shot Kitty a grateful smile.

'Take care of yourself,' Kitty said.

She took a moment to cast her glance over the shelves before she left the shop to return to her place in the queue.

'How is she?' asked the elderly lady. 'Coming over all unnecessary like that. It's this heat.'

'She's fine,' Kitty was pleased to report. 'Mrs Pargeter is looking after her.'

'Fancy not using her green book to go straight to the front,' said Mrs Headscarf. 'Daft thing.'

'Did you happen to notice what was on the shelves?' asked Mrs Straw Hat. 'I know you were looking after that girl, but – did you?'

'Did you see any boxes of suet?' the old lady asked.

'Or tins of corned beef?' asked Mrs Headscarf.

'Or tinned fruit?' asked Mrs Straw Hat.

Kitty laughed. When things didn't go according to plan, her lovely mam always used to say that you'd laugh about it one day, so you might as well save time by laughing now.

'I can't say exactly what was on the shelves, ladies,' she told them. 'All I can say is there wasn't much of it. I'm thinking of asking for a jar of gold dust because there's more chance of getting that than anything else.'

* * *

Kitty went to see Mr Tulip in his office to pay the money she owed for his men having carted furniture and other belongings upstairs a couple of days ago, using their expertise to store everything efficiently in the space available. The owners had paid her in cash, which was helpful because the petty cash tin needed a boost. Kitty maintained meticulous records and could account for every payment that came in or went out. She did this not only because it was the right thing to do, but also because she was all too aware that she was running this business absolutely against Bill's wishes, as he never failed to remind her when he wrote. Not that he was corresponding much these days. It was left to Kitty to send news from home, not because she specially wanted to keep in touch but because it was the done thing to send letters to servicemen. She and Bill might have fallen out over Dunbar's and he might have – in fact, he undoubtedly had – dealt her a severe blow by lying to his mother about her, but they still had their darling daughter to bind them together.

When Kitty entered his office, Mr Tulip not only stood up but came around his desk to greet her. As always, he looked dapper, with gold collar-studs and a silk hanky in his top pocket. When he shook hands, he placed his left hand on top in an extra clasp. Kitty didn't mind. There was nothing flirtatious or inappropriate in the gesture.

'My dear Mrs Dunbar, it's always a pleasure to see you,' he said.

'I've come to pay my bill,' said Kitty.

'You're always so prompt,' he replied. 'There's really no need to rush round here the minute my bill is presented.'

Kitty smiled. 'I know how much I rely on my customers to settle up on time and I like to do the same.' And, of course, living with Bill had left her with a horror of being in debt.

'How is business?' Mr Tulip asked, showing her to the chair in front of his desk.

She sat down. 'Doing well, thanks in no small part to you.'

Now seated behind his desk once more, Mr Tulip made a modest gesture. 'It wouldn't have mattered how much advice I provided, if you hadn't been prepared to work hard.'

Kitty acknowledged the compliment with a slight bow. 'I'm determined that Dunbar's is going to pay its way through the war years. Almost all the rooms are now occupied and it won't be long before we're full. Thank you for the customers you've sent my way.'

They talked for a while, then Mr Tulip escorted Kitty to his finance office, where she paid her bill. Folding her receipt, she put it carefully in her handbag, then walked home.

Home – yes, home. Dunbar's was her home now, and in a far more meaningful way than if it had carried on being a hotel. The new business was of her own making and she was immensely proud to feel she had put a roof over her daughter's head – and not just Abbie's but Beatrice's and Lily's too. The two of them were becoming increasingly dear to her and she couldn't imagine Dunbar's without them.

Abbie loved them too.

'Auntie Beatrice isn't going to leave here now that she's got another job, is she?' she had asked last month, her eyes filled with anxiety.

'Of course she won't,' Kitty had answered, and then had immediately felt a little thrill of panic in case she was mistaken.

It made her realise just how much she enjoyed having her new friend living with them.

Later that day, she had checked with Beatrice whether she entertained any plans for moving on.

Beatrice had looked anxious. 'Are you asking me to leave?'

'Of course not,' Kitty exclaimed wholeheartedly. 'That's the very last thing I want. You're welcome here for as long as you want to stay – which I hope will be a very long time. Abbie hopes so too. We both love having you.'

'That's a relief, I must say. For a moment there, I thought you wanted me out.'

'Never,' Kitty had declared, feeling warm inside.

Since then, it had delighted her to see Beatrice starting to find her feet in her new role working in welfare. She was the first to admit she had a lot to learn but she was the sort to apply herself and do her best.

Renee Shotton and Olive Judd had come to Dunbar's to apologise to Beatrice for the trouble caused by the unfortunate accusation that had been made against her.

'Unfortunate?' Kitty had exclaimed. She had stayed in the room for moral support, not intending to stick her oar in, but that word immediately got her riled up. 'That's one way of putting it.'

'I told you we shouldn't have come,' Renee had hissed at her sister.

'It's the right thing to do,' was Olive's reply. To Beatrice she said, 'We're both sorry, Miss Inkerman. We know you've had a bad time of it.'

'We weren't to know Ma really had given you that brooch,' Renee said defensively, 'so you can hardly blame us for thinking the worst.'

'Well!' Kitty said after she had shown the sisters out at the end of their short visit. 'I'm sure Olive Judd meant her apology but her sister obviously thought she'd been utterly reasonable in her behaviour from start to finish.'

'It doesn't matter. I've put it behind me,' Beatrice said with far more grace and generosity than Kitty was feeling just then. 'After all, if Renee hadn't reported me to the police, I'd still be an inco lady living in a poky half-bedroom.' She smiled and her brown eyes glowed. 'Look at me now. New job, comfortable home and good friends. What more could I ask?'

Kitty enjoyed the knowledge that Beatrice felt settled and secure in Dunbar's. Lily seemed settled too, though in a different kind of way. For her, Dunbar's seemed to be a safe place where she could hide away. Kitty's kind heart ached for the girl and the profound sadness that had overwhelmed her life. At least she was here at Dunbar's; that was one good thing. She had Kitty and Beatrice to keep an unobtrusive eye on her.

Kitty smiled to herself. Dunbar's was a good place for all of them. It was Lily's place of refuge. It was where Beatrice was blossoming. As for herself – her smile stretched wider. Dunbar's was where she had come into her own.

ACKNOWLEDGEMENTS

Many thanks to my agent, Camilla Shestopal, for introducing me to Boldwood; and to everyone at Boldwood, especially my editor, Francesca Best, and my friend, Maddie Please, for their warm welcome.

Thanks also to the editorial team led by Hayley Russell. To Jen Gilroy, who shares all the ups and downs; and to Beverley Hopper, always the first to review.

And a special hello to the readers of my Railway Girls series who told me they loved Fay Brewer and wished they could have met her earlier in the war.

ABOUT THE AUTHOR

Maisie Thomas is the bestselling author of the Railway Girls series. She is now writing a new saga series for Boldwood, set in wartime Manchester.

Sign up to Maisie's mailing list for news, competitions and updates on future books.

Visit Maisie's website: www.susannabavin.co.uk

Follow Maisie on social media here:

facebook.com/MaisieThomasAuthor
x.com/maisiethomas99

Sixpence Stories

Introducing Sixpence Stories!

Discover page-turning historical novels from your favourite authors, meet new friends and be transported back in time.

Join our book club
Facebook group

https://bit.ly/SixpenceGroup

Sign up to our
newsletter

https://bit.ly/SixpenceNews

Boldwood

Boldwood Books is an award-winning fiction publishing company seeking out the best stories from around the world.

Find out more at www.boldwoodbooks.com

Join our reader community for brilliant books, competitions and offers!

Follow us
@BoldwoodBooks
@TheBoldBookClub

Sign up to our weekly deals newsletter

https://bit.ly/BoldwoodBNewsletter

Printed in Great Britain
by Amazon